Are We A Band Yet?

by

Alexander Francis

Are We A Band Yet?

by

Alexander Francis

Arcus Verba Publishing
P.O Box 210
De Forest, Wisconsin
53532
www.arcusverba.com

Cover design by Alexander Francis

ISBN: **978-1-942420-16-3** print edition
ISBN: **978-1-942420-17-0** e-book

Table of Contents

Introducing the second and third Mick Grundy Thrillers

The shaking returned, and the shadow man stood there with

his hands describing small arcs in the night air. The shadows from the fence played across his face as he fought his body's urge to faint. In the distance, a peacock's cry hung in the night air. There was a subtle motion from the other side of the fence, and a woman's silhouette appeared framed by yellow light cast from tall poles standing guard in the parking lot.

"What are we supposed to do now?" Ahmed asked not too

quietly, continuing to play nervously with the safety on his rifle.

"Plainly, we are about to die. We have executed a plan doomed to fail from its inception. Mick Grundy will kill us, and we have only ourselves to blame. We came looking for him only to find his shadow, and now we have run out of options."

Read Excerpts from other novels by Alexander Francis
At afnovels.com

Are We A Band Yet?...Beware the Exit….The Green Scarf
Revenge of Jesus….Geminknot….Anthology of Childhood
Schemers and Dreamers…..Memory Gap

Foreword

When you reach your eighties, like me, you might think that you've seen and done it all, like I did. But, out of the blue, I was asked to write my thoughts about this book and that's a new thing for me, and a new adventure.

Most people know me as just an old jazz pianist, which suits me fine because that's all I ever tried to be and really all that I am. One fine day, this young cub approached me about trying to teach him jazz. The way I always thought about it, you have to be born with jazz in your blood. You have to BE jazz...you understand? Probably not, and he didn't either. Even after finding that he could play the piano fairly well, I realized that I had a long hard road ahead to actually make him feel the music, to make him really understand what he was trying to do.

But he did finally get it...he and his foxy lady friend are now able to put on quite a show and make an audience actually feel the jazz coming out of them...make it LIVE, you know, just as I wanted. Over time we became close, you see, and when I had taught them everything I know (well maybe not everything), I was sad to have it finished. Now, seeing them and their little band together on stage brings a little tear to even my tired old eyes.

So, back to this book and my comments about it. A lot of what has been written is the truth but a measure of it has been invented. The first time I read about myself saying something I never said, I tossed it across the room. After some time though, I finally admitted to myself that it WAS me in these pages, like seeing yourself in the mirror for the first time. This story is one that should have happened, even if much of it didn't. The real truth in this book is their love that jumps out of the pages and hits you squarely between the eyes. It's the musical chord that completes the emotion.

My last thought is about the name Daniel. It's not what I like to call him, as you are about to find out.

Solomon James
(Zap ... to my friends)

Chapter One

She Stepped Out Of A Dream

There should be no doubt, no reason to hesitate, really nothing to fear. After all, it was only for fun. But, logic and reason didn't matter and didn't assuage my apprehension. After standing in front of the door too long, I grasped the small knocker and rapped three times. I listened for any activity, any sound of footsteps getting closer, but other than the occasional burst of guitar music from some distant source, the place seemed devoid of human life. I clenched my teeth and knocked again, more firmly than before, the sound echoing in the room beyond the door and coming back as a hollow sound. "Now what?" I asked myself. I looked around the front of the house toward the windows, not really considering peeking in, more in a reflex of frustration. This was the place, written in Brenna's own hand, even the time was correct. I studied the paper scrap one more time while considering my next option. This was Brenna's doing, her scheme. She had made the connections for me, and she purred comfortingly that this was going to allow me to do something that I always wanted but was too timid to do on my own. It was true enough, and here I was, somewhat involuntarily, standing on the porch with my guitar case hanging from my hand as if I were an actual performer, one who actually knew what he was doing. The soon-to-be evident truth was that I was just an enthusiastic amateur, one who only knew a few chords and who stumbled over even that scant ability.

I knocked louder this time. The sound boomed back at me through the door, and I stood back a bit. An occasional stream of guitar music was coming from inside, and this time I heard the drums. Screwing up my courage, I tried the handle, and the door opened, allowing the band in the basement to fully envelop my senses. Nothing to gain by standing on ceremony, I thought, as I ventured inside following the sounds which led to the basement door.

The lower door was open a crack, spilling light and noise onto the staircase. Tentatively, I pushed it open and stuck my head in, causing the music to stop abruptly.

"You must be Dan," one of them said as he put down his guitar. The others looked at me in silence, and I could feel their eyes probing me, assessing my skills as if I had already started to play.

"I am. You're Tom?" I asked, venturing my hand and then looking at the other two fellows in case I was wrong.

"Close," he laughed. "That's Tom," He nodded toward the one behind the drums who waved back with a stick in his hand. "This is Doug," he pointed to the one standing close by. "And I'm Mike." As I shook hands with Doug, I noticed that he looked a bit rougher than the more normal appearing Tom and Mike. Tall and lean, he was wearing his long hair in a ponytail, dressed in jeans and a black tee shirt, which was adorned with a faded image of a former rock star.

I shook Mike's hand and found it to be thick and calloused, which fit with the blue tattoos on his forearm. He had a sincere smile and a friendly round face and moved quickly and surely, much like an oversized cat. Tom stood from behind his drums and nodded toward me, then sat back down.

"So we hear that you want to play some blues?" Mike asked. The others were listening for my response. "Played with a group previously?" he questioned.

"No. Not with a group. This is something new to me, and truthfully, I'm not sure you want me," I answered. It was a soulful remark, a bit too revealing, but they were going to find out anyway.

"That's fine. We all have to start somewhere. If you can play a few chords in a steady rhythm, that's all you have to do. Can you do that?"

"I think so. Love to try," I answered. There was a moment of silence, and the three glanced at each other. There was more to this, I realized.

"Brenna is *your* girlfriend?" Doug asked bluntly.

I suddenly felt wounded. Was I not good enough to have Brenna as a girlfriend? What was he getting at? "Yes," I finally answered. Doug flicked his eyes at Mike, then went back to tuning his bass guitar, its long battered neck adorned by untrimmed string ends which waved stiffly each time they detected movement.

"Don't feel offended," Mike said, his irrepressible smile coming back to his face. "We were wondering, that's all. We kind of thought she was going to be here. Just surprised, I guess."

So that was it. I was part of the package, the small give-away prize that no one really wanted. Brenna was the main ingredient, the reason the package was delivered in the first place. Tom was the one she mentioned when she told me about the band. He was her contact, but as yet he was silent, allowing Mike to speak for the group.

I turned to Tom, catching his eyes. "Did she tell you she was going to be here?" I asked, not knowing the answer myself.

"She led me to believe but didn't say in so many words," Tom replied.

"Why should she be here?" I wondered aloud. "You guys play blues, right?"

"Yeah, man," Doug answered for the others. He let go with a riff that drowned out any other sounds.

I waited for an answer.

"Say, Dan, just put your guitar in the rack. You'll find a cable to plug in just about anywhere," Mike said, pointing to the guitar rack which already held four electric guitars. Tom went back to tapping out a rhythm on the drums, as Doug commenced playing a steady blues beat. At least they ignored me as I set up my guitar and found a bare opening on the floor to stand. When I appeared ready, Tom stopped playing, and they looked at me again.

"Heads up, Dan," Mike said. "Four chords, that's all you have to know: Dm7 G7 C6 Am7. Like this..."

then he played the chords for me using an irregular beat and smiling the while. It seemed too simple until I tried. I knew the chords, but it was the pressure of not making a mistake that made me hesitant.

"You can do it!" he said encouragingly when I finished. "That's all there is to it. Now just follow us, and you'll see what I mean." They started playing in earnest, and after missing a few beats, I joined in, trying very hard to be on time with my strokes. It became obvious that in the din of noise being created, my additions made little or no difference, and once past that, I began to relax as I played and started to, at least, feel party to the music. After several minutes, they wound down and stopped, so I put my guitar back in the rack and approached the drum set with Tom waiting for me to speak.

"Tom," I said, extending my hand, which was taken. "About Brenna. Did you want her to come for some reason?" He looked sheepish for a moment, apparently wanting to dodge the question.

"I'll level with you. We want a singer. The way Brenna looks...well, I'm sure you know." Yes, Tom was right. She stops traffic. If she just stood on stage with the band behind her, she would only need to look like she might sing to attract an audience. I was used to it by now. She turned men's heads. She knew it, I knew it and so did Tom.

"Tom," I started. "So the idea was that Brenna would, or might, sing with your band. I am going to be standing around pretending to strum the guitar just to keep her around. Is that the idea?"

"Sorry, Dan, but yes, that's about it."

"You should have asked her. You would have learned that she doesn't like the blues and wouldn't dream of singing it."

"No kidding! She said she sang. Is there some reason she won't sing with us?"

"I'm trying to tell you. She is a very good singer, and she frequently sings while I play. Just not the blues."

"Then what does she like?"

"The classics. You know, Cole Porter, that sort of thing."

"And you actually play that on a guitar?" He asked incredulously, since he had just heard me struggle with simple chords.

"No, no," I protested. "I usually play the keyboard, but since I was a kid, I always wanted to play guitar in a blues band."

"Oh," Tom said. It wasn't what he wanted to hear. "Do you think she is coming here tonight?" he asked. Hope is such a hard thing to lose.

"Is that what she told you?" I asked.

"Not in so many words," he repeated.

"Hey!" Mike called. He was waiting patiently with his guitar at the ready, as was Doug. The question about Brenna was still in the air. As I put my guitar back on, I found myself wondering. She had been vague about tonight, where she was going or what she was going to do. Now I wasn't sure at all. She just might show up.

"This time," Mike said rather loudly, speaking over the other instruments which were warming up. "This time, you need to use B flat, E flat and F. Just mix up the octaves as you like."

I thought about it for a moment, trying to translate from the keyboard to my fretboard. "Yes, I've got it," I answered. I didn't, but I couldn't back down and strained to remember the hand positions for a variety of chords in different octaves. While I was struggling, the others started up, using a faster tempo than before. I missed several but got most of them and felt very good about it. I started to have fun, relaxing and enjoying the entire experience. It was just as I had imagined. Suddenly, Mike held up his hand, stopping the music abruptly.

"Did you hear something?" he asked. Was he kidding? Over that amount of amplification, we would have missed a tornado removing most of the house above us. The room grew quiet as we all listened obediently. Sure enough, there was a noise. It was the door knocker echoing around the upstairs. I was impressed. Mike's face lit up, and he rapidly put his guitar aside and took the stairs two at a time.

Doug and I stood like statues, immobile, made of bronze, but still clutching our precious instruments. Doug had a look come over him that I hadn't seen since I was a child when my brother and I were about to enter the living room on Christmas morning. It was a look anticipating some good thing, some very good thing, was about to happen. His prominent Adam's apple went up and down as he swallowed, barely breathing as he listened to the light footsteps coming down the stairs.

Brenna was first through the door and met my eyes instantly. She was freshly made up, her hair had that just-came-from-the-hairdresser look, and her outfit was new. I had seen her in every conceivable style of dress by now but seeing her walk into that room hit me with a punch. She was simply too beautiful to be there amid the cables on the floor, the scattered amplifiers and the fluorescent lights, not to mention four men in worn clothing. Brenna was a pearl floating in a basin of crabs. I couldn't take my eyes off of her long enough to see the faces of the other men.

Her lips formed the briefest of puckers, in an instant gone, but long enough for me to be told that she was mine and mine alone. Her eyes danced with merriment, but only I could have seen it. For the others, she was a curvy, gorgeous young woman entering into a cave of men: her perfume, her perfect skin, set off by her long blonde hair, shimmering even under the artificial light. They could never see past the woman standing there, but I could. She was the same fragile, shy, even introverted, little girl with big eyes whom my heart danced around even during my dreams.

"Hi!" she ventured, just a little too softly. "Can I come in?" It was a silly question, of course, but designed in that female way which would always bring males to give assurances that she was welcome. Of course, she was welcome. All of us, excepting me, were expecting her. Tom was sure to have added the visual description of her that intensified their expectations, and there was no way that anyone was disappointed. Not by a long shot.

"By all means!" Tom nearly shouted, and stood up waving her forward with his sticks. She didn't even look at him, her eyes riveted on my face. I didn't even notice her feet moving as she drifted toward me, her hair swaying softly from side to side wrapping her upper hips in glorious gold. As if by command, I leaned forward to receive a small, quick, polite, but not nearly long enough, kiss on the lips before she turned to face the others, her perfume enveloping me, as it always did, just as softly as an embrace from her arms.

"Are you going to sing?" Doug asked, his voice cracking a little, the words coming a bit too quickly and out of character. He was looking at her as if she was on the menu, an imported dessert right from Paris.

"Sing?" she repeated and looked at me for an explanation.

"Seems that Tom was under the assumption that you would not only come tonight but also would sing for them," I explained. She looked flustered. It was obvious that singing tonight was not even considered. I went on to clarify for her, "This is a blues band, Brenna."

"No, I don't think so," she said to the room.

"Would you sing if Dan plays for you? We would love to hear you, whatever you want to sing," Mike said. I felt her big eyes turn on me, a suggestion of pleading in them. It would take a lot of convincing to entice her to entertain them. So far, she and I had only performed for ourselves with no visitors permitted. At times, while she sang, I heard a voice emerge that should be heard by others. A unique talent was inside of her, but it was still shy and tender which is what made it so effective to my ears. Brenna's voice was an experience, not just its singing tone. Parts of her came with it, attached, inextricable, at times, too personal for me to share.

"I have a keyboard," Mike announced. Abruptly, there would be more difficulty for Brenna in refusing to sing. She turned and looked at me for guidance. It seemed to me that hearing her sing music that was so different in nature from blues would put an end to their imagining that they had discovered a compelling allure for the front of the band.

"We have a couple of numbers ready. I'll play if you'll sing." It was my turn to plead. It was the right thing to do, even though afterwards, they would likely want to re-think me as an addition to their band. Brenna studied my face for a moment, then looked at each of them in turn, meeting their hungry gaze with her innocence.

"Yes." Her answer was met with shuffling and commotion. A small keyboard was discovered in a corner and was quickly set up and plugged in. Their smiling, anticipatory faces were hard to resist. I sat down and started running through the keys...all 66 of them. It was a short, inexpensive keyboard, not meant for performance. It was a dabbler's, a beginner's or a MIDI musician's keyboard, but it would have to do for now. I adjusted the volume and began to warm up, while also attempting to create a mood for Brenna. She was never far from my arm, and I occasionally felt her make contact. There was no written music to guide me so we would have to do it from memory. I had played keyboard, actually piano, for many years, but I was only starting to learn the job of an accompanist. The role is very special, for sure, and requires a different skill set. The accompanist has to avoid the melody, that job is the singer's, and he has to provide fill, in the correct key, in addition to adding ornament when necessary. I wasn't all that good at it, I will admit.

She nodded to me that she was ready, and I began to play one of her favorites, the song, *You Stepped Out Of A Dream*, by Brown and Kahn. It amused me to think how entirely appropriate this particular number was this night of all nights. The truth of it self-evident, but I wasn't about to tell our small audience the name of this one.

At first, her voice was small and hesitant, but her notes were pure, and her emotions, genuine as the air she breathed, came out as well. I tried to concentrate on my hands, attempting to avoid running off the keyboard in spots, but I couldn't help steal glances toward her. It was a show, even for me, and I thought I knew every part of her by memory. But once loosed, this magical creation of feminine beauty combined with her emotion-laden voice became a life force of its own and penetrated the minds of our band members, enchanting them, not with the spell of the music but with Brenna herself. She placed her hand on my shoulder as we were finishing, a reminder of how she felt about me, that I belonged to her as much as she belonged to me.

They made a fearful commotion, those three, when she finished and each rushed toward her, wanting to tell her how much they were affected by her performance. I knew better. She was good, but it was the woman herself who was the attraction. I knew how they felt, because I had been under her influence much longer than they. The combination of sweetness and sincerity alone would be enough, but her stunning appearance, her curves, her lips, her hair, combined into a potent package.

"Could we beg you for one more, Brenna?" Tom pleaded for the others. Brenna turned to see if I would agree before she answered.

I spoke first, "Tell you what, fellows. I know that you three are nearly professional musicians, easily better than me, in fact. What about all of us accompany her this time. Just do what comes naturally for you. For your information, the key is E flat. I would change it for you, but I'm not that good. Is that agreeable?" It was, very much so, and Brenna and I waited until they got in position. I played some chords so that they could hear the key, because I understood that they played by ear and not by sheet music as I did. At the appropriate time, I started by playing the first few lines of Cole Porter's *What Is This Thing Called Love*. Brenna came in first, then I could hear the drums taking up the rhythm, mostly using snares. In the background, Doug supplied a deep rhythm using only four notes, and Mike joined in the breaks between phrases with little runs of notes.

This one was Brenna's favorite, and she was very accomplished with it. Now that their eyes were not completely fixated on her every motion, she was better, more relaxed. I couldn't help looking at her a second or so too long, then it happened. I made a glaring mistake, one that couldn't be ignored and, like an amateur, I stopped playing. They all stopped as well and four pairs of eyes were turned on the pianist.

"Goof. Sorry," was all I had to say before starting again at the top. No one minded hearing her again, and I'm sure we could have gone on for hours before anyone would have even noticed. At last the song was over, and I felt her hands on my neck, and her body against my back. She kissed the top of my head and murmured something that I couldn't hear because of the acclaim coming from the three mesmerized musicians standing in front of the keyboard, all applauding.

"We sound like a band, so we must be a band!" Doug shouted.

"We loved it, Brenna. You made a dream come true tonight," Mike said. "Didn't you enjoy it as well?" he hoped aloud. I could feel her nod behind me, and I patted her hand still on my shoulder.

"To play with you is an honor, Brenna," Tom said, something else on his mind. "Can we persuade you to try to sing a couple of blues numbers with us?" He was so convincing, I nearly agreed myself.

"No." A concise rejection came from her, a hard final blow, one that they should have expected since I warned Tom myself, not an hour before, regarding her feelings toward the blues. Tom didn't turn away though and wanted to discuss it with her more fully.

"What if we learned to play your kind of music? Would you sing with us then?" Tom asked.

"Only if Dan plays the keyboard," she answered. There went my life as a guitarist, right up the stairs and out of the house. I heard the door slamming behind it before it disappeared completely. But for her, anything. It was a small price to pay to have her company, to be able to make her happy. It would make the band happy, too, but I wasn't in love with them.

"Sure. Count me in," I said.

"Are we a band yet?" Doug asked. We laughed at him, because he looked so sincere.

Chapter Two

Meeting Another Band

Two days after our first contact with Tom, Mike and Doug, I received a call from Tom.

"Say, Dan. Are you able to give us a hand doing a little electrical work over at my place?"

The request was odd given that we had just met. However, I was impressed enough by their graciousness toward us that I wanted to give something back.

"Sure," I answered. "Just let me know when."

"How about now?"

I arrived within the hour, luckily not working that day. Tom and Mike were in the basement room, which was more cluttered than before, with boxes and wood piled up against one wall and a newly created clearing more or less in the center of the room. As soon as I came down, Tom handed me a canister light and a coil of wire.

"Could you put this light over the clear spot and hook it up?" It was a flood or spotlight for the soloist to stand under. I got the picture right away. They intended this area for Brenna, their new singer.

"I can, but we should talk this through first. It's for Brenna, isn't it?"

"Won't she look good under that light! And we have two more that you can install right beside the first one." He was so enthusiastic I hated to bring him down to reality.

"She didn't agree to sing blues. You recall that, don't you?" I asked.

"It's possible that she'll change her mind. Mike's building a small stage for her to stand on, and Doug brought over a crate of new electronic gear. You should see it." He started moving toward the boxes, his pride in their new endeavor heartwarming for me to see.

"I know that you want her to change her mind, but I have known her long enough to tell you that she'll put her foot down about this. No blues. Ever. Don't get your hopes up about it."

Mike stopped in his tracks, his face falling, "No chance?"

"She doesn't see herself in that image. As I recall, most, if not all, female blues singers are...well, earthy. Does Brenna strike you as earthy?"

"Not in the least," he agreed. "Then what do you suggest, Dan?" He tossed a tool to the floor, and it skidded away from us. His smile had disappeared as well, likewise spinning away from him.

"Is it really going to be so difficult for you to play the music that she likes?" As I was talking, he started shaking his head before I could finish.

"You can read music, I could tell the way you play. We can't. Blues are based on the pentatonic scale and the pattern of chords are fixed by tradition. There are only three things you have to learn to play blues. First, a few chords, the ones you can already play. Then the rhythm. The only difficult part are the riffs. Frankly, we just memorize a bunch and put them in as we go along. Next time the piece is played it might sound different."

"I heard you play. You are oversimplifying, aren't you?" I asked.

"Perhaps a little, but it is simple compared to what Cole Porter wrote."

"But," I started, "you did play for her, and you all sounded great. I mean, when she is singing, there isn't a lot of action from the instruments. We just help her along and fill in the dead spots."

"Now, you are oversimplifying, don't you agree?" Mike said.

"Now an admission from me, Mike. I learned to play by reading sheet music. You don't have to understand music to read and play it like it was written. A really good musician understands a lot more about music than I do. I just pretend to be her accompanist."

"What have we just said?" Mike summed it all up. "We have a great singer on our hands, and we're not good enough for her, none of us are. Don't you think that's the case?"

"Yes, I do. She's too good for us by talent and by appearance. But...what you don't know about her fragile personality would fill a book. She's not able to go off and sing with someone else and doesn't want to."

"You hope," Mike stated.

Yes, I did hope that it was true, that she needed me as I needed her. Being around her had changed my life, in that I cared more about her needs than my own. It wasn't a sensation of being captured by Brenna, rather an overwhelming feeling of devotion to her. At this point in our relationship, I couldn't conceive of life without her.

They were intent on completion of their project, and I helped where I could. In three hours, we could see the process nearly complete, and when Tom flipped on the lights for the first time, we stood back in admiration. She would stand on the small elevated stage and be lit by three colored spots from slightly different overhead angles. Doug had provided a professional mike on an adjustable stand as well as a sophisticated electronic voice processor unit for her.

"This must have cost a small fortune," I remarked, looking over the processor. "I'm sorry, but I took Doug for a fellow rather down-and-out. I must have been looking at another person."

"No, you got it right," Tom laughed. We call him Dangerous Doug. Neither of us actually knows much about him, and at times, we fear the worst." They both laughed knowingly. "We don't ask how he comes up with things like this. It's often better to be ignorant."

"So you haven't known Doug for very long?" I inquired.

"A few years, off and on. He disappears on occasion but then returns as if nothing had happened," Mike said.

"I've always thought that Doug is a gambler, but I'm not sure why I think that," Tom added.

"He plays well, nevertheless," I observed.

"You bet he does. He is the most experienced of the three of us, by far," Mike said. Then he turned to me in a more serious tone. "If you have the time, we can show you a few tricks on the guitar. Get you up to speed."

It happened that my guitar was still in the backseat of my car, and I rushed out to retrieve it. On my way out of the house, it struck me that it was nearly empty, only a few items of comfort were scattered around. A woman's hand was missing. The emptiness of the place depressing.

"If you just repeat what I show you, in short order you'll find that you can play lead," Mike said. He held the neck of his guitar gently, frequently swiping the length of the neck with his hand for no reason other than to have contact with it as if it were alive and would respond to affection. I noticed that his hands were muscular and thick but could stretch remarkably to attain a difficult combination of notes. He wore his hair long and swept back, not quite reaching his shoulders. Just enough to declare his masculinity and nearly enough to hide the obscene tattoo in the center of the back of his neck. His dark eyes were quick to notice me looking him over and wondering about his background.

"You noticed my tattoo, didn't you?" he asked, a wry smile on his face. He continued to play soft chords while he spoke like others would drag on a cigarette. He glanced at my face then back to his fingerboard, waiting on my answer.

"I noticed. It doesn't fit with the rest of you. You hide it, don't you?"

"It could be removed, but I keep it to remind me," he said without looking up. He softly played a run of notes as if his concentration was elsewhere. "I was in a rock band for awhile. We did some really stupid stuff back then. That's where I met Tom. He married one of the groupies following the band around." He nodded at the memory, recalling things he couldn't share. "Didn't last long, and now he has this empty house. She kept the kid and moved away." When he finished, he went back to strumming, a familiar blues melody emerging as if it was trying to be heard over his thoughts of the past.

A fragmentary couple of sentences and I was in possession of a capsule of their lives up until now. It was remarkable how everything fit together, like little pieces of a puzzle. Tom and Mike had had their flings early on, settling into middle life, trying to get through it but had not discovered that driving force which could direct them safely and happily into old age. They had each other's friendship but little else. It began to dawn on me how important it was to them to find a girl like Brenna. The grace hovering about her was something to feed on. It was the hope of something meaningful...a way out of a fog. I couldn't spoil their hopes, but I knew Brenna. She was a wonderful experience to behold or to hear but was also ephemeral. Tomorrow, she could decide that she was done with it all and want to move away. It was only me that kept her here, at least I hoped that was the reason. She was an amorphous vapor that you couldn't quite grasp and hold on to for very long.

The three of us spent nearly two hours on my guitar education. At the end, I was nearly able to repeat what I had learned about little jewels of string bending and hammer-on notes. I could start to feel the blues emerging in my hands, and I was on the verge of really getting it, of understanding the unique soul of it, the way the famous black stars of blues had felt all along.

"Would you be interested in hearing a live band perform tonight?" Tom asked.

"Where?" I inquired, thinking instead about keeping Brenna company, as I had planned.

"Downtown. About ten tonight. We know some of them, and we thought that you and Brenna would get something out of watching them perform. You would be our guests, of course."

"So, you want Brenna there?" I knew the answer. She was the center of everything at the moment.

"Yes, we do. And if she looks as stunning as she did last time, you'd better bring a bodyguard and a gun," Mike said. I laughed as I was supposed to at his compliment for her, but then again I wasn't so sure he was kidding.

"I'll ask. You'll know if we are coming when we come." It was a guess if we would be there, and if Brenna suspected that a fuss was to be made over her, it was a certainty that she would refuse.

"They are expecting us, Brenna," I persisted. Appealing to her indebtedness was proving as useless as outright begging, which had already failed. Brenna didn't like crowds or loud music and was stiff and silent around strangers. There was still time to take a different tact, one that I saved until the last moment. "You know what I'd like to do tonight?" My eyebrows went up in anticipation that she was interested. She wasn't. "We could go out to dinner at a nice place, then shop. After that, we can swing by the nightclub just to pay respects, just for a moment. There is a nice scarf I saw hanging around in a little shop not far away." She looked up and held my eye. I smiled broadly, innocently, and nodded encouragement of her acceptance.

"Ah, you are trying to bribe me, aren't you? I know all your tricks, little boy. First, you try to test my sense of obligation, then tempt me with food, now you are resorting to outright promise of gifts."

"How'm I doing?"

"It's pathetic. Transparent. I expect more from you." She looked huffy, if a beautiful woman can look really huffy, that is. "You didn't even try physical affection...yet," she added and looked away from my eyes. I took her hint as a clear invitation and crossed the room, went to my knees while leaning on her lap and oozing her hands into mine. I pulled her toward me, her hair spilling across my face as our lips met, the contact with her gratifying but leaving me insatiable for more.

"What kind of band?" she asked, pushing away from my face.

"Rock, I think, but before you say no, I need to tell you that Tom and Mike know some of them. They want to introduce us," I spouted out. She resisted being pulled forward again.

"Only if you promise that it will be brief and that the scarf is a very nice one."

"I swear that it's all true." I gently tugged at her until she bent for another kiss, and this time she put her arms around my neck. Knowing her as I did, when she gave me her trust, it was a sacred gift to me and me alone. Her belief in me was something so precious that I would die before abusing it.

Brenna sat between Tom and I on the bench at the back side of the circular table, a mirror behind her. An overhead spot was directly above her and highlighted her hair and face, which glowed like a piece of colored sculpture, placed on view just for connoisseurs of fine art. She was dressed in black, fine little flowers of silver threads danced around her neck line. I felt like throwing a concealing cloth over her every time a passing male did a head swivel toward us.

We had arrived just as the band, She Dog, started playing. Our seats were close, too close, and the music was loud enough to actually feel. Brenna covered her ears and frowned, looking at me as if she had been betrayed. She was right, the words were screamed, unintelligible, and the guitars were a blur of nearly continuous noise. The lead singer had long tangled dreadlocks which he slung over his shoulder by head jerk, more of a twitch, to emphasize some more dramatic part. To his sides were other guitarists who wore dark tank tops and long-brimmed caps. The drummer was awkward, his elbows sticking out at odd, crab-like angles, as he furiously attacked the drums. When they finished, the applause from the scattered patrons was reasonably sustained. Tom and Mike also clapped and clamored. The room went suddenly quiet as the next band came in and busily started getting their equipment in place.

"Weren't they great?" Tom beamed. Brenna was silent. I knew what she thought, and I knew that I'd better keep my promise and get her out before the next attack of music began.

"Loud," I observed.

Mike chuckled. "You get used to it. I thought that they gave the audience what was expected. What you don't know is that most of them actually are good musicians and well-educated. They look at it as making a living. The rock or heavy metal lifestyle is not really who they are or what they do."

Two young men approached our table, and Tom and Mike stood up to welcome them with smiles and handshakes. The moment it was over, both sets of eyes were glued to Brenna's face. My guess was that they could see her during their performance, and the anticipation of meeting her grew like a sprouting weed.

Mike put his arm over one of them and pointed to us. "These two are new members of our band. Brenna and Dan. Brenna is the singer I told you about." With his arm still extended, he said, "I want you to meet two old friends, Johnny and Fredrick. We call Fredrick, Freddie the Great, or sometimes just Great." They pulled up chairs to face us over the table. I barely recognized Johnny without his wig of dreadlocks, and Fredrick was serious and well-dressed, certainly both different than their stage appearance.

"I heard that you are really good, Brenna," Fredrick said, keeping his eyes locked on her. I started to feel invaded by his intensity. Brenna ignored the question, and I felt pressure grow against my shoulder as if she was trying to escape Fredrick's net.

"She is. A real angel," Tom blurted. This is not what Brenna wanted to happen, and I was sure to hear about it later.

"What kind of music do you like?" Freddie asked her.

"Oh, Porter, Gershwin, Rodgers, that kind," she answered softly.

"The American Song Book," he explained. "Yeah, I like that kind too. It's what every jazz great expounds on. It was what we used in music school for the basis of our jazz lessons."

"You went to music school?" I asked, wanting his eyes to leave Brenna's face, even for a second.

"Sure did. Got a master's. I play clarinet and guitar," he answered and went back to studying her face. A feeling of anger arose in me, largely protective jealousy I admit, but I wanted to take a punch at his arrogant head. Anything to get rid of his focus on Brenna. I think that Mike saw the anger building and wanted to intervene before something happened.

"Would you two like to come over to Tom's house some night and rehearse with us? You might be able to convince Brenna to sing. You won't regret it, I promise," he said.

"You guys can play swing?" Freddie asked, surprised at the invitation.

"No, not very well. You know that. We are trying though, because that's what our singer likes," Mike answered.

"Sure. I'll bring along a great saxophonist that I know." Freddie nodded toward Brenna, obviously expecting her approval. As I anticipated, she didn't move or even blink. This also, I would hear about later.

"Only if Dan plays as well," Brenna said, surprising all of us.

"Well, sport, if you are up to it," Freddie winked at me, a little smile of victory on his predatory face.

Chapter Three

Perspective

My keyboard and my guitar were waiting on me to do something. A world of music awaited exploration, and it was up to me to bring them to life. I sat down and looked at them, and they looked back, the obedient tools which were capable of creating joy, sadness, nostalgia or any other human emotion. It was in the hands of the creator...me. Only, I was in a funk, a state of mild depression. It wasn't for lack of effort on my part, for I had diligently given every spare moment to practice, jumping back and forth between the keyboard and the guitar. One for Brenna, one for me. It wasn't working, and I felt more and more lost and despondent about my ability.

Our last practice with the band was not satisfying. Brenna did her part and, in truth, would have done better without any accompanying instruments. We, the instrumentalists, just couldn't harmonize or keep a consensus regarding who was in charge and which instrument would be heard, so we ended up competing with our little singer, and the result was atrocious. We just had to do better.

I picked up the guitar and started running through the chords I had recently learned, but thinking about Brenna and how I was letting her down. We were happy when I played and she sang and only we could hear the results. Now that the business of creating music was becoming serious, it was no longer fun and exposed my inadequacies.

My phone signaled an incoming call, and I picked it up. "Good morning," she said sweetly. Her essence pouring over the phone into me. I love the sound of her voice.

"Well, I was just thinking about you," I responded. A remark always true, no matter time of day or circumstances.

"What are you doing today?" she asked.

"Just sitting down for practice. You?"

"About the same. I was just working on a number, that's all. Miss you."

We were currently only eighty miles apart, just ninety minutes by car, but far enough that I couldn't touch her, inhale her, or bury my nose in her neck. Her little "miss you" was painful, because it was so much the case for me. "Miss you, too. What number? Do I know it?" I didn't want her to be fluent on some piece that I couldn't play.

"*Come Rain or Come Shine.* You play that one. I know what you are thinking, and you shouldn't worry." She could read me like a book. I was never opaque in her eyes, not the opposite though. Brenna could look right through me with those blue eyes, and most of the time I had no concept of what was in her mind until she told me. Was it true with all women or just this one? Her perfect but blank face turned toward me, at times filling me with awe, other times with lust, but almost never with certainty of what was inside. My stark fear that she would find me inadequate in some way and move on frequently took over any rational thought.

"Yes, I know that one. How's it going?"

"Good. Ready to play next Thursday?"

"I will be. Anything else?" I asked.

"It was obvious that you weren't happy last time. Was it me?" she said softly. Her? I couldn't think of anything she could possibly do that I would find fault with. With one critical exception, of course.

"Never with you. You were magical as you always are. It was the rest of us. We were terrible, and the worst part is...I don't know what to do about it."

"No, Dan. It's me. They want to play blues, not jazz. It's my fault. I think they picked the wrong singer." She was right. It wasn't the right band at all. How did this happen? I regretted taking an interest in the guitar and not concentrating on the keyboard as I should have. Trying to be master of two things and failing at both was accomplishing nothing.

"Let's give it a couple more tries before we call it quits. We owe them that, after all the expense and work that they did for you and all the lessons I have been given. Everyone is disappointed, I think."

"I want you to know that you never let me down. You always come through, and you will again. Don't fret about it so much."

After she hung up, I was left feeling hollow. Already I could see that she had potential with her singing and combined with her remarkable appearance...well, she was a star in the making. I just hoped that I could keep up, but I had a nagging sensation we had started something that was to take over our lives, that ultimately I was destined to be left behind.

Imagine finding the greatest treasure of your life by accident, not by design or hard endeavor. We met by serendipity, by chance alone, a thousand things could have prevented our ever crossing paths. Even after we met, it took several times being around her for me to acquire the nerve to actually speak to her as a person. It was simple intimidation, fear of rejection, all the male excuses for avoiding the very woman we are most attracted to.

We both signed up at the same time for tango lessons given at a local studio. She was there with a close friend...another woman, thank God. When I looked at her, I was stunned into silence. A woman with her looks couldn't possibly be low enough to speak to me, I thought. The instructor eventually got around to pairing us, and when I looked into her eyes, I knew. Perhaps she did also. That was the ice breaker, because we were natural together. Our timing and balance were complementary, and her hand in mine felt like it had always been there. I recall some clumsy attempt to ask the obvious...was she taken? She seemed to divine my thoughts and, in a few concise sentences, told me that she wasn't seeing anyone. Neither was I, and that was the very reason both of us had taken those classes, to find someone.

Brenna was married once, for just 8 months. It was a college romance, one that became a marriage before they really knew each other, and especially before Brenna knew his parents. They were married and moved to Buffalo, to be under his dominating parents' wings and supervision. A Catholic wedding, with children expected. After half a year of trying, it was obvious that something was amiss. Testing proved that Brenna was barren. She was quickly thrown aside, and the marriage annulled. She told me that she received the divorce papers and the letter of annulment on the same day.

She had been cast adrift with no relatives to help, no job, and no place to live. Her mother was still residing in Texas, her home state, returning there after Brenna's father died. Brenna and her father had been close, but her mother was raised hard and never formed close loving bonds, even with her only daughter.

Brenna's roommate from college, Ruth, is a headstrong woman, quick to make decisions and to take chances. Together, on a whim, they traveled to Hawaii looking for work, and they found it. Both were educated in customer relations and marketing and quickly excelled at creating advertisements for travel companies. The predatory Ruth married her boss, a May to November pairing. Brenna is shy by nature and, lucky for me, avoided any commitments. Ruth's divorce and extravagant settlement came in twelve months, but by then, she had her claws into another successful man who craved the attention of a young, attractive and aggressive woman. The three of them, by the most impossible chance, moved back to Brenna's hometown, my hometown. Brenna was promised a good job with Ruth's husband's company. As it turned out, the job lasted about as long as Ruth's second marriage, or about a year. That's where I came in.

Our meeting in the dance studio would seem to have been fate. Thinking about our beginnings made me remember an embarrassing event. The second night of dance instruction, I was paired with Ruth. She was married again at the time, but as always, aggressive, nearly pathologically so. After our dance she offered to take me aside and strip to her waist so that I could see her in the au natural, something that she was proud of and likely with good reason. While this rather forward and indecent proposal was being made, I caught sight of Brenna out on the dance floor. She was watching closely, her face serene but her intelligent eyes taking in every detail. I refused Ruth's offer politely, actually several times. Later, I wondered if it was a test they had worked out. Even if it were, I'm convinced that Ruth would have followed through. Nevertheless, I passed the trial, unfortunately or fortunately, never getting a look at the shapely Ruth. I rather prefer that it turned out the way it did.

Once our relationship started, it quickly became hot. The only catch...Brenna hated our city, despised her memories of late childhood when they had moved from Texas. Her father was a big man, a Texan, loud, opinionated, but gentle as a colt. He was an officer in Air Force Intelligence, and he and his much younger bride had moved around the planet as they were assigned to do. When Brenna came along, the moves became more difficult, and he elected to retire and settle down. Because of his aerospace connections, he landed a job easily.

Reading between the lines, so to speak, I inferred that Big Matt was never happily married but was raised with principled morals and strong religious convictions. Instead of straying, one hot summer afternoon he hung himself in his own bedroom and Brenna was the one who found him. I'm not sure what effect that had on her development, but when I first met her, she was in agony, not sure of where life was taking her. She told me many times that I had "saved my life," as she put it. We are close and grow closer with each day. We live apart for now, but there is a story there as well.

After we met and I found out more about Brenna, I wanted to help her find some meaningful job that would make her happy. In addition, there was no keeping her in Rockford any longer. She had a belly full of bad memories and unfulfilled dreams. I knew that she liked Milwaukee because of her happy college days, and when we went there for events, she seemed to know the town very well. I made some calls to some old friends at the local health department and was given the name of a politically connected official in Milwaukee.

I can't take full credit for the subsequent chain of events other than the fact that I got it started. She was eventually hired to work in the Public Relations section of City Hall. The mayor seemed to be drawn to her, and she was quickly singled out for favorite treatment. I should have worried about her more than I did, but she can handle herself with men and has had lots of practice fending them off. She eventually bought a house in a near suburb of Milwaukee which meant a lot of driving for me.

For a while, things went well. I was at her side for numerous events she was involved with or was expected to attend. Two things happened to change the atmosphere for her. The mayor tried and failed to move along politically and suffered severe power loss and so did all his appointees. This event also created a change in the atmosphere around Brenna who, unfortunately, became a point of friction for others at City Hall. We quickly and simply decided to "get out of Dodge," and she moved to Madison.

She is working two part-time jobs but appears to be as happy as she gets. Tom recently compared her to the strings on the upper octaves...taut. Yes, she is, but as long as I am around, she won't break. One more thing, Ruth is now four husbands down, but she has managed to acquire a large house, a new German auto and doesn't need to work any longer. She and Brenna have remained close friends.

Chapter Four

Professionals

It wasn't a long trip to Tom's house, about twenty minutes, and we were halfway there. Brenna hadn't said a word, just rode silently beside me, looking forward with no outward sign of emotion or stress. "Brenna?" She turned and looked at me, but I couldn't hold her gaze because of the traffic. "Want to talk?" I asked.

"There's nothing to talk about," she declared levelly. In my peripheral vision, I could see her look away from me again.

"Are you angry, hurt, afraid, or anything? Do you wish that I was an astronaut circling the moon right now? Can't I get anything out of you?"

"I'm going. It's what you wanted, so just let it go."

She was giving me what I call the night-and-day treatment, moving from her tender look of affection, her hypnotic female traits, to the old cold shoulder. I preferred being beaten with a stout club. I had aroused her pique when I delayed telling her that we were going to Tom's house this night instead of out to dinner. Brenna hates surprises, especially this kind. The news sent her into a frantic mode of choosing the right dress, the perfect shoes and, of course, dealing with her hair. After changing her mind several times, she was wearing it "up". I watched in wonder as she braided her long hair into two long strands and wove them in opposite directions. The result was stunning, but the effect wasn't about her hair at all. It was the exposure of her long luminous neck. I couldn't take my eyes off of her, and I made her turn around several times, catching my breath each time her head swiveled back to me, until she tired of it and pushed me out of her room.

She chose a simple, unadorned dress of pale blue with matching shoes. Around her neck was a slender gold necklace that I had given her on her last birthday. Her choices were perfect, and it made her incomparably wholesome, delicious in fact. A slinky, stylish and sexual outfit would have sent the wrong message and portrayed her as someone she was not. This was the girl next door, the beautiful one whom you'd never noticed before but suddenly discovered that she was a world-class beauty. After she walked out of the bedroom, she stood there, letting me take her in with my eyes, roving up and down from her feet to her head and back again. It was an advanced form of torture, because I knew better than to rush over and encapsulate her with my arms and my kisses. My punishment was to wait until her punishment was over.

I took her advice and didn't utter another word until we arrived. Leaping out of the car, I rushed around to her side and held her door open, my hand suspended in the air for her, in case she needed an assist. Not a chance. I was not allowed to touch her at the moment, and she gave me a glance that said as much on her way past. Without knocking, I opened Tom's front door, and we went inside, following the voices to his kitchen where they were waiting for us while having a beer or two.

When she walked in, the chatter stopped abruptly, and the three men, Doug, Tom and Mike, acted as though they had never seen a woman before, only read and dreamed about them. They backed against whatever was behind them and held on, afraid to speak or breathe lest she disappear.

"Hi!" she said, looking at each one in turn. Since none of these men were strange, it changed her mood, and her face took on a pleasant, inviting look.

"Hi!" they said back, unable to think or even remember their previous conversation.

"Don't I get one?" she asked, nodding at the beer in their hands and laughing a husky laugh as Tom rushed toward the refrigerator. I suddenly remembered that my music was still in the car, and I left to retrieve it. When I returned, the situation was changed. This time, all three men were talking at once and had more or less surrounded Brenna, who looked happy that I was back.

"Now, boys," I suggested. "Give her some air at least." They politely backed away and looked a bit sheepish. I understood completely. Brenna was magnetic, she couldn't help how she looked, and she told me many times how burdensome it was. If she ever did succeed in getting into the public eye, she might receive a surprise. Onstage, they couldn't touch her or crowd her, but she was bound to cause a male audience to devolve into some state of rapture. And offstage, her life would never be the same.

I stood there waiting for their party to end, my music under my arm. The fellows got the hint. We adjourned for the basement. Once there, Brenna and I were surprised to see one of the walls painted a flat black. The one right behind her little stage. I could already see that it was going to work as they planned, and I gave a thumbs up to Tom.

A flip of several switches, the murmur of working amplifiers, and the hum of florescent lights made the background come alive. I noticed Tom checking his watch, something that I had never previously seen him do. He looked at Mike until he caught his attention and tapped his watch face. Something was up, and I knew what it was, but Brenna didn't. They were expecting Fredrick and his saxophone-playing friend, and they were all expecting Brenna to sing. Another battle was brewing. This was going to put her on display in front of admitted professionals. I thought she was ready, but she didn't. Frankly, I was more worried about my playing than her singing. I didn't think I was ready, and I wasn't.

"Dan," Mike called, waving me to him. Before I came, I found a small chair by the keyboard and held it for Brenna while she sat down.

"We've got a little time," he said. "Does she know?"

"Not yet," I admitted my cowardliness in not telling her. In truth, if I had, we would have been at dinner about now.

"Want to join in a quick little jam session? You can play my spare guitar," he asked. I glanced at Brenna, who was watching, sitting in her little chair with her back straight and her slender arms folded on her lap.

"I would. It'll be less awkward that way." I picked up his guitar and checked its tuning. I smiled at Brenna, nodded toward her agreeably and pointed to the guitar. She never flinched, just continued to hold me with her big blank eyes. We started abruptly with Tom's drum call to arms. I played rhythm along with Doug. He was in the bass range using single notes while I played chords one or two octaves higher. I was hoping that Brenna was impressed with my playing, because her eyes never left my face, and I could sense that her attitude was softening. Mike signaled for me to take the lead, and I went into the routines he had so patiently taught me. Success! I was most happy with the sounds we made. When the piece wrapped up in a flourish, Brenna started clapping for us.

"I think we better warm her up, Mike," I whispered to him. He agreed, and I put away the guitar and went to the keyboard and Brenna.

"Will you sing for us? Any piece you want," I asked. She stood, and everyone watched her to see what she was going to do.

"I want to sing *Night And Day*," she responded.

Tom reached behind him and switched on the stage lights and turned off the fluorescents. It was waiting for her, bathed in colored light, and when she stepped up and turned around I nearly gasped. It was like seeing her on a real stage with throngs in the audience all around us. The light played off of her hair, rendering it a brilliant gold with red and blue streaks. Her face and body contour were enhanced with sharp, deep shadows, completing her visual transformation into a professional singer.

Cole Porter's famous piece has been played in every possible style of jazz, and, often, the tempo is slow with a lot of feeling and other times played with jump and jive. I like it slow and so does Brenna. It gives her time to give it the perfect sentimentality and gives me an opportunity to study the beautiful woman singing it.

I started with several bars of introduction, as Cole Porter intended, and then nodded to her to come in. She started, hesitantly at first, still intimidated by the others and thrown off by her new circumstances. The other instruments and the drums came in quietly and then played around the edges of her voice. She obviously felt the power and support of the four of us and started to relax and put her emotions into the words. I looked up at her when I could and realized that she had turned toward me, her eyes were on my face, her smile directed at me and me alone. The moment welled up moisture to my eyes which caused a brief bit of panic when I had difficulty seeing the sheet music. At the end of the song, the climactic moment, she opened her arms toward me and smiled as the last word poured out of her, her head and body arched backward in a natural but stunning way.

We applauded wildly and then I realized that there were more hands clapping than we had. Through the door emerged Freddie followed by a large bearded fellow grasping a big brass saxophone. They had been quietly lurking on the stairs, listening, until she finished. She turned to see who it was just as they both bowed toward her and continued clapping.

"Marvelous!" Freddie said. "You were right. She can sing." His large companion seemed to also agree and was smiling and nodding about it. "Nice touch, the stage. Makes her look pro already," he added, fixing her with his little ferret eyes. We all knew why they were here. Not to play with us or to show off their skills. It was to scope out Brenna.

Freddie nodded toward me, a brief acknowledgment that I was alive. He held up his arm and pointed to his friend. "This is Pete. You all know him, I'm sure. He's simply the best horn player in the area and sought by every band for a hundred miles." Pete grinned and looked around the room for approval. I had never heard of him or seen him play, but I was never a frequent in the kind of places he likely performed. The others knew him, it was obvious, and given his reception, he was respected for his skill.

Brenna stood still, watching Freddie silently, as he stood a foot below her, looking up at her face which was shrouded in colored light from above. I didn't understand what she was thinking but found myself hoping his little barrage of compliments weren't getting through.

"Well, Brenna. As I recall, you agreed to sing for us, and we are here to play any piece that you choose. What will it be?" He stood waiting for a reply, and I saw her glance at me. Was she asking for my approval or a suggestion of music?

I ventured a suggestion, a number that we both had played many times and were both comfortable with. *"Love For Sale,"* I called out. Another Cole Porter piece which, when played and sung with emotion, was perfect for her. I saw a hint of smile when she heard me.

"Know that one, Pete?" Freddie asked. Pete swayed his head from side to side indicating that he either didn't know it, or more likely, didn't like it. Freddie turned back to Brenna, shrugged and smiled. He ignored me. From somewhere, Freddie produced a couple of pages which he handed to Brenna. "What about this one?" he asked. I had the feeling that these two boys were only going to play their own numbers, no matter what they had promised her.

She took the music and studied it for a moment before answering. She handed the music back and said, "I have heard it many times but have never sung it." I was dying to know what the piece was, and I got up and took it from Freddie. It was the *I Left My Heart In San Francisco* number which we had all heard Tony Bennett sing so many times. I had never played it either. Besides, Freddie's music was written using guitar tabs, making it nearly impossible to translate to the piano keyboard on the fly.

"Don't worry in the least, we will guide you along. All you have to do is sing the words as written, and we'll do the rest," Freddie suggested smoothly, his black little eyes flashing at me then back to her. To my surprise, she took the music from his offered hand and, with one last look, nodded that she would do it.

"Got some extra copies. Need one Dan?" he asked, flashing his tight little smile at me.

"That won't work on a keyboard. No...you can manage without me, I'm sure," I answered. Brenna had voiced one demand and only one. That I play with her. It wasn't like her to change her mind easily, and I was intrigued to learn what was going to happen.

After a few minutes, they were ready to go, with Freddie wearing Mike's spare guitar and big Pete standing against the far wall. Doug, Tom and Mike were also ready but looked a little lost. They had no music and were expected to play a relatively modern jazz piece in a yet unannounced key. Our guests were about to show off for all of us, and that included Brenna.

Just as they were warming up their instruments, Brenna reached behind her head and pulled something, and the result was a cascade of shimmering gold hair which fell behind her back and swayed there, catching all the males by surprise. She didn't have to say a word. With the removal of a simple stay, she had taken control of the room. There was something about her, the way she was holding her head level, even a little up, and the way her smooth face presented itself. It was the classic female method of domination on display, creating a humbling lust that cannot be fulfilled. She was the most important object in the room, not the professional musicians. Brenna innately knew how to use her potent good looks when she wanted to, but it was the first time I had actually seen her do it. We were all forced to take another appraisal of her, and this time we saw the curve of her hips and the swell of her breasts caught in the sharp light, but it was the subtle way she moved that was spellbinding.

The music started, Freddie leading with the melody and Tom's drums forcing a rhythm. Brenna started singing while holding the paper up in the light. Her voice was pure and clear, and when she took a breath, the saxophone broke in, spinning the melody in another, but harsher, direction. Yes, Freddie and Pete were pros, no doubt about it, but they were secondary to Brenna. It was her presence on stage and her voice that entered our brains, her emotions which entered through our skin. She owned the room.

At the second repeat, she dropped the papers on the floor and took hold of the mike, pulling it away from the stand and turned to face me. The last remaining bars of this romantic number she meant for Dan and nobody else. I felt their eyes on me, the jealousy about our moment evident. She had allowed them to feast on her for a too brief instant, but she was mine for life. Now I understood what she had done. She had taken revenge on them for their arrogance and rewarded me in front of them.

When she finished and the instruments came to rest, she stepped off the stage and came to me, finally standing behind me, resting her warm hands on my shoulders and pulling herself against my appreciative back. "You were a wonder up there,

Brenna. I am in awe of you," I said so that only she could hear. Her hand patted me softly.

Pete was first, and he stood in front of the keyboard trying to look through me to her. I could tell that he was sincere, like a little boy who had just seen something he didn't clearly understand. "That was really excellent. If you ever want to go professional, I can make it happen," he said. "I'd consider it a great honor to play with you again tonight or at any time." After he spoke, he just stood there as if he was out of words. It softened him in my eyes, and I began to like him after all.

"Thank you, Pete," she said over my shoulder. "No more tonight though," she added, to his disappointment.

They all filed up, with Freddie the Great not looking so arrogant this time. "Fantastic. The best I've discovered in a good while. I wasn't expecting anything like what I've seen and heard," Freddie gushed. "I don't know where you learned all that..." he paused trying to form the idea more clearly, wanting to avoid the explicit mention of her sex appeal. "But if you can do that in front of an audience, you'll become a sensation. Is there any chance I can introduce you..."

She didn't let him finish. "Nope," her small voice said from behind me. There was no malice in it, nor simple dismissal, just a statement of fact which didn't allow or require explanation.

With frequent backward glances at Brenna, Pete and Freddie picked up their gear and slunk out, giving everyone a last wave, and giving Brenna a wistful last look as their heads disappeared up the stairs.

"I'm glad that's over," Doug admitted. We all nodded the truth of what he said but, at the same time, realizing there was something which had come to us as a result. We felt closer as a group. It was an us moment, where we felt protective of one another, valued each other all the more because of the attempted humiliation. It was our little singer who had carried the day for the men. We owed her.

Chapter Five

Emergency

*H*er call came as I was driving north, on my way that fine Saturday morning with so many plans for the day ahead, all spent in Brenna's company. Little did I know how plans can suddenly change.

"Are you almost here?" she said. I detected some stress, a crack, in a heretofore always melodious voice.

"Thirty minutes, depending on traffic. Something wrong?" I asked, but my heart knew there was something amiss.

"Just not feeling well. I have a tummy ache and had a bad night. I'll feel better when you are here." It was a lot of information, a ton of it. She would never complain to me of a minor problem. My mind raced ahead and dozens of horrors, each worse than the previous, whorled in my vision.

"Have you thrown up?"

"Not yet, but I have that feeling."

"What's your temperature?"

"Didn't take it, but I feel hot."

"Had anything to eat or drink?" I wondered.

"No…nothing." The list was still long and included such temporary afflictions as transient viruses all the way to life-threatening emergencies. I felt myself becoming agitated, and my speed increased.

"Can I bring you anything?"

"Just you."

"On the way." I shortened the trip by breaking the law, but I arrived safely in front of her apartment and bounded up the stairs. I used my key instead of knocking as I usually did. She was on the living room couch, and I could see her pale color from across the room. I knelt beside her and felt her pulse as I affectionately touched her face. Her skin was hot, and she had the glint of perspiration on her forehead as well as a rapid pulse.

"Anything hurt?" I asked.

Instead of answering, she placed her open hand lightly across her lower abdomen. I pulled it away and gently touched the area using the tips of my fingers. It was lower abdomen tenderness, mostly on the right side, and when I pulled away suddenly, she gasped in pain. The symptoms of appendicitis were notorious long before treatment was available, but removal of the appendix has become common over the past hundred or so years. Of course, there are other pathologies which present as similar, but they all have one thing in common; diagnosis and treatment should be undertaken quickly.

"You have to go to the Emergency Room...right now," I said. She didn't register any surprise, just resignation, combined with distress. She had been thinking the same thing, I believe. I stood up digging for my phone, wondering if I should look up the number for an ambulance and considering where she should go.

"You take me in, Daniel," she murmured. I stopped in thought. Could I carry her safely down the stairs, and could she ride in the backseat comfortably? There was no time to waste trying to decide. I bent down and scooped her up, finding that she was light, a small precious package, more valuable to me than any other thing I could possibly hold. She held onto my neck, and we started down the stairs toward the car.

"You'll stay with me?" she said in little gasps.

"Every second that they will allow."

We arrived safely at the University Hospital's emergency entrance, and before I could even open the door, an orderly arrived with a wheelchair, ready to assist. I insisted on being the one to lift her from the backseat, and even then, I managed to cause her to cry out in pain. She was in trouble, and the process, whatever it was, was accelerating. I felt my mouth go dry even though I had seen my share of emergencies. It was different when the victim was so close, so…all those thoughts.

It was an efficiently run facility, and they quickly got her into a treatment room to be examined as I hurriedly filled in the necessary paper work for her. When I returned to her room, there was a tall young man bending over and going over her with his stethoscope. He turned toward me with concern as I came in.

"You related?" he asked the necessary question.

"Not yet," I admitted.

He paused for a moment, then asked, "Is there a next of kin?"

"I'm it," I lied, but there may as well not be a next of kin. Anyway, I wouldn't have any idea of how to get in touch with her mother, not that it would matter.

"She's a sick gal," he expressed the obvious. "We're going to get a lab profile, CBC and radiographs...and an ultrasound. She will likely need surgery today. Any prior medical history?"

"Unexplained sterility. That's all as far as I know."

He frowned. "That's interesting. She appears to have a typical appendicitis, but I've been fooled a few times. We'll see what General Surgery says." He folded his scope and put it way, nodding to me on the way out. I reached for Brenna's hand.

"That's what you thought, isn't it?" she asked.

"Yes. If that is it, they just cut it out, and you go home. Very routine." I was trying to be somewhat flippant but didn't feel that way at all. I was scared. So was Brenna. Her brow was wet with sweat, and she had lost the sparkle in her eyes. The IV dripped endlessly and silently as we waited for something to happen.

We didn't have long to wait when the enclosing drapes snapped back to show a gurney and a couple of nurses who efficiently moved beside her and started making preparations to move her over. "You can wait in the waiting room or in her room, sir. She's going to radiology and then straight up to her room." She handed me a slip of paper with the room number. I stood back and watched Brenna's face as she did the transfer. She arched her back in pain and grimaced but never cried out. It was one of those moments when men have to re-learn what they should have always known. Pound for pound, women are much tougher than men. They can handle pain which will make us pound the bed and scream for our mothers...or our wives.

I walked beside the gurney holding her arm as long as they would let me, finally stopped by a set of double doors and a hard look from the nurse. As Brenna disappeared down the hallway, my heart sank in my chest. I knew that a simple appendectomy is, in general, trouble free, but I couldn't relax and accept things until it was over, and I had her back in my arms again. I knew enough to realize that disasters often occur when you least expect and that simple things can be complex in the end.

I waited alone in the empty room assigned to Brenna. Waiting is the worst part, that is, if you are not the patient. Waiting and worrying is yet ever worse, and that is what I was doing. I looked out the window at the parking lot four stories below, and over the roof installations of a lower adjoining building, and at my watch, and at the hallway as people and staff went by, and thirty-seven minutes went by in agony. The worn lounge chair was uncomfortable, and each time I heard a gurney go by, I jumped up. Lost in thought and worry, I thought back about our time together over the past five years. It seemed like a dream or fantasy which had passed too quickly. Life is like that; you only get a string of little intense fragments either good or bad to remember, and the rest is a blur. We had had some great times together and never any bad ones. If something happened to her, I could never get past it. I tried to put despondent thoughts out of my mind. The problem was that on this issue, I knew too much, and the possibilities kept on ticking past. I was helpless to make any difference or change anything. My part had been to recognize the danger and get her to care quickly, but now that it is done, I know she is going to surgery, and I can't stand to think of her being cut.

A head appeared in the doorway looking at me. "She's on her way back up," she said and disappeared again. Thank goodness. I started to pace, wondering about the results of the test and what was to come next. From down the hall came the familiar sound of the elevator door, and I leaned out to watch. It was her. I could see the lustrous hair and the top of her nose. The IV bag swayed back and forth as they moved forward. At the nurse's station, it paused, and one of the nurses came out to inspect her, and I could see her conversing with Brenna. I moved out into the hall just as the nurse held a clipboard for her to sign, then allowed her to start moving forward again.

"Hi," I said trying to be warm and cuddly. She looked worse and didn't respond except to look at me briefly. The nurse still holding the clipboard saw me look at her in a questioning way.

"Consent for surgery," the nurse answered my unasked question. The gurney started moving toward Brenna's room, and I held back for a moment.

"She going down soon?" I inquired.

"Ask the surgeon, Dr. Grimes. He'll be along shortly, I expect."

I hurried to the room just as she was being off-loaded again. More agony this time, and she had at least one or two more transfers to make. I was impatient to see the surgeon and wished that she was already in surgery to spare her any more pain. Two nurses came in and busied themselves getting her properly admitted. A pain pump was placed and activated, and I watched as Brenna relaxed.

An older physician in a white lab coat swept into the room and looked around. "You her family?" he asked.

"Yes." And I was, at least in my soul I was.

"I'm Dr. Grimes, the surgeon. The laboratory and radiographic studies support the provisional diagnosis of appendicitis. We are shortly going to surgery with her. Do you have any questions?" He stood there and patiently waited until my head cleared. One glance at him and I knew that he had done this procedure more times than could be counted. He was authoritative in the surgeon's way, but his face showed his kindness and his humanity. Dr. Grimes inspired immediate trust. I had no questions so he rapidly departed, the pressing needs of his specialty on this Saturday evening demanding his attention elsewhere.

I sat by the bed in the provided chair and couldn't take my eyes off of her. As many times as I had seen her, I never had as long a time to study her face. Over and over, I traced the contours of her lips and nose with my eyes and then moved on to her perfect ears. I spent some time on her forehead and her hair which lay in exquisite disarray. What a perfect creation she was, lovely beyond any words and lovely beyond any attempted creation of her image in any media. Only occasionally could I get a glimpse of her open eyes which flickered only long enough to know that I was still there. Ah, the eyes are said to be the key to the soul, and I sense that it is true when her eyes look back into mine. She knew that I was there, because occasionally her hand would open expectantly, waiting for mine which would quickly arrive. It seemed to go on forever that way, and the only interruption was the coming and going of the nursing staff.

Finally, an anesthesiologist appeared, clipboard in hand, to evaluate her for anesthesia. "Hi, I'm Doctor Bigings," he said with a smile. "Some of the nursing staff call me Dr. Big, but I won't admit to it or answer to it." I didn't think it was very funny, and Brenna was out of it, so his humor fell awfully flat. He briefly listened to her chest and aroused her for a response and then turned to me. "We are about set to go on this, and it will be within the hour. Cases like hers are unpredictable for time, but I assume it will take about 45 minutes for the surgery and then some time in recovery. She will be gone from the room for about two or three hours, and you can wait here or go down to the surgery waiting area. That would be better, of course, and her surgeon will be able to come out and tell you what happened."

I already knew this from experience but thanked him as if I didn't know anything. I didn't want to know anything and was trying to erase what I did know from my mind. More waiting, but soon I could hear the OR gurney coming for her. She aroused in anticipation but soon was holding her abdomen again. They moved her to the gurney and, with a few nods to me, took off down the hall with her, me in tow. I held her hand until the last moment, until she disappeared into the maw of the open OR doors. The last thing I remember was her attempting to look at me until the doors came between us. I have been through similar doors thousands of times, and I would have been comfortable just walking in, but I knew I couldn't. Even if I was allowed in, I couldn't bear to watch her surgery.

I asked for directions to the waiting room and proceeded to it. In such an area, you can spend a lot of time just watching people and trying to figure them and their situation out. Anything for distraction, to not concentrate on what is happening to someone you care about just yards from where you are. I paced, read, thought, nodded at people, drank a cola and worried. One of the OR staff finally came out to tell me that they were getting done and not to leave since the surgeon wanted to talk to me. She said that was all the information she could tell me at this time. I watched for movement at the door like a predator waiting to strike.

One of the staff eventually came along and, since I was the only one remaining in the waiting area, led me to a conference room. Shortly, Dr. Grimes came in and shook my sweaty hand. "Well, it was appendicitis just as we thought, and I feel that we caught it before it ruptured. Because there was a lot of swelling, we made an incision in the abdominal wall and removed the appendix that way, but the incision is small. We didn't see any perforation, but we are going to keep her in for a while for observation and for antibiotics." Just as I thought he was finished, he seemed to recall the other item of interest. "Because of her history of sterility, we had a good look at her reproductive organs from inside, and one of the gynecology staff who was available examined the pelvic area. There are no abnormalities that we could see. If you are the male involved, I suggest that you get tested. She appears to be normal."

He efficiently covered all that needed to be said in an unbroken monolog. No need to tell him that I wasn't the one concerned about her reproductive capacity...at least not yet. I nodded approval but didn't say much. I didn't voice any of my many worries. I didn't tell him how anxious I was to have her back to her old self. He didn't care anything about that and who can say that he should? I thanked him for his efforts, and he left without further comment. After all, it was now one o'clock on Sunday morning, and he was still down here at the hospital. Even surgeons have to sleep some time.

Now that I knew she was out of the OR and her condition treated, I realized how hungry I was. The cafeteria was closed, but I found some vending machines and loaded up on snacks and another cola. I ate some, and the rest I took to Brenna's room to wait for her.

By the time she arrived, I had dozed off in the chair, and I awakened with a start, stumbling a little when I got up, drawing a little chuckle from the orderly pushing her bed into the room. I shot him a hard look for I was not in a forgiving mood. He and the nurse moved her to her bed, and I saw that she was still heavily sedated and appeared to be mostly unaware of where she was. She looked up at me once and then fell back asleep. Her beautiful hair was matted from sweat and the hairnet. Some dried drool was at the corners of her mouth, and adhesive tape residue was still on her face. You could expect her not to look her best under these conditions, but I promise you that she was more stunning than ever. She was a porcelain casting by Michelangelo, sort of a fallen angel, slain but perfect.

I had time to kill, and I used up the battery in my phone looking up post-operative care of the appendectomy patient. There was also plenty of time to think about her and us that night. One of the things I often ponder is the nature of attraction between men and women. Songs are sung about it; plays and dissertations are written about it, and history is rife with it, but I still didn't understand it. Each time I glanced at her, I felt overwhelmed with affection and attraction. Never had I tired of looking at her. There must be a switch which gets turned on in our heads when the right person comes along. Best yet is when her switch goes on at the same time yours does. Her sleeping form, turned slightly to her left, made me realize that she was the most attractive living creature I had ever seen. Or did I just think so because I loved her? Parting from her even for a day was hard, but for forever, I couldn't even contemplate. I suddenly felt the need to reach out and touch her, but I resisted in order not to awaken her.

As I stood there, I recalled the time that I impulsively insisted that we catch the ferry across Lake Michigan. We had no luggage and just walked on, two carefree lovers on an adventure together. It was a two-hour ride across the cold lake in the early spring. Before we left the dock, I conceived visions of her hair blowing in the wind as we peered across the empty vastness looking for the Michigan shoreline. It didn't turn out that way because of the strong, cold wind generated by the forward motion of the ship. We hid in the windless area on the rear stern behind the passenger compartment and huddled together until we could no longer stand the cold and went inside. Once disembarked, we had a full day just walking around and seeing the sights and later were fortunate enough to get a room in a small bed and breakfast perched on a hill overlooking the lake. Brenna had to get back for a political event on Sunday, and we were able to hire a small plane for the crossing Sunday morning. The memory of her happy and smiling as we strolled along holding hands will remain with me for the rest of my life.

Finally, sleep came over me, but the nurse returned several times, gleefully turning on the overhead lights, so by morning I felt as drugged as Brenna. She slowly awakened, and by the time sunlight streamed in, she was quite alert.

When the time was right, I got up and leaned over so that we were face to face. "Welcome back," I said with a grin.

She continued to look into my eyes and slowly put her hands to my cheeks and held my face softly. "Thanks for saving my life again, Daniel. Without you, there are no tomorrows." She stated this with precision and had obviously been thinking about the words. My emotions were so strong that I couldn't say anything in return, and after a moment, she reached across my cheek and brushed away a tear without comment. I would do anything for her, even die for her, so this was a small thing, and it was what anyone would have done under the circumstances. To have her back, out of danger, was all the thanks I wanted.

She still had not had anything to eat or drink, and I was sure no orders had been written until rounds were made. I heard several voices in the hall outside the room, and I got up to check it out. It was the surgery resident staff making morning rounds and heading our way. There were about a dozen of them, and they appeared to range from medical students to senior surgery residents. They moved as an attached mass and floated from room to room, busy in conversation.

I quickly explained to Brenna what was going to happen. With concern on her face, she asked, "All of them are going to examine me?"

"I'm afraid so. This is a teaching hospital, and that's how it's done," I explained.

"Is my surgeon with them?" she inquired.

"I didn't see him," I answered. I could see a set look come to her face which told me that she was going to have a say in this.

In they came, all of them. With a rustle of footsteps and ruffling of white lab coats, they formed a circle around the foot and sides of her bed. One of the older resident surgeons asked if I would mind stepping out of the room. I understood the drill and complied, but I couldn't help thinking that they would be better off with me in there. I was standing just outside when one of the residents partially closed the door in my face. Catching glimpses of her face between elbows, I could hear most of what was said. She was half-sitting up and looking from face to face, placidly but with intensity, and fully awake. They were being given a synopsis of treatment by one of the younger ones and were all looking at her or intermittently at Brenna. When the visit came around to an actual physical examination, things evidently changed, because the door suddenly opened, and all the young doctors streamed out of the room, the door closing behind them. Knowing what had happened, I smiled at them as a group, because they had clustered on the opposite side of the door from me. Brenna had no intention of letting herself be exposed or examined in front of a group and had them thrown out. Suddenly, the door opened again, and the senior resident beckoned me to come in. He graciously accepted her resolve and was very polite about it. Her quiet determination and tight lips meant that she had reached her limit of cooperation. She glanced at me, but there was no softening of her face.

Dr. Tremonti introduced himself as chief resident, and explained that he needed to change her abdominal dressing, but she had required that I be present. I nodded and went to the foot of the bed as an observer. He was very gentle and talked to both of us as he removed the bloodstained dressing to get a look at the wound. I was struck at the short length of the incision over the appendix area which had been closed meticulously and definitely was not typical of abdominal closures that I had seen.

Before he left, Dr. Tremonti added, "She needs to be here until about midweek for the IV's and to look for any complications. I want to inform you, though, there are some risks of GI problems associated with aggressive antibiotic therapy, and we may need an infectious disease consult for her."

After Dr. Tremonti left, I returned to sit beside her, but she crooked her finger for me to come closer. As I did, she used it to sweep across the stubble on my chin while inspecting me closely. "You look worse than I do. Did you even sleep last night? And when did you last eat?" she asked.

"I'm fine; don't worry about me. I'm here for you, and nothing else matters," I responded.

"Here is what you are going to do, Daniel." She was looking very intense and serious. I had a hard time not smiling at her. "You are going over to my place to eat, clean up, and also to rest. And don't come back until you do! And, by the way, bring me back some personals like underwear and toothbrush and so on.

You know what I need." She reached up and patted my cheek, none too delicately to make her point. One thing I have learned is that when she makes up her mind you might as well do what she wants. Not only was I really bushed, I could smell myself. She was right. I had to eat sometime, and she really needed some things from home. I leaned over and kissed her on the forehead, then over both closed eyes and lastly on her nose. Touching her head, I reluctantly left, resolved to return as soon as possible.

It was about two hours later when I returned, clean but not rested nor fed. I had gathered up some personal things for her and had called Mike, informing him of what was happening. It was amazing how much emotion came out of him, and he was very relieved to know that it was largely over. That's what I thought until I rounded the corner and turned into her room. The smell hit me like a punch. I recognized the odor of diarrhea, and I knew that it was not a good sign. She was lying there looking pale and fragile. Dr. Tremonti and one of his resident staff were standing by the bed looking at her records.

When he saw me, Dr. Tremonti motioned for me to go back out into the hall. He followed me and pulled me out of earshot of Brenna. "She is having some problems associated with the aggressive antibiotic regimen, as I feared, but we caught it early. We are going to get a culture and look for Clostridia and treat accordingly, but I am afraid she is in for a rough post-operative course." He looked sincere and concerned. There was no choice but to accept what he said and hope for the best. Dr. Tremonti pointed to his resident and instructed, "Take a stool and blood culture stat and get her started on Metronidazol. And stop the other antibiotics right now." The resident nodded and quickly headed for the nursing station.

I returned to her side and slid my hand into hers. She was warm, and there was a hint of blue around her eyes. She told me that she started having problems soon after I left, and her abdominal pain had worsened. I knew I shouldn't have gone, but I also knew that I could not have changed the course of events had I been with her full time. The poor thing hadn't eaten since this started about 48 hours previously. This time I was going to rot there if I had to instead of leaving. With her new problem, I knew she should not be visited, and there was a chance that she would be put into isolation. While she was looking at me and not protesting, I called Mike to prevent a visit. He seemed to understand and said that he would be checking in with me frequently to see how things were going.

The surgical resident and two nurses descended on the room and commenced following Dr. Tremonti's instructions. The nurse informed me that Brenna had to go to radiology right away for an update.

After she left, I sat alone, despondent. My new little friend, Nurse Benedict, came walking in and stood in front of me. "I thought you were on the night shift," I questioned.

"It varies," she replied. "Say, we are all impressed how you are sticking with Miss Christensen without a break or food."

"I'm loyal," I offered.

"Yes, you are." As always, she was very direct. "We have a couple of trays left over from patients who were discharged early, and we would like to invite you to come back to the break room and get something to eat."

She was right. I was getting weak from hunger but couldn't pull myself away from Brenna, and I just couldn't eat in front of her. I slowly looked her over and saw for the first time the strength of personality in this small woman. "I would be grateful; please lead the way," I finally answered. She led me back to a small room behind the nursing station and closed the door behind me.

On the table were two food trays containing a variety of dishes, bread and juice. There were also two young nurses sitting and working on their paperwork. "I hope I won't bother you," I asked them before sitting down.

"No, no, we have been planning this for a while, and we are glad you agreed," they twittered together. It was delightful eating with them and talking. There was a great depth of knowledge and interest in Brenna which reflected much discussion about her. They were all concerned but confident that she would be better soon. I gathered that Dr. Tremonti was very well thought of professionally and also had developed a female fan club. A nurse opened the door and told us that Brenna was on the way up from radiology. I thanked each of them, especially Mary Benedict, for this act of kindness and headed back to the room.

Brenna was pale and limp but seemed to want to talk to me. I pulled my chair up as close as I could and leaned over and grasped her forearm and listened. She wanted to talk about Tyler, her mother, and how their relationship fell apart. Some time ago, I met Tyler, and I had no doubts about the nature of their mother-daughter friction. Brenna had been close with her father, who was a big gruff teddy bear and would do anything for his little girl, sometimes to the irritation of his wife. To judge someone, however, you need all the facts, and Brenna, for some reason, wanted to tell me her mother's history.

Tyler was the fourth of seven children and grew up on a small chicken farm in the Texas Panhandle. Her father was an alcoholic and eventually wandered off during her childhood, leaving the family to fend for themselves. Her mother took in a friendly but jobless male as a companion, and together, both of them took out life's hardships on the children. One by one, as they neared their middle teens, they left for good without looking back. About fifteen, Tyler left also, catching a bus for San Angelo. She had no money, no belongings but was leather-tough from her upbringing. Forced to lie about her age, she landed a menial job at the Goodfellow Air Force Base. She lived in the back room of a gas station for a time before she teamed up with another worker and got a small room together. Since she was born at home and her mother had since moved on, there was no birth certificate. A friendly clerical worker at the base helped to create her history, somewhat fictionally, and she acquired a State of Texas birth certificate with her age posted ahead about three years.

Now legal, she went on the prowl for a man and found the kind and generous mate she was searching for in Captain Matt Christensen. He was an intelligence officer, much her senior but fell madly in love with the little dark-haired sprite from west Texas. Even his great capacity for love and his big bear tenderness couldn't soften Tyler, who had been raised without affection. She remained aloof and withdrawn throughout their life together. Matt and Tyler managed to produce one child, Brenna, and Matt poured all his love into her. He quit the Air Force so that he could spend more time with Brenna and her mother and eventually found work at an aerospace firm. At any event in Brenna's life, Big Matt was there for her. They sometimes traveled together, just the two of them, and if she ever needed anything, it was Matt who gave it to her, without any questions. As far as I can tell, both Matt and Tyler had no contact with other relatives while Brenna was growing up, and now that Tyler was back in Texas, Brenna was alone, except for me, and I wasn't going anywhere. She still couldn't talk about her father's death or any precipitating event leading up to it. Someday, perhaps, but I didn't want her depressed at this time, so I was eager to avoid this topic.

She looked at me for a long time, then asked, "Daniel, am I going to die?" She was very serious, and the question had to be answered without platitudes.

"No, Brenna, not now, not yet," I said with gravity. "No one dies from appendicitis these days. They will straighten this out soon, and you will again amaze everyone with your singing."

She smiled, and her eyes teared, but she didn't look away from me. I didn't want to show anything but confidence and steadiness, and I didn't want to show the fear that I actually felt. It wasn't the time to tell her that I loved her, adored her and couldn't live without her. She knew that anyway just by looking into my face. That kind of communication, straight from the soul, is evermore intimate than physical contact. Brenna only had one thing of value in her life and that was her beautiful self. There were few friends and only one uncaring relative in the world for her. But she had me, for whatever I was worth, and in my heart, I had already taken the vow that I would be with her for life or for as long as she wanted me.

Time went by without any more conversation, and she gradually drifted off to sleep, relaxing her hand over mine. She would frequently awaken, experiencing bouts of diarrhea, abdominal pain with spiking fever, which seemed to diminish as the day wore on. Later that evening, I heard a noise at the door, and I turned to see one of the young nurses that I had conversed with while eating. She motioned for me to come out into the hall, and I complied without waking Brenna.

"Some men are here asking about Brenna. They say that they know you both. Do you think they should come in or should I send them away?"

Instantly I knew who they were. "Are there any orders regarding visitors?" I asked.

"No," she replied.

Pausing and thinking for a moment, I felt that she could see them for just a short time if she was prepared. "Could you see if she needs the bed pan now and signal me when she is ready?" She said that would work, and I headed toward the nurse's station to meet Doug, Mike and Tom, who were milling around in the hall.

"Gee, we are sorry, Dan, for coming over anyway. We know that you didn't want visitors, but Brenna is important to us also," Tom explained. They all were fidgeting and looking around nervously, unfamiliar with and uncomfortable in hospitals. Tom had two drumsticks tucked into his pants, and Doug was carrying a small black instrument case. I held off saying anything until the nurse stuck her head out of Brenna's room and gave me a chin up.

"I appreciate your coming very much, but this can't be a long visit."

Mike spoke for the three of them, "We know, but we would like to show her that we care. We'll leave soon, I promise."

I put my arm over Mike's shoulder, and we walked down the hall to her room and went in. The nurse had done wonders getting her cleaned up. She was sitting more upright, her hair had been brushed out, and the coverlet was straight and pulled tight. She didn't look as desperately sick as she really was and seemed happy to see them. They lined up at the foot of her bed, grinning from ear to ear. She smiled back, and the energy in the room had to be good for her. When they looked at each other awkwardly, it was apparent something was afoot.

Doug pulled out a nice little uke from its case, and Tom drew out his sticks, and with a quick count, he started tapping a rhythm on her bedstead. They started singing, all three of them, accompanied by Doug's picking and strumming of his uke and Tom's rhythmically tapping on the bedstead, the drapes, the chair and occasionally on Mike's head.

The song they had chosen was *You're The Top* by the magical Cole Porter, and Brenna's hands went to her mouth in exclamation, eyes wide open.

By the end of the first stanza, Brenna was streaming tears of joy and smiling as broadly as I had ever seen her do. I noticed that a small crowd, consisting of three nurses, a resident physician, and standing behind them, an elderly male patient pushing an IV pole, had gathered in the hall outside the room. I was amazed at the antics, the joy and the respect they brought to Brenna that night. They continued, without hesitation, to the delight of everyone in earshot.

As soon as they finished, Brenna threw up her arms in that distinctively female way, her arms slightly hyperextended and her palms facing forward. One by one they came around and bent over for an embrace and kiss. The little audience applauded briefly and went on their way.

All I could say was, "Wow, how did you manage that in a few hours?"

Mike answered, "We didn't; we've been working on it for two weeks. It was always meant to be a present for Brenna."

This was nearly the most cool thing I had ever witnessed, but poor Brenna was visibly worn out. They all noticed the change and nodded to me with recognition and resignation that they would have to leave. Doug pulled me aside and whispered privately, "We know that you have been here almost full-time with her, and each of us would like to give you a little break this week."

What a nice offer, and timely too, as I was due back to work the next day, and my obligations made it hard for me to not come in. I decided that if she was worse or still the same by 5:00 AM then I would stay with her. If she was better, I would be grateful for some help. Other than me, she had no one but this small group of friends to rely on, and it would be a comfort to have someone with her.

Tom and Mike were nearby and agreed, giving a thumbs up to indicate that they were supportive also. I went around, shaking their hands with gratitude, and after a quick goodbye to Brenna, they left together. What an amazing group of people we had found. You can go through your whole life knowing a large number of people but without finding true friends, and here we had three. The PA system was instructing all visitors to leave, and as the lights in the halls dimmed, I sat down again, held her hand and settled in for a little rest.

Except for the nurses coming and going, we had a quiet night. I helped when I could, and when she was allowed to get up to go the toilet, I guided her there and back. Mostly, we both drifted in and out of sleep, and there was little conversation. About 5:00 AM, I decided that she was better, and I asked her how she felt about me going to work.

"By all means, go to work, Daniel; I'm really feeling much better, and you shouldn't worry about me at all." She had those big eyes which reminded me of a little girl while she spoke. Of course, she would say that, I thought, but should I leave? After talking to her more at length about how she felt and a quick call to Doug to make sure he would come in, I decided to leave. Doug gave his assurances that he would call me if anything changed and would arrive by 6:00 AM. Brenna and I exchanged a long, lingering kiss goodbye, and our hands slid apart with fingertips reluctant to part. I said goodbye to the nurses on my way out and tried not to think beyond the now.

Chapter Six

Multiple Personalities

There was a lot of time to think as I drove the eighty miles back to work, and being alone, I could choose the topic, but the only thought I could think was of Brenna, and she went around and around in my head as she often does when I'm awake or asleep.

I smiled to myself as I recalled the many times she pretended to be someone from another country. One of the crazy things she does that I love her so much for. She has rather high cheekbones and has been told that she looks Russian or Czech by several people. At times she suddenly becomes Russian, complete with accent. She carries her head high, adopting an aloof attitude as she becomes Sasha, the beautiful Russian émigré, who is both sought-after and wealthy. Everyone is her servant. "Danyeel, don't you like your leetle Sasha eney mooore?" She looks down her nose at me, and I break up, but she doesn't skip a beat. "Yoour cooontry es so hard to understand. Your peepole so deeferent." I nod with resignation, and we go on. She can stay in this mode for hours, causing me to beg her to stop and act normal. She won't and ignores me. She is completely unconcerned what people think during these episodes, and I have learned to dread them. For some reason, she always wears darkly tinted contacts over her naturally blue eyes when she is Russian, but she wears green when she is "petite April", the French girl.

The absolute worst for me is when she becomes Southern. She is either "May Belle" or "Mary Jane", and they are very different. I would characterize May Belle as poor white trash and Mary Jane as a Southern belle. The May Belle character is loud, has poor manners and wears cheap clothing and sneakers. At least Mary Jane is feminine, even though she faints easily and calls everyone "honey child." I hate to go shopping with May Belle, who stops at every window, points and acts awkward. I can't believe this sweet, attractive woman will act like she does in public and then can be so sophisticated and dignified the next day. She revels in my embarrassment. If I ask her which is the real Brenna, she just looks at me with her big eyes and says, "Which one do you want me to be?" The answer, Brenna, is that I love them all, because, in some way, they are all you.

As the long road goes by under my tires, I have an inspiration. The answer to the band's problem with Brenna could be easily solved. What if we could get May Belle to sing the blues? Why didn't I think of that sooner? I continue to drive, lost in thought, occasionally laughing aloud at my wild ideas. Suddenly recalling that I should call Doug to make sure he actually came to the hospital as he promised, I clicked on his number while I drove.

"Yup?" he answered.

"Hi, Doug, this is Daniel." No response. "Say, are you at the hospital or not?" I asked.

"Sure, I am." He sounded slightly offended. Another pause. He wasn't going to elaborate for me, I could tell.

"Everything OK with her?" I probed.

"She's eating breakfast, and I am looking at her," he answered. Something about his answer gave me some unpleasantness.

"Have the doctors been there yet?" I asked, trying to draw him out.

"Yeah, a whole bunch came in about fifteen minutes ago and chased me out. I don't know what they did," he said.

"How long are you going to stay with her this morning?" I asked.

Doug seemed to be preparing his response, eventually saying, "I don't get tired of looking at her." That's not what I really wanted to hear.

"Could you pass the phone to Brenna?"

There were some rustling sounds, and at last, Brenna's sweet voice came into my ear. "Hi, are you still driving?" she asked. There was a very slight crack in her voice.

"About halfway. You OK?" I answered.

"Dr. Tremonti was in and says that I am getting better. You could tell that, couldn't you?" she asked. There was a hidden compliment in there, but the truth is that I took a chance leaving her, and I am already regretting it.

"Are you dealing with Doug?" I inquired.

We both knew that Doug was hopelessly enchanted with her, but neither one of us would have guessed that he came just to stare at her. "Well, he's so cute, and he just sits there and looks at me without talking much. He's to get a break at midmorning, and Tom is supposed to take his place." I knew that she was looking at Doug as she spoke, but I doubted that he would get the hint.

"Say, I left my tablet computer there by the bed for you in case you've recovered enough to want to use it. It might take your mind off of Doug for awhile," I suggested.

"I can use your computer? You mean it?" she said in her little girl voice.

"Now, you are kidding me. You have a good day, and be sure to call me if you need anything. Another thing, please don't give Doug any encouragement, will you?" I pleaded.

"Y'all don't have to tell me that, honey child," she said and hung up.

Chapter Seven

Saved By A Nurse

My ninety minute return trip started about five that evening. Tom had called an hour earlier, explaining that he had to leave the hospital but for me not to worry, because she was better and eating. Doug had stayed until noon, relieved by Tom for a couple of hours, so she had company most of the day. When I was nearly there, I decided to stop by the shoe store and pick up a pair of shoes she had previously expressed interest in. I knew her sizes by heart, and I also knew exactly which ones she wanted. This diversion took only half an hour longer, and I was walking into her room by seven with the shoebox under my arm. I turned the corner into her room, expecting her to be waiting in bed, but she wasn't even in the room. I backed up, checking the door again for its number, just as I spotted her flowered personals case by the bed. It was her room, but where was she?

Frustrated, I looked around again, noticing my computer on her bed stand, and dimly wondered if she had managed to get into this very novel you are reading, a possibility I had overlooked. Of course, this story is mostly about her, and as you already know, Brenna is essentially placed on a pedestal in it, nearly worshiped by me. But...within those pages,

I had disclosed confidential information about a very, very, private person, and one who is easily wounded. I had been writing down what I experienced to get it out of my system and to record my memory of our lives together, and at that time, I really had not considered, even remotely, publication without at least extensive revision. No doubt I did the deed though, and if she had read it, she would not only be deeply hurt but also feel betrayed. I had only written the truth about her, and nothing I had put down would put her in a bad light, even the contrary. Forcing myself to believe there was another explanation for her absence, I sat down to wait.

Sitting there alone, I drifted off, but was awakened by a premonition that Brenna was returning to her room. I stepped into the hall to have a look, and there she was, shuffling along, using her IV pole as a support. A young nurse was alongside, helping her. One look and I knew that she had been crying. Not only that, she wouldn't look me in the face. There was an aura of hostility radiating from her nurse, who did want to catch my gaze and stared back with latent violence, but I avoided looking at her as I backed out of their way. She tucked Brenna in, and after a couple of final nasty looks in my direction, thankfully left. The room went dead silent. Brenna looked at the ceiling or kept her eyes closed to avoid me, willing me out of her existence.

No man lives long enough to avoid female wrath, and there are no known ways to avoid the associated pain. I just sat there, saying nothing. Saying nothing was better than an apology which would provoke an immediate emotional assault. Offering her the gift of shoes at this moment would show weakness and invite attack. I sat still and didn't dare to blink. Under such circumstances, silence has to be the best strategy, because you are demonstrating how much you care by just being there, and you don't try to get out of anything, because, in your view, you didn't do anything wrong. Inevitably, though, one of us had to speak first. I was genuinely concerned how she was doing, other than her probable anger at me, but asking about her health would appear as if I was avoiding the main issue. Not that I, for certain, knew what the issue was. I sat there in painful silence looking at the black TV screen. Waiting for the action to begin was agony.

At that critical moment in walked Nurse Riley, Brenna's experienced and wise senior nurse. One look and I knew she was fully aware of the current issue. She undoubtedly had talked to the young nurse who had wanted to string me up by the neck or cut me into little pieces. Her eyes darted around the room taking it all in as she quickly advanced to the bedside. She picked up Brenna's wrist, while pretending to take her pulse. "How are you, my dear?"

Brenna turned toward her, and I could see a slight tremble of her lower lip. She couldn't respond with words yet. Nurse Riley spotted the package of shoes, remarking brightly, "Well, Daniel, have you brought a gift to cheer Brenna up today?" She got my nod of permission and picked up the shoes, rattling the box. "May I open the box for you, Brenna?" she asked.

Brenna nodded, without looking at her. Amid a bit of rustling, she reached into the box and pulled out a pair of sleek purple stilettos. "Ooo! And from Italy, I see. Wow!" then she turned to me and exclaimed, "You have incredible taste for a man!" Continuing without a pause, she leaned over Brenna and said lowly, "You know, he is a keeper. He has been here two nights in that chair without sleep and has been pacing the halls in concern for you. I happen to know that he's the one who brought you here for treatment. Any one of us would run away with him if we had a chance." Her little sermon had its desired effect because, at last, Brenna turned her eyes on me, tears streaming freely down both cheeks. I could see a soft look returning in her face, a sort of pleading mixed with forgiveness. Standing up, I took her hand in mine as Nurse Riley silently withdrew.

I love those make-up-kisses, the tears, the puffy lips and hot breath kind. I quickly decided not to inquire about whatever grievous wrong I had committed that had upset her so, because it was so obviously about the book that I was writing. The shoes were still lying on the bed between her legs. "Color OK?" I asked.

Brenna wiped at her face with her palm and picked up one. "Perfect," she said with a little crooked smile and a shining moist face. She carefully extracted her feet from beneath the covers but couldn't bend forward enough to reach them. I helped, and there she lay in bed wearing a wrinkled hospital garment with ties in the back complemented by high heeled, spiked, purple, high fashion shoes. I suppressed a laugh which would have been an insanely stupid thing to do at that moment.

Without warning, Dr. Tremonti and his resident flock surged into the room. He is about the quickest person I have ever met and, in one glance, sized up the situation, then with one hard glance at his staff, he issued a silent order for them to control any mirth. They were all well-trained and not one even glanced at her ridiculous shoes. Ever all business, he quickly assessed her and while speaking softly, palpated her abdomen and inspected the incision site. Stepping back, he said to the air, "Vitals?"

One of the group spoke up, "Normal temp, normal pressures."

He glanced at me and then back to Brenna. "Want to leave this place tomorrow?"

"I'm expecting to," she answered, smiling her bewitching smile at him.

"OK, in the morning then." He gave me a quick wink and thumbs up. As he was nearly out the door, he paused, twisting at the hip, "Real nice shoes, Brenna, real nice."

I knew the moment had arrived. She looked at me for a long time before speaking. "Daniel, I trusted you, and you let me down." Her lip quivered just a little as she fought for control.

"You read my story," I guessed.

"You, the only one in the world who knows all about me inside and out, and you are going to share me with the world."

"I wasn't thinking, I guess," I responded, "but have you ever seen anyone so revered as the way I feel about you? I mean, I even teared while writing it down, and I love you so intensely that I can't begin to put my feelings into words. Since I can't really describe how I feel about you, my novel is already a failure before it's finished. I'm truly sorry if you were hurt by anything I said, but everything I wrote is true, especially my love for you."

She pondered on this a bit, and I could tell that she had softened. "As long as you assure me that it won't ever be published as it is, I'll forgive you."

"I promise...I do...I do, with all my heart."

"Come here, I want to thank you for the shoes." She smiled that little girl smile with her head down and her eyes up, beckoning to me with her index finger.

Chapter Eight

Another Opinion

By 7:30 AM, I was on my way down the, now familiar, hospital hallway path to Brenna's room. I had spent the night, actually three hours, at her apartment, and I had brought some of her street clothes for her expected discharge. At the nursing station, I nodded and smiled to the staff scattered around the small area. Just passed, but still in my peripheral vision, I noticed a nurse motioning toward me with her head, and before I could get much farther, I heard rapid footsteps behind me. I stopped and turned.

The fellow approaching me was slightly shorter than me and was wearing a loosely fitting white lab coat. He was smiling and came up close before speaking. "I was told that you are Brenna Christensen's companion," he began, using an inappropriately low voice. I noted a vague accent which went along with his grooming. He was tanned, his longer hair combed back in a continental style, and he sported a very well-groomed short beard and mustache. I guessed his age to be 50 or so. A quick glance at his ID badge provided his name, "Dr. U. Gast, Hospital Administration."

"What can I do for you, Dr. Gast?" I responded. I sensed a slight delay in his answer, but his eyes never left mine.

"I require a brief interview with you, if you please," he responded, smiling and beckoning me to follow him. There was the accent again, and I started processing where he could be from.

Shrugging, I said, "Sure," and gestured for him to go ahead of me. He led me back to the small meeting room behind the nursing station and closed the door. I couldn't imagine where this was headed. Could it be about some financial or insurance problem?

We sat down across the small work table while he took his time silently appraising me before speaking. He took out another ID badge from his lab coat and threw it on the table. "I have also another role at this institution, and so today I can speak on both sides of my face, if you will," he said, again with the same penetrating look accompanied by a disarming smile. This badge identified him as a psychiatrist. I tend to take in some people at a glance and form an opinion. Others take more time, and this was the case with Dr. Gast.

"You can call me Udi; may I call you Daniel?"

Dr. Udi Gast was well-informed, I could see. "You may, Udi, if you can summarize why we are meeting about Brenna without her being present." I smiled back at him.

He settled back and stroked his beard as he spoke. "Brenna's surgeon called me about some concerns that he and the nursing staff have about Brenna's behavior on a couple of occasions. Dr. Tremonti had a rotation under me early in his training and was really outstanding in his grasp of psychiatry. He wanted me to have an informal look at her prior to his writing a formal request for consultation. You see, with psychiatry, you frequently meet resistance before you begin. Occasionally, I solve the problem with an informal talk to see if there is a need to formalize the process of consultation, as I did with your friend, Brenna."

"Dr. Gast, what, if I may ask, prompted all this concern? After all, I know her better than anyone, and I have no knowledge of any issues along those lines." I tried to smile, but I had some inner, protective reflex irritations welling up at any mention of mental problems regarding Brenna.

"I can sense your defensiveness, and it is understandable, even necessary, that you feel that way," he said after his usual contemplative pause. "I visited with her in response to two episodes, each dutifully recorded by our staff, during which she appeared to be assuming a new identity, complete with accent. Each was different. In reviewing these reports, I discovered she was in this mode for some time and only came back to her normal self following sleep."

I started to interrupt with a "But," before he cut me off.

"Your thoughts on this in a moment, if you please, but let me finish my presentation." He resumed, "As you are aware, I visited in my capacity as a hospital representative, and we chatted for some time. I attempted to obtain answers along the line of the

SCID-D, but as soon as I delved into any questions traveling along psychological paths, she abruptly redirected the conversation. I would venture that she has had some training in this field in the past." I nodded that his assumptions were true.

He continued, "Your Brenna is very intelligent, and she simply cannot be deceived nor can she be given any mental health exam without her cooperation. She began to manipulate me during my short visit. As you know, I am certain, she is aware of the depth of her attractiveness and seems able and willing to use it as she needs to. The combination of her physicality and her IQ makes her a formidable patient for a simple psychiatrist like me. This is where you come in. I need to ask you some questions that, either she won't answer, or I can't ask. In return, I will give you my working opinion about any need for additional investigation on a more formal basis."

Dr. Gast sat back, stroking his beard and looking at me with a placid, unrevealing face. While he was speaking, I had formed an opinion about his country of origin. Germany. I started by asking, "I assume your training was in Germany?"

"Yes, I practiced in Germany and taught there for years. Most of my publications have been in German. I was known mostly for my work with dissociative disorders." He gave me a penetrating look to determine if I had ever heard of this diagnosis.

I avoided giving away my ignorance and stated that I was willing to be interviewed on Brenna's behalf. There could be questions that, in respect for someone I cared about, could not be answered, but I would decide this at the time.

"To begin, have you noticed any episodes of identity change previously?" he asked.

"She likes to assume a persona and has several different ones. It is all a big game for her, and I am sure she knows what she is doing." I was somewhat defensive, because, to me, it was always a game she was playing. Why she had chosen to take on one of her personalities during her hospital stay was confusing however.

"Does she remember doing it?" he asked.

"I have never asked her that, but I am sure she does." I wasn't actually sure, and after I spoke about it, I was even less sure. I couldn't remember anything that happened during one of her personalities that we discussed later. As I remembered, she would go on and on with her little game even when I grew tired and asked her to drop it.

"Another question, please," he said. "Are you aware of any unusual trauma in her life?"

There was the one big elephant-sized trauma of her father's suicide, but she had never discussed it with me in any depth, and because of the obvious, I never pursued it with her. Best forgotten, I felt. "Her father committed suicide in their home," I reluctantly answered.

"Was she the one who discovered him?"

"Yes, but I don't know any more details. The subject is too personal and painful for her to discuss, and I have seen no need to pursue it."

He thought and stroked his beard, looking away. "What age was she when it happened?" he inquired. Again, the penetrating look.

"Sometime in late high school, probably her senior year."

"You said that she viewed the body?" he asked.

"Yes, she found him hanging." There was a long pause, and he seemed to be reluctant to explore other areas he had concerns about.

"Was she close to her father?" he asked.

"I understand that she and he were very close. Her mother is very standoffish and remote," I explained.

"Please, don't take any offense at my next questions," he said while giving me one of his long looks. I agreed that I wouldn't. "Have you ever, even slightly, suspected that she and her father had an inappropriate sexual relationship?"

Wow. No, I can't even think that way. I couldn't even bring the image up. "No," I answered as firmly as I could.

"Does she have any sexual dysfunction?"

"No."

"Does she have any unusual fears or phobias?"

"She refuses to ride on my motorcycle with me, but that is only common sense. She is fearful of high places, but there is no phobia. She, so far, won't go in the water in small boats but rode across the lake on the ferry last year."

"I have learned that she was previously married; can you tell me anything about it?" he continued.

"Well, there was a brief marriage of a few months to a classmate. There was an annulment when it was determined that she was unable to have children."

He thought through this new information, stroking his chin and staring into the ceiling. "Do you know the reason for her sterility?"

"No, and according to her surgeons, there is no obvious pathology. They seem to feel that she is normal."

Again, he was lost in thought. I felt that he had more questions but was reserved about asking them. We sat in silence for awhile until finally he spoke. "My field of interest is dissociative disorders and, specifically, what you may know as multiple personality disorder. I have published several papers on this syndrome, and I feel that I am as knowledgeable as most on this particular topic. The whole diagnosis is questioned, because other experts feel that there is no such disorder. Many physical causes have been proposed that are associated with measurable data such as EEG, MRI, PET SCAN and so forth. There is a long list of possible psychological etiologies which usually relate to a specific traumatic episode, and sexual molestation is frequently discovered. I am not suggesting that this happened to Brenna. The prognosis is not known, and some patients go on to acquire other, more familiar, diagnoses, such as schizophrenia. My belief is that most patients eventually throw it off when they are in a stable situation, surrounded by love and support. One therapeutic suggestion is that the other personalities which emerge not be courted but gently discouraged."

He gave me another very long appraisal. I said nothing, absorbing what I had heard. He continued, "I don't have enough to pursue this at this time, and I am certain that she would resist and also be offended, but I offer you my card in case there is a need for me to get involved." He handed me his business card which I put away, silently.

Dr. Gast abruptly resumed speaking, "During our conversation, I was made aware of the close relationship you and Brenna have. If there is actual pathology dormant in her, you may be filling a need which could be temporary. As I mentioned, she is both very beautiful and marvelously intelligent, and such women have many options. It is possible that your time with her will run its course, and she could abruptly change direction."

This time I took my time answering. "Dr. Gast, this is true for any relationship, isn't it?"

He nodded that it was true, and I got up to leave.

"Thanks for your time and interest. I hope you are wrong and that she is just a game player with a troubled past, but for the present, I will continue to love her and treat her as good as I can while she permits it." With that final comment, I strolled back to her room to await her discharge.

She was up, sitting in the bedside chair with her breakfast tray in her lap. Her face was bright and happy, and she smiled up at me as I came in. I sat on the edge of the bed, very glad to have her back again, and watched as she finished her breakfast.

She offered me her coffee, and I accepted gratefully. "When am I getting out?" she asked.

"Have they made rounds yet?"

"One of the residents came by and said that he was going to start the discharge process, and soon after, the nurses came in and took out my IV," she answered.

"Well, there is the paperwork, but I would say by midmorning, at least," I guessed.

"Is that my clothes bag?" she asked, taking it out of my hand. She peered inside and started smiling. "I can count on you to dress me in style, can't I?" she beamed. I just smiled at her happiness.

"You are going to go out in grand form, and I may have to beat off the young medical staff to keep you safe."

She pushed the tray back and stood up easily. "I'm going to take a shower and change," she said, gathering her things.

While she was in the shower, I headed up to the nursing station, looking for familiar faces and found one. "Excuse me, but is Nurse Riley working this morning?"

The nurse told me that Mary was down the hall and would likely be right back. After a short wait, I saw her coming and walked forward to meet her. We stopped in an area of the hall without patient room doors adjacent. "Mary, I want to thank you for all your help this week. You know, I thought I felt some antagonism from you at first, but I was so wrong. You are a very special person."

"No, we didn't hit it off at first, did we?" she said while smiling up at me. "You are a special person also, but I am afraid that you have your hands full with Brenna."

"Were you one of the ones who wrote her up for strange behavior?" I asked.

"No, I wasn't on duty those times, but I read the report. She was always normal during any exposure I had with her. I will say that I found it strange also. The hospital is an unusual place for that kind of game, and either way, it raises some concerns."

If I had a beard, I would have stroked it just then. I respectfully touched her shoulder. "I am really glad you were around. It was great to meet you." She nodded, smiled and hurried off.

When I returned to the room, Brenna was just emerging from the bathroom, looking transformed. The change was from a child to an adult, and she was again in charge of herself. Of course, I had forgotten her hairdryer, and she had put her damp hair back in a ponytail. She sat up on the bed, and I sat in the much lower chair. It was like a power shift, with her in control, and I noted that she had a blank facial expression and was looking intently at me. "You want to tell me what you talked about?" she asked.

"Whom and what are you talking about?" I naively asked.

"You and your pal, Dr. Udimein Gast," she said, without a flicker of emotion.

That was amazing. Did she have the nursing station wired, I wondered? There was no reason not to tell her anything she wanted to know, and I already knew from experience that she could always tell when I'm not being truthful. "We talked about you, Brenna. I never met him until this morning in the hall, and as far as I am concerned, our meeting is no secret."

"He is a psychiatrist, a leading authority on multiple personality disorder, and was born in Germany," she capsulized. "Yesterday, he tried to pull off an interview with me by posing as a hospital administrator, and I am not exactly happy about being deceived."

I was not about to get trapped in this vice, because I had no hand in it. "He told me that," I answered.

"Please don't make me drag it out of you. You understand what I want to know."

"Brenna, the whole thing started because you went into one of your accents, and they took it seriously," I answered. She didn't admit or deny it. Did that mean that she didn't remember it? I bucked up and asked the question I had to know the answer to. "Do you remember doing that?"

She responded instantly, "You know I am not crazy, Daniel. There is nothing wrong with me except a little scar on my belly, and if it doesn't bother you, it won't worry me."

Skillful, I thought. She managed not to answer and turn the conversation to another topic. "He had questions about incidents in your life which could have caused emotional stress, but I don't actually know much and didn't give him what he needed. I think he will have to talk to you more directly, as a psychiatrist, to satisfy his questions, but for now he is not going to pursue it."

"I assume that he told you to call him if I go nuts," she asserted. I could sense that anger was boiling just under her skin, and I wanted to avoid provoking her.

"Brenna, I would never do that behind your back. You know I am here for you as long as you want me in your life. I am the nutty one, and it is all about you."

Chapter Nine

A Surprise Trip

*E*ven two weeks after her discharge, I would say that we were still not back to normal. She was moody past the normal female moodiness and slightly depressed. We were still working on music, which was nearly our only entertainment. A pattern had been established that Brenna, on her own, would pick a new song to learn, then give me the name, and I would be expected to learn it to perfection before we rehearsed it in her apartment. Her nearly deaf landlady lived beneath her and was accommodating to the noise of our practice during the day, even up until 10:00 PM. Past that time, we would considerately use the keyboard and not the piano, because we could both use earphones, and she could sing in sotto voce. My problem was that she almost always chose Cole Porter pieces which can be difficult music to learn to play accurately in a short time. I partially overcame this problem by using a simple melodic line which she sang for correct pitch and rhythm, and later, I would play in the same key just to provide some fill. Playing the piece as written overwhelms the singer, which is why you almost never hear the piece in its original form.

Our band had fallen on hard times with Doug gone again. The rumor circulated that he was a professional gambler, and we speculated that he had acquired some debt which required taking off for parts unknown for awhile. Too bad, because he was very important to the group, and although I try, I cannot take the place of an experienced bass rhythm guitarist. At least not yet. I had been putting in most of my practice time on the piano for Brenna, so I made little progress on the guitar or my theory and jazz studies. But, Brenna appeared content, and she continued to make progress.

One day, I read about the continuing presentation of Cole Porter's, *Anything Goes*, musical at the Stephen Sondheim Theatre in New York, and it was getting very good reviews. I had never been to New York or a Broadway musical, and I started plotting about it. In the space of two days, I purchased tickets for good seats in the orchestra section, made airline reservations, booked a room in the famous Waldorf Astoria, and even had advanced placement tickets for the ride to the observation deck of the Empire State Building. In addition, I discovered how and where to get a coach ride in Central Park. The plane was to leave from O'Hare in Chicago late on a Friday night and return late Sunday night. I had surprised Brenna previously by taking her unexpectedly to unusual places, and this time I was delighted with my idea and couldn't wait to spring it on her.

Friday morning, the day we were scheduled to depart for New York, I called Brenna and asked if she was free for the weekend. Her antenna went up immediately, and I was glad that we were separated by distance, because she would have been able to pry it out of me. I am so weak with women, especially this one. When I suggested that she might want to pack a small overnight bag, she insisted on knowing where we were going so she would choose the right clothes and shoes. I told her not to worry, that we would probably be camping and any clothes were acceptable, expecting that she knew me well enough not to take that seriously. That night, I arrived early at her apartment for the trip to the airport, and we took off in the car. She was still in the dark about our destination but willing to have any adventure that I would give her. When we arrived at the airport, she mocked surprise, saying, "I wonder where we are going to pitch a tent around here?" jerking my chain a little, too. I held on to her ticket as long as I could to prevent her from uncovering where she was bound. At last, she made the connection, "New York! Is that where we are going?"

"Yup," I answered, still silent about the reason.

"You are in for some trouble, my little man. Because of your stupid trick, I have no clothes with me for New York."

"Don't worry about it, my little girl. It's taken care of."

She took my hand, and we went to the gate together. I could tell that she was loving this and trusted me completely. The whole trip turned out to be magic, and I described it to someone later as like being in a movie.

There was little sleep for us Friday night. After arriving in New York early Saturday morning, we left the airport, quickly enveloped by the hustle and bustle of the big city. When the cab pulled up at the entrance to the Waldorf, Brenna asked, "Isn't this the hotel that Cole Porter used while he was in New York?"

"Yes, he actually died in his Waldorf Tower apartment," the cabbie answered for me.

You want to know anything while in New York, just ask a cabbie, or better, just wait for his unsolicited remarks. After I paid him, I said, "I knew that!" and we both smiled. We approached the doors at the main entrance carrying our small bags. A uniformed doorman on each side of the double door pulled his side open with a smile and greeting, and we strolled together in high style. I paused to look around the large lobby and found what I was hoping to see.

On an elevated stage in the front of the lobby sits Cole Porter's grand piano. We went up to the short iron gate and peered over at this impressive reminder of Cole Porter. As I looked it over with lust in my heart, I became aware that Brenna was watching my face. I turned to her, and she gave me a big smile. "You really love that big piano, don't you?" she asked.

"Sure. You know that he wrote a lot of the songs you sing on that very one," I informed her.

She continued to study my face. "Would you ever want a piano like that for yourself?" she asked sweetly.

"Any pianist would," I said and then turned back to see it once more, adding, "I could never afford anything like that, and even if I could, I would never have any place to put it."

After checking into the Waldorf, we caught a couple of hours sleep and were on our way back out as soon as the stores opened. We caught a cab straight to Macy's where we spent a very delightful time shopping for clothes, as I had promised her. She was able to get a great outfit complete with dressy, but comfortable, shoes for walking the streets and seeing the sights. I insisted on looking for a tangerine color because of the old song, but she rejected it. We had lunch at the store cafe, and while we sat, we looked over at each. Neither one of us could suppress a smile for very long, because the excitement was so intense. After shopping, we headed back to the Waldorf to freshen up and change clothes.

"My, you have this all planned to the smallest detail, don't you?"

"You'll see," I said with a smile. She was still in the dark about my plans for the musical until our cab pulled up at the entrance to the Stephen Sondheim Theatre. There it was on the marquee, *Anything Goes*. The music had been written and designed for Ethel Merman in the thirties and has been performed off and on many times since. There have been three movie versions as well. Brenna was so happy that she almost quivered. We took in a wonderful afternoon performance.

We took a cab from there to the carriage stand on the south end of Central Park. The ride goes into the park a little way and moves very slowly out and back in a circle. It was a warm summer afternoon, and a lot of folks were out enjoying the end of the day. Not so romantic as you would think, because we really had no privacy in the carriage, and the driver talked the whole time. At the end of the ride, we walked in the park for a little while to catch the sunset and then caught another cab back to the Waldorf. We had dinner fashionably late at The Bull And Bear, one of the more famous restaurants in New York and which is located in the Waldorf. Then, after a couple of drinks and tired beyond belief, we went to bed.

Since I had acquired 7:30 AM tickets for the Empire State Building, we awoke early, dressed, and grabbed a cab so we could get there on time. I was grateful that the crowd was small and polite because of the early hour. We were quickly whisked up to the observation deck in the fast elevator. Through the glass windows was the panorama of one of the world's largest cities from of one of the world's most famous buildings. Brenna stayed in the inner glassed area, and I went out to walk on the outside viewing area to take some photos. What a view, and what an experience to be in New York. I felt very happy, and I turned my back to the overlook and spotted Brenna through the glass. She was evidently following me around from inside, and she smiled broadly back at me. I motioned for her to come outside and join me, but she made a puckered expression, rolled her eyes and put both hands to her ears. I got the message. I leaned back against the concrete rail and thought about her and our future. Udi's warning came back to me that she has lots of options, and he didn't even know about her marvelous singing. Was it going to last? I knew that I wanted it to, and I knew that if I asked Brenna today, she would say the same. Then there was the question about her mental stability. She had been depressed since discharge, but there was no sign of any serious problems. She needed this trip and so did I.

She understood my finger pointing down and nodded yes. After getting our fill of the experience, we went for breakfast at a little place near the Empire State Building and lingered over coffee. We could see the massive tower from the window seat. Sitting across from her over coffee in that little cafe was the stuff of dreams. I was so happy that she was having a good time, and it was such a privilege to be in her company. Some of Doug's infatuation with her must have rubbed off on me, because all I wanted to do was look at her lovely face and listen to her soft voice. The light streamed in and streaked across the small table, lighting up the linens which in turn gave a hypnotic glow to her face and neck. Brenna finally urged me up to my feet, out the door and on to new adventures. We spent most of the rest of Sunday walking up and down Park Avenue in the warm sunlight until our time ran out. Returning to the Waldorf for the last time, we retrieved our small luggage and hustled off to the airport.

For the next week, all she talked about was the good time she had in New York, and of course, it refreshed her appetite for Cole Porter. To be honest, I was starting to be more demanding about trying other equally good music from the thirties and forties, but I met with limited success. After all, how could I complain when she could sing these pieces as well as anyone I had heard. As far as Brenna singing the blues, I had pretty well given up for the time being. She was narrow but very good at what she wanted to do. The idea grew in my head that if she developed a more expansive repertoire, she could have a professional singing career. I would be happy for her, if that is what she wanted, but I knew that I was sure to lose her, because I felt that I was doomed to stay an amateur. The best thing I could do for her was to expand her interests in music. I started finding and watching old movies with her, the ones with music by Jerome Kern or Gershwin and singers like Crosby, Sinatra, and Fitzgerald.

Chapter Ten

At The Recording Studio

We went through the glass entrance door of the recording studio together. I was nervous and apprehensive about playing the piano this morning, and I desperately needed some time to warm up, but so did Brenna. Pete had called me the previous week to pressure us to come in this particular morning. Apparently, a former buddy of his had become a recording producer based in Atlanta and was going to be at the studio. Pete told me that Harvey was always looking for new talent, and well, you never know.

Brenna was calm and looked determined. Good, at least the one who mattered was okay. Neither one of us had ever done anything like this and didn't know what to expect. We introduced ourselves at the desk and were quickly shown in. As directed, we went down a hall toward the rooms with a red light outside, noticing how the place smelled of old tobacco and sweat. Before we entered, I glanced nervously through the glass window and could see both the studio and the adjacent control room.

The sound room had a well-worn black grand piano off to the side with several mikes dangling overhead. There was a stack of folding chairs against one wall and scattered acoustical baffles attached haphazardly to the other walls. The floor was dirty as were the walls and molding around the doors. The control room had a long glass window looking into the studio, and I could see two technicians with earphones already moving about inside.

Pete was there and met us in the hall. "You have about an hour to warm up and then we will see what happens. Harvey Silverman is upstairs, and I'll get him when you're ready to start. Listen, my friends, I know that both of you are going to do very well, and I want you to relax and enjoy this experience."

Enjoy this, I thought, you must be insane, Pete. Talk about pressure. On the other hand, what did we have to lose? A short balding fellow holding a clipboard came up to us, looking back and forth between Brenna and me. "Hi, I am Randy Fellows, the supervisor of the recording studio. We want to welcome you both here, and we will try to make this a rewarding experience. By the way, can I see your union cards?"

"What union cards?" I asked, perplexed.

Pete leaned over and said, "Your Musicians' Union cards. They won't let you record here without them."

"We don't have any union cards, and I don't know the first thing about it," I said.

 While Brenna stood silently looking at me, Randy tapped his pen on the clipboard and frowned. "Look, you still have an hour. Let me make a phone call, and you can write a check for dues for you both, and we can move forward this morning." It was apparent that we had no choice. Before he left, he turned back around and said rather absently, "Oh, and you can pay for this morning's studio time with a separate check." I gaped at Pete, because I thought that this was a freebie this morning because of his friend, Harvey Silverman. Pete looked sheepish and shrugged, then turned and walked away. Randy was waiting for my response. I was trapped, having no choice but to pay up, and it ended up costing $859.00, paid with two checks. This was before any note was heard in the actual recording studio.

A small blonde girl wearing oversized glasses unlocked the studio for us and left without a word. The first thing I did was to examine the piano and test its tune. It seemed to be close, so I sat down and put the music Brenna had selected up on the stand. You guessed it, Cole Porter. She chose to sing *It's All Right With Me*, which was sounding pretty good yesterday in her apartment. I started playing and getting the feel of a new piano, while Brenna went to the corner, singing scales and warming up. She knew the words by heart, and I knew that she would be superb once we started. I watched the clock and about ten minutes ahead of the hour motioned to Brenna that it was about time. She chose to use this time to visit the restroom.

During her absence, the door opened, and Pete and his friend came in. "Hi, Dan, I am Harvey Silverman." He appeared affable and stuck out his hand. I stood and shook it. He was heavy, dressed in a black short sleeve shirt ornamented by a silver tie, black slacks and black shoes. A large diamond ear stud was on one side, and a gold Rolex flashed light and called for attention. The lower part of Harvey's round face was covered by a full beard and mustache, and his thinning hair was pulled tightly back into a short ponytail. His eyes roamed around the studio, obviously looking for Brenna.

"She'll be right back, Harvey," I informed him, saving him from asking.

He nodded. "You come with praise from Pete, whose opinion I have learned to respect. I am eager to hear what you have," he said.

Brenna made her appearance through the door. She was dressed elegantly in a black shift, laced with gold thread, as if she were in a nightclub rather than the studio. I could see Harvey and Mike ogling her from head to toe, but she was used to it and ignored them.

"Brenna, I am Harvey Silverman, and I am sure looking forward to hearing you sing." She smiled back at him and just nodded. There was a tapping on the glass, and the techs motioned that they were ready. Harvey and Pete went into the control room, and as I watched they were handed headpieces.

I gave Brenna a quick hug and said, "Knock them dead."

She looked placid, steady, and confident and smiled at me. We both put on our headsets and suddenly the sound was different. I could hear what I was doing, but sounds were now hollow like we were in a much larger space. I briefly wondered if I should have been warming up with this gear on. A voice came into my head, "Just feel comfortable. No one plays just once, and you have a whole hour for one piece." I looked through the glass at them but couldn't tell who was talking to me. There is a short piano introduction to *It's All Right With Me*, and I started playing. After a few seconds, the voice came on and said, "Sound check complete. We'll let you know when to start over." I stopped as requested. The voice came back on and said, " Brenna, could you sing a few bars just to get your mike set up?" She nodded and started her part. After a much longer time, the voice returned, "Thanks, now both together please."

I decided that I would start at the beginning, trusting she would know when to come in. The music came more easily now, and she started right on the beat. Again, the voice came on and said, "We've got it now; you can start over any time. Try the whole piece, and we will all listen to it and decide on any changes. Relax and enjoy." Brenna shrugged and nodded that she was ready.

This little song carries a lot of nostalgia regarding a previous lover and grudging acceptance of his/her present company. Generally, Brenna won't sing any song which implies dumping a lover or jilting a lover, and I like to think that she is being considerate of me and how I feel about her. I love this particular piece of music and, after some effort, finally persuaded her to try it. She always, and I mean always, reminds me that she is not singing about us. She looked over at me and mouthed, "I love you," just before turning to face the mike.

I began slower than usual, using more feeling with considerable rubato, creating more emphasis on the tune. It's hard to do this style of playing with a group, which will demand a more even tempo, or a singer that's new to you. I have memorized Brenna's style of singing, and we both understand where the emotion lies and how to bring it out. She started singing, and I had never heard her sound so good. There was a great deal of enhancement being electronically added from the control room. My piano boomed like we were in a large orchestral hall with resonance creating a sort of hollow sound.

Our music died out and faded away, sort of like the feeling you get after having satisfying sex. A voice came on, and I recognized it as Harvey Silverman's. "Say, could you do that again, but somewhere in the middle, say before the 'wrong chips' segment, let the piano go solo on the melody and then Brenna can come back in to finish."

I answered, "How long should I play until she starts?"

"Look over at me, and I'll tell you," he advised.

Brenna overheard our conversation and smiled at me with squinty eyes, telling me that she was happy with her part. As for me, I had played a very sparse accompaniment to give her all the focus, and I would be happy to be heard and was most anxious to try. I started again and right away got lost and stopped.

"Quit trying so hard," came a stereo voice into my head. I started once more and got it right.

"Hold it, Dan." I looked up at the control room window. Harvey's face was looking back and said, "You will be able to express yourself in the solo part, just keep it simple until then."

It was a criticism, but I nodded acceptance. After all, we were new at this and had a lot to learn. I started again, and this time there was no reproach. Brenna came in just like before, and just before the stanza Harvey pointed out, she looked at me. I had the full score on the stand, and I played a little louder, with a lot of feeling, sort of letting the music linger in the air. When I reached a repeat I looked at Harvey and he nodded. Brenna was watching and came back in like a pro. We finished and the last piano note died out slowly.

"Hey, that sounded very good." It was Harvey again. "Want to hear yourselves?" Before we could respond, the music started in our heads. I had never heard us enhanced that way, and it sounded official or professional or something like that. I closed my eyes, concentrating on the piano. No mistakes, but did I get the timing right? Brenna was as good as perfect and was looking at me with moist eyes. She was happy.

"Okay, kids, that's a wrap." Different voice.

The door opened, and Harvey and Pete came in. "I want to invite you both upstairs so we can discuss this a bit," Harvey said in his gruff smoker's voice, loud and direct, his true opinion of us withheld for the moment. We followed them upstairs, Brenna ahead of me. We were led into a conference room which was decorated in a contemporary style featuring a large oblong black glass table with a gold stripe slightly off center. The walls were decorated with autographed photos and several gold records displayed in small walnut cases. I pulled out a heavy leather chair for Brenna and sat down beside her. Four other men sat down across from us, Harvey, Pete and two I didn't know.

As ever, Harvey was in charge and started the conversation. "Well, I got what I came for and that is to hear you, Brenna. Pete has a high opinion of your possibilities." He stopped to look down at his papers for a moment as if to gather his thoughts. We sat silently waiting, but I reached for Brenna's hand under the table. It was cool and moist, reflecting her anxiety, but she didn't show any emotion on her face.

Harvey continued, "In the recording industry right now, there is a bit of a revival of the old jazz standards, and we must have at least 20 or more really great young female stars who are also gorgeous. You have a lot of competition. The thing that makes one succeed over another isn't always talent. You need something different to stand out, and you have to be heavily promoted by someone like me. There are a lot of successful singers who have no talent, no training and no style but are there because someone like me told the public that they were special. There have been some outstandingly talented singers who haven't made it because their personality didn't click with the audience."

We sat there listening and holding hands. There was nothing Harvey had said to comment on, and I could tell that Harvey knew what he was talking about. He continued, but held Brenna in his focus, "Pete told me that it is his understanding that you only sing Cole Porter at this time?" Pete was also looking at Brenna and nodding affirmation but also, with his eyebrows, asking Brenna to confirm or deny. I tried to catch her eye, not wanting her to respond with anger, but she was looking at Pete and back to Harvey. There was no way of knowing what she would say or how she would react, could be tears, could be anger, but I was pleasantly surprised at her actual response.

"To that comment, I will agree that I am narrow and only do what I want. I never claimed to be a big talent or to have aspirations to be a national personality. Instead, the only thing I ever wanted was to sing love songs with Daniel. He wanted to join a band and play guitar, and I arranged that, but I never said I wanted to be a part of it. I don't like the blues, just like you probably don't like gospel. The question at hand is do we have enough talent to entertain anyone? The second question is what do we do next?"

There were four instant responses, and the consensus of the group was that our performance was done very well. After they were quiet, and after an uncomfortable pause, Harvey resumed his critique. "I have been around a lot of singers and a lot of beautiful women, but I was physically aroused watching you perform. You weren't trying to appeal to me or anyone else, and I doubt if you were aware anyone was even looking at you. Your singing was sexy, involved, compassionate, clear. I liked it. A lot. Even without spotlights or effects you are impressive, because you are not pretending; you are the real thing. If you could repeat that performance for the right crowd, you would have instant celebrity."

He turned to me. "Daniel, you are interesting. I can see that you and Brenna are a team and tuned into each other very nicely. I briefly attended a music college as a piano major so I can tell that you have had some classical training. Your tendency is to stick to the original music and do very minimal experimentation. Is that roughly correct?"

No reason to deny what was absolutely true. "Yes, I have stuck pretty close to the original score, and there are a couple of reasons. First, I think that there is a lot of great harmony and theory thrown away with arbitrary changes, and it is difficult to improve on a piece this simple and elegant. The other reason, I admit, is that I am weak on jazz improvisation. I have been studying music theory lately and trying to learn jazz chords, but I am still not up to speed."

He was quick with his answer, "Don't get me wrong; I like your style. It is different. Remember, I said that we are looking for anything different. The laugh is that by playing the original, you have created a different sound. Excellent!" He reared back in his chair and roared at the ceiling. When he sat back up, he looked more serious, "Okay, I want to tell you both that I enjoyed this morning, and I feel hopeful that we can go someplace with this. With your permission, I want to take this recording with me to Atlanta and have some people play with it and do some electronic changes to enhance the sound. You may not know this, but this kind of tinkering can be taken too far. You may get a really great sound out of it, but when you are heard live, there can be a let down for the audience and subsequent problems with your career. What I want is to get the most out of it and preserve your personalities and your stamp on this music. Here is what I suggest for you both, and I want you to get working on it."

He took out a business card, wrote on the back, then slid it across to Brenna. "Here is the name of a good voice coach in the area. Mill had a fabulous career at one time, but it was stopped short by an unfortunate accident. She has a second shot at life helping people like you, but you should be warned that she will demand a broad repertoire from you and a lot of effort. She is worth putting up with and will transform you into a real stage singer." Then he turned his attention to me. "Dan, if you want to get in this business with Brenna, you have to become a versatile jazz pianist. There are people who can help, but most individuals interested enough can do it on their own, especially if they have a background like yours. You only need to apply yourself and learn to be able to play from a fake book, because I guarantee that you eventually will be required to do it."

Harvey was right, and I had come around to the same conclusion. Brenna and I were still holding hands under the table, and she squeezed one last time and let go. She reached across the table and offered her hand first to Pete, then to Harvey. They shook and were all smiles. She said, "Thanks to you both for the support, encouragement and kind remarks today. I am inspired by the possible opportunity ahead, and I promise I will do what you suggest and get some help. I also promise Daniel," turning to me and clasping my face in her hands, "that I will give him more time for study." She said this while looking steadily into my eyes. God, I so loved this woman.

When she let me go, I half-stood and also shook their hands. "Thanks a lot to you both. I feel that your advice is right on target, and I will make every effort to improve myself. I am also looking forward to hearing the improvements you make to our recording."

"Well, that may take awhile. Don't get too anxious. I want to play around with it until I get it right," Harvey said. I nodded acceptance.

As we got up to leave, Pete put his arm over my shoulder. "By the way, I heard a rumor that Dangerous Doug is about to come back."

Interesting, I thought. It made me wonder who Pete's contacts were. "The band is alive again," I surmised.

"I would guess yes on that," he answered.

There was good and bad in this new information. In my heart, I wanted to resume playing the guitar, but any time spent with the blues would take away from my promise to learn more jazz. Earlier, Brenna had reminded me that she has no intention of ever singing the blues and suggested that our band should really go on without her. To separate from her would be unthinkable. The blues would have to wait. We went out the same glass doors into the September coolness.

Chapter Eleven

Mill Elbers

Outside, while walking to the car, I looked at my watch, " Brenna, I am starving and no wonder, it is almost two. Want to get some food?"

She looked up, her brow wrinkled in thought. "I see a little Indian cafe over there. Will that do?"

"Perfectly. At this time of day we should have the place to ourselves," I answered.

We entered into a small, rather dark room filled with scattered tables. There were no customers and a couple of the kitchen staff were at one table eating lunch. We selected a small booth hidden away in a corner. After ordering, I asked Brenna about her feelings concerning the day's recording session.

"I felt pretty good about our performance. The advice Harvey gave was very close to what you have been saying, so I want to tell you I'm sorry I didn't listen. I can be pretty stubborn."

"No problem, my dear. Are you going to call that instructor he suggested?"

"Right now," and to my surprise, she pulled out her phone and dialed the number. After connecting, she started telling the person on the other end that she was given her name by Harvey Silverman, and I could tell that made all the difference. They talked briefly and when Brenna clicked off, she said, "This afternoon at three. Want to come?"

"I wouldn't miss it, but do you think she will mind?"

She ignored me as she was busy with her phone looking up some information. "There she is," she said and slid the phone over to me.

"Mill Elbers," I read. There were a lot of musical recordings under that name, and it appeared that she was an up and coming singer in the late 80's, even made a few albums. There were no records after 1989. "Well, that is about what we heard Harvey say," I said.

"What do you think happened to her?" Brenna asked.

"I guess we are about to find out." After lingering over lunch, we studied a map and found out where to go. It wasn't far, just a couple miles west of the city. We timed the drive over there so we would arrive at exactly three.

The address turned out to be a small cottage-style house with a couple of bird statues crookedly perched on the front lawn, an older SUV in the drive. The property showed a general neglect, with the house needing painting and perhaps a new roof. When we arrived at the door, it opened before we could ring the bell. Through the screen, she looked youthful, even attractive, but then she opened the door.

"Hi, you must be Brenna and Daniel!" she said. She stood back and welcomed us into the living room. "Harvey called me just after you did and told me all about you."

In the room, I got a better look at her. She was dressed in a plain, faded cotton dress, her dark blonde hair pulled back into a tight bun. Her bright blue eyes burned in a youthful way and, combined with her slender form, made her look younger than we knew she was. She held her left arm in a funny way, and when I looked closer, I could see why. Burns. Her left hand was shriveled, apparently useless and permanently retracted, indicative of burns along the whole arm. When she turned, smiling at me, the left side of the face including her left eye was a mass of scarring and contracture. In spite of her deformity, her smile was warm and inviting. "Car accident, years ago," she clarified. The subject was never again mentioned.

At Mill's request we sat down, and I surveyed the rest of the room. The west end was taken up by a massive black grand piano which had a perfect, unmarked gleam about it. I strained my neck a bit and saw the distinctive profile of a Steinway. This was a concert grand worth as much or more than her whole house, a piano that was nearly nine feet long, weighing in at a thousand pounds. It was breathtaking, even on a large stage, but in this small room, managed to look menacing. Mill clearly could not play this piano, at least the way it could be played, and I wondered why she had it.

"Daniel, you play the piano, don't you?" she asked, knowing the answer.

"I try, but I am not allowed to even touch a piano like that one." I was serious. That would be like being invited to drive a Ducati motorcycle on a racetrack when you only qualified on scooters.

She smiled a tight knowing smile. "The first thing I want to do is to hear you sing, Brenna, and you both can just repeat the performance from this morning for me, if you please." She saw me wince and added, "Please, Daniel, it won't hurt you, and you can't hurt it." She gestured toward the piano, effectively commanding me to play her massive instrument.

"Just a moment, I have to go to the car and get the music," I said, and started to get up.

"You have to use sheet music?" She looked surprised as I left without an answer.

Was Mill being sarcastic or trying to be helpful? But, since I was asked to play her piano, I still needed the music. Walking to the car, I knew that she was right; it didn't look very professional to use written music, but we had been playing a lot of different pieces lately, and I just couldn't memorize them in the time that I had. I came back in and sheepishly put the sheet music on the stand. While at the piano, I noted all the framed and signed photos on the wall behind the piano. I didn't have enough time to look for faces I knew, but I did notice that the photos were all professionally done in a studio or live on the stage.

The big lid for the piano was shut, gratefully, because a piano this size will produce a formidable sound, even when closed. I tested some octaves and found that it was perfectly in tune, and there was not a scratch on it anywhere. Just a touch of a key produced a sound as clear as a bell ringing and resonated as long as the key was held. If I hit a wrong note, it would feel like hitting myself in the head with a hammer.

Mill asked, "Like my piano?"

"Of course, who wouldn't?"

"Gift from a friend," she offered. "You don't need to play very forcefully, you know," she said, pointing out the obvious.

"I can sure see that, and I will try to just tinkle a bit."

She turned to Brenna, "Ready?"

Brenna stood and walked over to the curved area on the right side of the piano and turned to face me, faintly, just faintly, smiling, but her eyes sparkled. Mill gave a sharp up motion with her good hand as an indication to start, and I did. What a great feel I got from this piano. I heard that the concert grands were stiff, and the rumor was true. It took a firm touch to play, but after a short time playing it, I was reassured, because it appeared to resist slips or inadvertent touches. Brenna came in on my nod, and we played straight through instead of using the piano solo as we had done on the recording. After all, I was not the point of this visit. When we finished, I felt that we did pretty well for a strange circumstance, and I could tell by looking at Brenna that she felt the same. There was a long pause, and we sort of looked around awaiting the critique.

"Well," said Mill, flatly. "There is enough here to work on, and I am willing to take you on." We had no idea what that meant, but I suppose we were being complimented in her way.

"Let's go into the kitchen, have a cup of tea and discuss this a bit." She didn't sit during our song, and when she abruptly moved out toward her kitchen, we followed. The small kitchen was a bit confining, but it was clean and bright. We sat at her small dinette table, and she efficiently prepared the tea. While her back was to us, she asked, "Do you know anything about me?"

Brenna answered, "Only what Harvey said and what I found on a search at lunch. I know that you had a singing career and now mentor selected singers."

Mill placed each item on the table one at a time. I felt like I should help her, but I didn't want to be insulting, so I just sat there. "It may help you to hear some of my recordings, and I suggest it. I only work with people who have a lot of potential, and I also trust Harvey's judgment. By the way, we were once lovers. It happened a long time ago, and I have known him in good times and bad, and he always tells it to you as he sees it." I felt in the way, because Mill was only talking to Brenna. She continued, "I have had a hand in bringing out a few stars. You saw the wall. I require that you do what I tell you to do or find someone else."

Talk about blunt. The clipped speech and the directness told us that she was not to be taken lightly. "What do you have in mind for me?" Brenna asked.

"What do you want?" Mill asked. "Do you want to just sing to your lover over there or to an audience of thousands? If you want to be known, be famous, and be rich, I think you can do it. It will take a couple of years of hard work from you both." She turned to look directly at me for emphasis.

"Daniel, you are crucial to this, because you already work well with her, and she trusts you, I can tell. You will provide the accompaniment, the encouragement and the financial help she will need. Are you up to that?"

"I would go to Hell and be dragged around in the hot coals for her," I said, without any emotion.

"Good, then we can plan for the future; drink your tea," Mill ordered.

"Excuse me, but I still don't know what you expect of me," Brenna asked.

"I expect you here three times a week for one or two hours, and I expect you to practice constantly and only on the work that I'll give you." She turned to me, a hard look coming to her face. "I'll expect you to come with her at least once a week, to practice with her and only play the pieces that I give you. I expect you not to use sheet music and to play from a cheat book, if anything. You will not use any written music for accompaniment in this house, and I expect you to pay for the sessions at my rates."

Mill was the hardest woman I had ever encountered. I sat back and wondered if we could live up to her expectations and if we could tolerate her demanding personality. Mill got up suddenly and left the room.

After she was gone, I whispered, "What do you think? Is this what you wanted?"

"Let's give it a try; we can always change our minds," Brenna answered in a whisper.

"Brenna, I wonder if I can learn what she expects of me so quickly."

"Well, there is nothing like pressure to kick-start you, and I will be under similar pressure, so don't complain to me," she said with a smile.

Mill came back in with a large stack of papers which she put on the table in front of us. She separated the papers in three stacks. One she pushed in front of me and said, "This is the sheet music for the pieces, but don't play them as they are written; just use it as a guide for rhythm and harmony. Use the chords noted above the treble cleft. By the way, they are in order, and we will start at the top next week."

She turned to Brenna and pushed a similar stack to her. "Can you read music, dear?"

"Some," she answered.

"Can you sing a melody by looking at the score without accompaniment?"

"No," Brenna answered.

"That's what I thought. Here is a list of the pieces. Find recordings of these by several singers and practice along while the recording is playing. Also, you can use the sheet music and sing as you play a single note melody on the piano. When you two get together, sing to his playing. Do you understand?"

"Yes, Mill, I understand," Brenna responded.

"Daniel, here is the list of dates that I want to see you here with Brenna, and here is a list of approximate costs per month. I charge two hundred per hour for amateurs like you two, but in a few months, we will see if we can get her a contract which will pick up the fee. Then I charge one thousand for each hour of time. I am willing to accompany you to concerts or recording sessions, and the record company will usually pick up my fees."

I did the math in my head. Mill was making some pretty big bucks if she had several apprentices. It didn't jive with her living quarters, and I couldn't understand her living here at all, given her earning potential. A mystery.

Another sheet was placed on the bundle before me. "This is a contract you both need to sign which obligates you for six months."

I took the paper up and saw that this was a self-inflicted prison that you also had to pay for. She was going to make twenty-five thousand from us in six months, and we were going to pay whether or not we even showed up or could not be trained at all. This morning I thought the recording session was going to be a no-charge affair and was presented with several hundred dollars of fees. We had only just met Mr. Silverman and really knew nothing about him. Now here was his former lover hitting us up big time with promises of stardom hanging over us like bait. And Pete. I played with him once and saw him once or twice after that but only briefly. We didn't know him either. From the looks of this house, I concluded that we were about to be taken for a ride. My intuition told me to back away, and I studied Brenna to see what she was thinking, but I could see that she was utterly enthralled with Mill.

Just before I said no way, Mill interrupted, "I don't want any signature or money from you today. I have provided a list of former students with both their phone numbers and email addresses, and I expect you to contact at least ten of them for recommendations prior to any commitment. Take your time, because I want a full effort from both of you. Go make love and talk it over afterward when your head is clear and then let me know. Harvey will send me your recording when he is ready which will help me know how he feels about direction. This is a tough business, kids, and I want to tell you that it's not all roses and glory. By the way, Daniel, given Brenna's looks, if she makes this happen, you will have to work really hard to hold on to her. Every wolf around will be sniffing at her butt, and they will come from every direction."

This from a woman who has been there, and not only something I have feared all along, but what Udi warned about as well. Suddenly, I didn't want to go there any more. Couldn't we just stay in Brenna's apartment and create love music for ourselves? I would be happy with non-success if it meant keeping Brenna. I wanted to turn back the clock, wishing I had never mentioned any interest in music, wishing that I had never met anyone here, and Brenna had remained in the little Milwaukee suburb in the nice little house we bought together. All I wanted was to be around her, feel her touch, her breath and look into her eyes, forever and forever.

Mill spoke first, "I don't want to hurry you off, but it's approaching five and I have another client coming along soon, so I think that this is goodbye for today. By the way, Daniel, next time you can help me serve the tea, because I know I am handicapped, and I would appreciate the help rather than look clumsy."

Wow. I felt like crawling out on my hands and knees, slithering to the car and limping home.

On the way back to Brenna's apartment, I suggested take-out food, and we stopped for some quick Chinese and went home to eat it. We sat there and ate without talking. So much to think about. I couldn't tell her what I feared about this endeavor, because I could hardly bring myself to think about it. My mood became depressed, and I withdrew inside myself. Women are naturally adept at sensing emotional swings in men, and Brenna was quick to pick it up. I could see her intermittently looking toward me, noticing that I was lost in thought.

"You heard the same thing from Mill today that I'll bet you heard from that silly Dr. Gast in the hospital. That I'll leave you someday for someone else." She continued munching and was looking intently at me for a response. I looked down at my food as if it was going to get away.

"I have no hold on you, Brenna. We aren't married or engaged, so I can't expect anything. Even if we were, you could still change your mind," was all I could come up with. Inelegant. I wished that I had more power with words. So cornered, Shakespeare would have been brilliant.

Are We A Band Yet? *by Alexander Francis*

Chapter Twelve

New Friends

*B*renna did call every single one on Mill's list, but several had to be contacted by email. To a person, they all agreed that Mill was worth the time and money as far as preparation for a singing career, but worth immensely more just for her contacts. After considerable thought and discussion, we decided to go ahead and start with her. I think I was under more pressure than Brenna because...well, because I worry more. I put $25,000 into an account that Brenna could draw on for payment, which was due weekly. I really started concentrating on my jazz and theory and quit playing anything except the piece for the week. I was struggling a lot and decided to find some help.

It was long overdue for me to contact Mike or Tom, and I called Mike one morning. As soon as I spoke, he interrupted.

"You! Hey man, it's about time we heard from you. Did you know that Doug is back?" he said enthusiastically.

"Yes, I heard it from Pete, but I have been tied up in this thing we brought upon ourselves. I would like to see you and tell you about it in person."

"We were filled in by Pete, and I want to tell you that we would be delighted to see you both again any time, but we know what's up right now. Your plate is pretty full."

"That is real understanding of you, and I want to let you know that I haven't forgotten you guys, and I would like very much to come back and play with you as soon as I come up for air."

He responded with, "Hey, you gotta do what you gotta do. How can I help you?"

"I am trying to learn to be a jazz pianist in short order, and I would like to get instruction from some local talent, if you know anyone."

"Let me make some calls, and I'll get back to you soon. By the way, Doug sends his regards to Brenna. He didn't mention you," he said while laughing crazily.

"I get it. I won't take it personal," I said.

The next day Mike called back and had a name for me from some friends. "The guy you want is Solomon James. He goes way back, and he was told that you would contact him. I don't know him personally, but I have heard that he is a handful. Be prepared to be called some names, and he is impatient, critical and hard to work with, but he knows his stuff. He was in Chicago for years with the jazz scene and now is in poor health and mostly retired. He plays part-time out of the Roundup which is on the southeast side. Not a great neighborhood for you, so I would be a bit careful."

"Thanks for the contact, Mike. I'll check it out and let you know," We chatted for a bit, mostly about Brenna and Mill. "Thanks again, and I hope to see you soon," I said and hung up.

There was no information on the Web about Solomon James, and I drove by the Roundup before I called. There isn't a great deal of crime in Brenna's city, but what there is, is usually found in a four square block radius of the Roundup. Formerly, it was a seedy cowboy bar, very shoddy on the outside. The sign sort of hangs down on one side and is left over from an earlier era. There was parking only on the street.

When I finally worked up the nerve to call, I talked to someone who said, "He ain't here, leave a message," in a not very friendly tone. I explained that I wanted to talk to him about some instruction and was not after him for anything else.

She responded with, "Yeah, I'll tell him when he come in. Call back tomorrow an ax for Lulu."

I did call back, and Lulu told me that if I really wanted to see him I could go to the Roundup on Sunday morning about 11:00. Well, a particular Sunday morning found me driving around looking for a safe parking spot. Lucky for me that, on a cold blustery early October Sunday morning, there was no one in sight. I parked, gathered myself up and went in the unlocked door.

The place was dark and smelled of years of spilled beer on the wooden floor. A small elevated stage dominated the end of the rectangular room, which also held an upright piano with the front of the case missing, its strings and hammers visible above the keyboard. A small group was seated at a round table in the corner, and on the other side of the room was a long, empty stand-up bar. I walked toward the table while they silently watched me come. Cigarette smoke was suspended like a horizontal cloud in the air above the table.

When I reached the table, four dark faces were turned toward me with no welcoming comment and no smiles. "Mr. James?" I said looking back and forth to see which one answered.

"You mean Zap, don't you?" one answered.

Guessing, I said, "Are you Mr. Solomon James?"

"I go by Zap to my friends, but you can call me Mr. James." The others laughed a guttural laugh and nodded approval.

"My name is Daniel, and I understand that you are expecting me. Can we talk?"

"Ain't we talking now?" More laughs.

"I was hoping to get you to teach me something about jazz," I said.

"Me teach a white boy something about jazz, you say." He paused and looked at the others. "I don't think that it's possible, and what is that you have in your hand?"

"Sheet music," I answered, holding it up. I had brought some of the music Mill assigned me to learn.

He leaned back and shook his head. "I've been playing since before you were born, and I NEVER used any damn sheet music. You might as well throw it away now. I don't use any music, never have, never will."

I looked perplexed. I couldn't throw this away even to impress Zap or, excuse me, Mr. James.

"I'm willing to learn and willing to pay."

"How much you pay?" one of the others asked, smiling at the joke.

"What are you expecting to be paid?" I asked, ignoring the previous questioner, and continued looking at Zap.

"I get $30 per hour, $40 if I do a good job. I'll always do a good job," he answered. The others laughed again.

This time I waited a bit to answer as if I was thinking it over. "OK, when do we start?" I finally said.

"Today. Come back in an hour. What kind of car you in?" he asked.

"BMW."

"You go back home and get another one. You gonna lose that one here. Shit, I should have charged you more." The others nodded affirmative. "This place okay today, but I don't want to see you down here at night unless you with me, got it?"

"Sure, can I call you Zap?"

"No, it's Mr. James to you, White Boy," he answered. "By the way, this be Maynard, Joy Joe and Peaches," he said, pointing to his friends one by one. "They good boys, and they all know music, and if I'm not around, they can take care of you."

"Pleasure to meet you," I said and offered my hand, which was ignored. At this point, they resumed their private conversations with each other and pretended that I was gone. Getting the point, I left.

I did what Zap suggested and exchanged my car for Brenna's which was more invisible in the neighborhood near the Roundup. When I returned, Zap was the only one in sight, and he was at the piano playing some jazz. It was a demonstration of the joy of music, arising effortlessly out of his hands, and continuing for some time without any written music in sight. When he finished, he spun around on the swivel stool to face me. "Play some music that will impress me." He was thin and slightly stooped, his face reminiscent of a bloodhound's face, full of sags and jowls. The whites of his eyes were more yellow than white, and there was a hint of lip and chin hair. He got up, and I sat down.

I still had my written music with me, but I knew better than to use it. Two pages of Cole's *Begin the Beguine* were still fresh in my memory, but this piece is generally rated high in difficulty for a modern piece, and I certainly found it so. It has an underlying Latin rhythm with a melody switching hands. After playing it for him, I felt that it sounded acceptable, even given the poor quality and tuning of the piano at hand. I turned to face Solomon James, trying to get an idea of how he felt from watching his face. He frowned.

"Listen, boy, you can't play that and expect anyone to sing to it. It's too complicated. No one, and I mean no one, plays it that way. Get up and let me show you," he said, while standing up and moving toward me. Adjusting his stool, he looked me over. "Assume that there is a singer here, and she wants to sing it straight," he said, not waiting for my response. "What you played was in B flat major?" he recalled, while starting to move thru some chords.

"Yes, two flats," I answered belatedly, wanting to demonstrate that I knew something.

"Mostly, I keep the melody on the top, but here we won't put any melody in because your singer is doing dat, and I won't put much rhythm in because your drums gonna do dat." He started humming as he played to simulate the singer. He played sparsely, but the smoothness and the unusual chords he played were very pleasant. "We can do better; let's change keys." He abruptly started over and was adding additional notes between chord changes. "This is C minor; sounds better?" It did sound better. "Hey, Peaches," he yelled. "Come out here and play a beat." One of the fellows I saw previously came out from the kitchen area. He was ample around the waist and didn't move quickly.

"Wat you need, Zap?" he asked.

"This piece we workin on needs a beat, but make it some syncopation with exception, and not very loud," Zap said, without pausing his playing.

Peaches drew the cover off the drum set and sat down. Previously, I never even noticed that the set was there. Someone flipped on the overhead lights for the stage. Peaches started with a bump bump bumpedy de bump.

"More," Zap commanded. Peaches responded with a more complex irregular beat and occasionally hit the bass drum. "Yeah, that it," Zap said. He hummed louder, and they went on for about four minutes. Zap spun on his stool and said, "That what you want to do?"

"Exactly, you both were great; thanks for the demo."

Zap nodded to Peaches who slowly got up and covered the drum set. Zap was watching me closely. With a humorous expression, he asked, "When yo momma taught you to talk, did she make you read it out of a book?"

I laughed, because I could see where he was headed. "Of course not," I answered.

"She just said the words over an over and you talked, ain't that right? You shortly knew which words went together and how to use them, didn't you?"

"I did."

"Then you could tell a story, and you could put meaning in how you said your words?"

"Absolutely," I agreed.

"You learned that you could add or take away some words, and everyone still know what you say?"

"Right again."

"And you found out how you said your words, faster, louder and such, made a difference in what happened after you said them?"

"I did."

He spun around again to the keyboard and struck a chord. "Know what dis is?"

"Sure, that is a C major," I said.

He struck another.

"That is a minor seventh," I said without prompting.

"And this?"

I couldn't identify that one. It could be inverted or augmented; I didn't know. "I'm blank."

"We don't want to get boring so we change things. Use a seventh for a minor third, and before you go back to the one chord, use an add chord. Know what I mean?" He looked at me to see if I was lost. "Another thing, White Boy, I watched you pedal when you played. You like that pedal too much. When you play jazz, let up the pedal before each chord, always, got it?"

I thought about it. In classical music, we are taught phrasing and the use of the sustain pedal across measures in a phrase. I did see that because of the frequent discordant sounds in jazz, you have to let the air clear. I said, "I noticed that you were doing that."

"Alrighty now, what I want you to do is get a circle of fifths and start at C and move up or down a fifth and play the three, sixth and one chords. Learn that for all the keys, and then learn them backward sos that if I play the three chords you can tell which key I am in. You gonna have to learn the seventh and ninth and to invert the chords as you need to. One other thing you should know. Music is a lot like color. You start out with only red, blue and yellow, but as you get older, you can handle mixes of color, and you might even use some honky name like periwinkle. You will find that the more you learn, the more color you can put into the music."

I did remember that the musical spectrum is frequently compared to colors. Both are types of energy. A chromatic note is part of the spectrum of music. I acknowledged what Zap was saying and promised to work on what he wanted me to do. That didn't help me a lot at the moment, to play for Brenna or to meet the demands of Mill, but I can only learn so fast. Brenna's needs came first, and in my other time, I would work on the jazz. Guitar will be put off again for someday farther and farther in the future.

Zap gave a look that told me that the lesson was over, and I said, "When should we meet again, Mr. James?"

"That right, White Boy, Mr. James." Laughter erupted from someone unseen in the distance.

"When will you be ready for me?" he asked.

"Well, let me work on it for two weeks. Then maybe...."

He nodded, fingering his facial hair. "Okay, two weeks, same time, same place. You can pay me now. Forty bucks, I was worth it."

Yes, he was. I agreed and paid him.

"Thanks, Mr. James, I'll see you next time."

"You better be ready, White Boy, or I'll give you hell."

I don't think he was kidding.

Chapter Thirteen

Digging In

Life for us settled into a pattern of trying to get by with the necessities, such as working for a living, shopping for food, and, for me, driving a lot. Brenna and I were both over our heads, and there was occasionally friction during rehearsal together. Nothing significant happened, other than moist eyes, curable by a little kissing, but our stress was becoming apparent. We never got out of her apartment for entertainment or had time for friends. Mill was a relentless advisor for Brenna and was giving me a hard time each time I came with her. She was short-tempered and exacting. It was as if she expected us to show up and play perfectly. Not likely I'm afraid, so we got chewed out almost every time we went. Brenna didn't fare any better alone, and some nights cried herself to sleep after a lesson. She was making progress though, and she rarely sang Cole Porter any more. The variety was good for us, and I found some other compositions were easier to play than I had been used to. I was following Zap's advice more and more, and it was taking less effort as I understood my role better. After two months of this, we needed a break. I felt that a getaway from music would let us return with fresh vigor, but I knew that Brenna would not go without permission, so I decided to talk my idea over with Mill first.

I felt uncomfortable calling her, because I just couldn't decipher her frequent silence and decided instead to drive over and see Mill in person. There was no way of knowing if she had a client or was even home, but since the distance was not great, I took a chance. The driveway was empty, so I parked on the street and walked up to the door and knocked. No answer. Well, I had taken a chance; she wasn't there, and it served me right. Just then, she drove up in her beat-up little SUV. I stood watching as Mill got out and waved for me to come over to her car.

"Just in time! Help me take the groceries in, please," she asked. I hefted up her four bags from the backseat, and she carried a small package hanging on her good arm, her handbag over the other, her crippled arm. "Well, this was a stroke of luck, Daniel. You must be clairvoyant to know just when to arrive." She smiled a rare smile at me. "Come on in, and we can talk. I think I know why you came, anyhow." We went into the kitchen, and I began to unload her bags without much conversation. "Enough of that, sit and talk," she suggested. After we sat down across from each other at her small kitchen table, she said, "I'll bet you want to get away with Brenna for a break, don't you?" I nodded yes. "I have the pressure on both of you, don't I?" she asked. Again, I nodded affirmative. "Where did you have in mind going?" she asked. I felt that I was transported back to my mother's kitchen, and I was again about ten and had pimples.

"I was thinking of Las Vegas. I have been there and sort of know my way around, but she has never been there. There is a lot of entertainment which she would love to see, but I felt that I should seek your advice before surprising her with it, because I know that she won't go otherwise," I waited for her to comment.

Mill gave me a long look without any emotion or even blinking. She rocked back in her chair and reached for her purse and a cigarette. After lighting up and taking a deep lungful of smoke, she turned her attention steadily on me. "No, Daniel, I can't let you take her yet; I have some more work to do with her, and I have some plans for her which may unfold shortly." She exhaled, and the room filled with smoke. Mill had a way of looking at you with her steel gray eyes that always felt confrontational. It was obvious that she was beautiful once, but never soft.

Disappointed, I said, "Can you let me in on what's up?"

"Not yet," she answered. Her look didn't soften. There was no other option for me except buckling down and continuing to support Brenna emotionally as much as possible. I hoped that she could take it, but I was worried about her emotional strength. Mill was never comforting and always demanded more. We knew the way it was in advance, but taking it was the hard part.

"By the way, I hear that you are seeing Zap James," Mill commented. I must have looked surprised at her knowing about this little bit of private tutoring he was doing for me. "Yes, I know him," she admitted, "and I sang to his accompaniment once or twice. He is really good, and he could teach you a lot." She was smiling at something, finally adding, "Does he do the White Boy thing on you?"

"Yeah, several times each session."

"Don't let him get to you. If he allowed you to come back after the first time, he likes you. By the way, he is not who he appears to be." Whatever did she mean by this, I wondered. "He went to Juilliard for two years on a scholarship until he was drafted to serve in Korea, then quickly joined the Marines instead. He is quite the musician, but he likes to pretend to be an old wisecracking jazz player." She paused briefly lost in thought. "Perhaps by now, that is what he is," she added.

"I never would have guessed that; thanks for telling me," I said. So much for Zap not being able to read music. He evidently knew more about it than I ever did.

Mill suddenly got up and left the room. I could hear her rustling papers, and she returned with several pages of sheet music. "Take these to Zap next time and tell him that I want you to work this up right away," she said, extending her good hand full of papers.

Looking at the titles, one was a handwritten page of chords and melody titled *Sing, Sing, Sing*. The other one was a Cole Porter number, *Just One of Those Things*. I knew and loved that one, but Brenna would never sing it. Any song that was about dumping your lover, she wouldn't touch, even though I told her that I knew that it was just a song and not about us, it made no difference. "She may not do this one, Mill," I warned, holding it up so that she could see.

"Yes, she will, Daniel, because this song may lead to a big break. Trust me on this one. You and I together will make her do it, and anyway, she has to cast off the childish impulse she has about relationships."

I never thought that love was childish, but in Mill's world there was only success or failure, not love. Brenna had been through a lot in her life and held onto me as I held onto her, as a buffer to the rough and tumble of the outside world. Yes, it was childish of us, but since Brenna was so considerate of my feelings, as I was to hers, I was downright grateful to be in love with her. "What's this about, Mill, can you tell me?" I asked.

"Not yet. There is really an outside chance that it will happen, but I believe that being ready for things eventually pays off. By the way, I have an apartment in Vegas that sits empty when I'm not there, and when you go, you can use it."

"Thanks, Mill," I replied sincerely. There was always more to Mill than you could see at any one time. "Mill, I wondered why you stay here in this town when all your contacts seem to be on the Coast?"

"My mother's house," she explained, while giving a sweeping motion of her good arm. "She is in a nursing home, and I share responsibility with my sisters to watch over her. I'll stay here periodically until she dies."

Her simple answer cleared up a lot of my questions. "Do you stay in Vegas the other times?" I asked.

"No, I have a house in the Hills. It's still the center of the entertainment industry," she responded.

She must have meant Beverly Hills, I thought. Nothing cheap there. "We were lucky to catch you here, Mill," I observed.

"Yeah. By the way, I am going to leave again in two months. You have that long to get ready. After that, you are on your own again," she gave me a hard look accompanying her words.

Chapter Fourteen

Connections

Again it was Sunday, and I was searching for a parking place for my lesson with Zap. I had quit working on anything but the latest music that Mill supplied, which I had with me. After parking, I pulled open the door of the Roundup, and the strong stale smells hit me with familiarity. Zap was already at the piano and without looking up, he called out, "Ready for action, White Boy?" I mounted the stage without answer. Zap sensed in some way that I was carrying several pages of sheet music. "Please tell me that you ain't bringing any sheet music to this holy place." He went back to playing some improvisation and shaking his head. "White Boy just can't live without his sheet music," he said and continued to ignore me.

"Mill Elbers sends her regards," I said.

He stopped playing and swiveled around to face me. "So you know Mill," he nodded as he spoke. "I thought that the music you wanted to learn sounded familiar, and I should have guessed. She tell you about me, then?"

"Some... enough," I answered.

"What a babe she was in the day. Couldn't touch her though. Guys who tried called her the Ice Cube. She was never in my league, so I escaped being cut in half." He looked off into space while he talked. There was no trace of ethnic accent in his voice. "Bad, what happened to her. Haven't seen her since, but I hear that she's still connected," he mumbled, trailing away. "About you, though. I hear that you have a real honey of a singer on your hands." He smiled showing his gold front tooth and turned around to take a long draft of his beer which was sitting on the piano. I could see that he was putting it all together now. "Let me see what she wants," he said and reached for the sheet music. There were only two short pieces, and after flipping through them, he took on a look of recognition. "They are from the Benny Goodman era." For clarity, he added, "Both of them were played at the same concert back in the fifties. This was before your time, but there was a group of three luscious girl singers called Rare Silk..." He paused in mid-sentence, remembering, and then continued, "The Gillaspie sisters and one other that I don't remember now. They sang with Goodman frequently." There was another long pause, and he continued to look blankly at the sheet music while he thought. "There is a group out of Canada that I heard is playing around, and I hear that they are doing a lot of Goodman. What I don't get is how your singer is connected to that group."

"She's not," I said, "and as far as I know there isn't going to be any connection." The idea made me pause though. Mill has many links and knows what is happening. Of course, there may be no connection. Still.

Zap put the music on the music stand above the keyboard and turned to face it. He gave me a quick side glance. "I am a jazz player by choice. Jazz players play by ear and not by sheet music, and that is what I have been trying to teach you, White Boy. Playing this music with other tight-assed White Boys, you need the music because any experimentation is out. They want to sound like Goodman. Exactly like Goodman. You have made progress, and I can tell that you are listening to the music and not looking away from the keyboard. You are getting better but still have a long way to go, and this will set you back. You know that you are only learning this to help your singer and not for yourself, don't you?"

He was right; all the work I had done was for her career, not mine. I enjoyed learning and making progress with music, but I never imagined that I could ever make a living with it. Brenna had the talent and the looks though. I wondered if she had come to grips with what success would mean to her. She was pretty, but fragile emotionally, and I really worried about what the industry would do to her. It was selfish of me to think negatively about her career, because I know what I'm really afraid of is losing her. In my nightmare, I saw myself watching TV somewhere with her on the screen and not beside me. Such thoughts made me sick inside, so I usually tried not to imagine past today.

Finally, I was ready to give him an answer. "Yes, I know what is likely to happen, and I can't talk about it. Just show me how you would handle these two pieces." Zap seemed to me to have experienced this situation previously, and he gently nodded to me, and I felt his support almost like a pat on the back.

"There is no one way to play jazz accompaniment for a singer. You have many options. You can stick close to the original melody or chord structure, you can go off into space with it and only occasionally come back to the original tempo and melody, or you can do almost anything in between. We have to assume that this music is going to be played by an ensemble and not on a single instrument like the piano, so the tempo and melody are untouchable. Just like Goodman," Zap kept saying. After a while, he turned to rest and said, "How about a beer, White Boy?"

I needed one, and we moved over to a small table. A couple of his friends that I had met on the first day also sat down, and we cracked open some bottles. Peaches, the drummer, spoke to me for the first time, "You getting better!" I smiled back at his grinning face. This was a profound compliment, and I took it to heart.

"Don't go swelling his head, Peaches, I have to keep him down sos he can learn right," Zap quipped. We sat and drank our beers, and I felt accepted for the first time.

"What do you think of a little real time down here with your singer, White Boy?"

"You mean bring her down here and perform live?"

"That exactly what I mean. We can bring in the whole group, see how she does and how you do," he said loudly.

The other two, Peaches and Maynard, spoke up, excited at the new idea. "Yeah, jam session. We get Joy Joe and William, too!"

Zap cocked his head and gave me a knowing look and explanation. "Willie play the Clarinet."

"You mean on a Sunday like this?" I asked.

"No, man," Peaches said. "Zap means on a Saturday night! This place be full then, lots of action, you know." No, I didn't know at all. I didn't want to refuse such a generous offer, but from what they said about crime in this area, I couldn't risk Brenna for any reason.

"Do you think it would be safe for her down here at night?" I asked.

"Man, I come get you in my Cadillac, in person. You be safe wiff me," huffed Peaches. He was about three times my size, and I could tell that he meant what he said.

Zap was smiling, gold tooth sparkling in the dim light. He leaned back and took another pull on his beer. "Got the number for Mill?" he asked me.

"You going to call and invite her, too?"

"Yeah, I want her to sing, too. We were good together once, and we don't care how she look down here," he said. I looked at my phone and got the number for him. He called while sitting right there and immediately made connection.

"Mill, this is Zap... Well, I'm glad to hear from you, too. I hear that you got Daniel's, I mean White Boy's, singer shaping up... Yes, I want to see her do her thing.... We are thinking of having your singer and White Boy putting on a show for us, using your music, sometime soon, and I want you to come sing too... Yes, that's right; you sing, and I'll play, just like old times. It would be so good to see you again and hear you sing, just like an angel.... Now don't say no to me, because I'll have to beg you and a poor old jazz player don't like to beg.... OK, I'm begging you, Mill, please, please, please; now, how can you resist that?" There was a long silent pause, and Zap rolled his eyes and shrugged. "Well, I think White Boy will be ready in about three weeks, and so let's plan for the 15th.... Good. By the way, if you go to White Boy's house, Peaches will pick you all up and take you home after. Thank you, thank you, Mill. We all will be real honored to have you here."

He hung up laughing like, "Hee, hee, hee," and clasped his hands together. "Another beer for everybody," he shouted at the ceiling and soon more beers appeared. We sat and talked for a while about nothing really. Zap leaned forward toward me and spoke confidentially like he was telling me a dark secret. "I met Benny Goodman when I was in New York. He came to Juilliard one fine day and played jazz for us. I was always leaning toward jazz, but that day clinched it. Little did I know that it would be three blood-filled years later that I could begin to take it up again." He looked wistful and became silent.

"Get up, White Boy; we have some work to do, and I need to earn my forty dollars," Zap said as he moved toward the stage. "Come over here, White Boy; I have to learn you some things," he said while moving away from me and motioning with his hand for me to follow. After seating himself at the piano, he gave me a knowing look. "Listen up. I know that you like to play the original music, and that's expected, because that is how your teachers taught you. The way all formally trained pianists are taught is to play the music exactly as written. You also should know that your favorite composer, Cole Porter, wrote for the stage, and listen up here... HIS PIECES WERE NEVER PLAYED AS WRITTEN!" He paused and continued to observe me, then started again. "Your foxy singer cannot sing to the original; there is too much music there. Our job, your job, is to provide a framework for her to sing. We are in the background, a long way back in the background. Fortunately, your composer provided the framework for us. He wrote the music; we didn't, and we need to use his chords to play his music. That's all we have to do! The singer will sing the melody; the drums supply the rhythm. Now, there are ways we can get fancy if we want to. One way is to use the chord tones, that is the notes from the chords. You can play all you want of them, and it will always sound good. You can sneak in some chromatic notes as leading tones, or you can take off and do your thing with the music. I suggest that you keep to the chord structure as written at first, and stay in the background."

I knew this, but I was stuck on an idea which I decided to explore with Zap. "The thing that concerns me is how much of the incredible harmony you loose the farther you get from the original music. These pieces were worked on at some length to get the harmony and tension right, and I don't think I could ever do better than Cole Porter."

Zap looked frustrated and pursed his lips before speaking. "No, White Boy, you can't do better than him and neither can anyone else. It's been awhile since I tried, but as I remember, you have to practice for months before you can perfect one of those difficult pieces, and then if you make a mistake during play, the error is glaring. This is nearly concert stuff, and he wrote it to impress and to sell the sheet music. The stage versions are simple and use several instruments. There are very few recordings not using a singer, because all the pieces were written for a singer. Any instrumental recording you can find will always be altered from the original."

He was absolutely right, and I had already encountered that.

Chapter Fifteen

Getting Ready

"Did you talk to Mill about me?" Brenna asked.

"When?" I answered.

She pouted her lower lip and lowered her head, "Don't give me trouble on this, just answer."

"I confess. I did."

"You are getting deeper than you want to be, Daniel. You think this is a game?" She lowered her voice and furrowed her brow this time.

"Hold on now, I was saving a surprise for you, but since you are going to beat me up about it, I'll tell you," I said, feigning terror. "I went over to her house last week and was going to beg her to let me take you out of town for a break, but she wouldn't do it, and then things changed."

"What things changed?" Brenna asked, using an artificially sweet voice. From experience, I knew the cat was coiling up for an attack.

"The short story is that you are singing in a nightclub in two weeks. It's off-Broadway, far far far off-Broadway, in fact, in town here," I smiled, knowing that she was just sharpening her claws.

"I'm what?" in a much higher pitched voice. She got up and came toward me in a menacing way. Suddenly she leapt at me, getting her hands around my throat and putting her nose to my nose. The rest of her was astride my lap.

"Normally, I really like to get you in this position, but your hands on my throat is a bit off-putting." I was trying not to laugh.

"Unless you get quick with the details, this is the last moment of your life, you heel," she said, eye to eye now.

"Okay, I know when I am beaten, and I officially give up, but before you do me in, I have one last request," I said, squinting at her with nearly closed eyes.

"Make it fast," she commanded without letting go.

"Could you please kiss me to death instead of strangling me? I would look so much better dead with a smile instead of with my eyes bulging out." We started kissing, laughing so hard that our front teeth kept hitting. She took a deep breath and quickly planted her lips on mine. I should have copied her, but I didn't think about it in time. She kissed me so hard that my nose was compressed by her cheek, and after a few seconds, all I was thinking about was breathing. She finally broke it off and rolled off to her back beside me on the couch.

She propped her feet and legs on my lap and was about to try to tickle me with her toes when I squealed, "Okay! Here is the whole story, but first I have to know some things. Did Mill give you some new music this weekend?"

"Yes, and she said I had to sing it or...," she answered. Her eyes seemed to moisten a bit. "She acted like it was a big secret and told me to ask you about it." I could see some actual tears forming.

"Hold on now; there is no reason for stress. Mill wouldn't tell me why either but gave me the same music, so I asked Solomon James to help me work it up, and while I was there, he arranged for you and me to perform at the Roundup for one night. The best part is that Mill is also going to sing, and she will be accompanied by Zap himself!"

Brenna sprang to her feet with her eyes and mouth wide open. She clasped the sides of her face with her hands and danced around the room. "I can't believe it!"

When she stopped for a moment, I interjected, "I have no idea what Mill will sing or for how long, but you and I are going to do both songs. As far as the reason she chose these particular songs, I'm sure only Mill knows. She is betting on something happening, and it might not, so she doesn't want to disappoint you by generating false hope. Our job right now is just to do what she wants. She is getting you up to speed on these two pieces, and Zap is getting me ready. Sometime soon, we'll have to rehearse with Zap and his band. I got a hunch from something Zap said, and I am sending you two YouTube links of those two pieces performed by Benny Goodman back in the fifties. One of them uses three singers, and that one I want you to study closely, because I have a feeling that you will benefit from copying that style, but I have no hard information, just a gut hunch."

"I have news for you. You're right, because I got the same links from Mill this morning." Perhaps two plus two does add up. Interesting.

"Has she started the scat stuff?" I asked.

"Well, she gave me some printed copy with the scat words I am to learn," she said while digging into her purse. She came up with a music score using single melody notes with the scat words below. It was just like the old video recording of the Rare Silk group with Benny Goodman. We looked at each other, trying to decide what it all meant.

This would be our first actual performance! The wonderful thing is that we would be together, and I had a feeling that all the musicians from the Roundup would be on stage with us. Brenna was to be the star, though, and would be center stage, the very center of attention. I made a mental note to ask Zap or Peaches for suggestions of what she should wear.

The music Mill handed me included my old favorite, *It Was Just One Of Those Things*, and was not particularly difficult, mostly consisting of piano jazz chords. I needed to get a feel for playing with a group to get the timing right. The old videos I had discovered were not very helpful, but it started me thinking about how to put this together. In the era of Benny Goodman, selected members of the group would be allowed to solo during a performance, and the singer was treated about the same as an instrumentalist. Brenna and I had used that style during our only recording session. This time, all the instruments would be there for only one purpose, to prepare Brenna, and therefore, our performance wouldn't really matter. I decided to do as Zap demanded and stay totally in the background. That got me thinking about the recording that Brenna and I made. So far we had heard no word about it or even when we might expect the results of digital enhancement, as promised. I reminded myself to call Harvey Silverman the next morning.

I could hear Brenna in the other room practicing scat as well as she could by using the video recording she was given. Previously, I was only dimly aware of scat singing but never thought much about it. It turns out that scat is difficult, certainly isn't easy as it sounds. The intention is to make vocal sounds mimicking an instrument rather than words and as such is closely tied to the music. There have been some notable scat singers in the past, such as Louis Armstrong or Ella Fitzgerald, but more recent jazz stars do not have a high opinion of scat. Today, it is more a novelty, but mastery of scat is mandatory to reproduce some of the old style of singing. I had been of no help to Brenna learning *Sing Sing Sing*, because the piano just wasn't like an ensemble for this piece, so she was singing with the video of the Rare Silk girls, essentially becoming the fourth member of the vocal troupe. We had begun to rehearse *It Was Just One Of Those Things* together and were making progress. She was being well-coached by Mill, and it showed in her poise and projection, because now she looked relaxed, smiling through the entire piece, and was using her graceful arms to emphasize the music. I was struck by her level of professionalism for such a short period of training.

"Would you be willing to go with me to the Roundup on Sunday to rehearse with some real musicians?" I asked.

Brenna looked at me with some surprise and said, "Can I?"

"They'll love it, and you can also meet the group. It will make you more relaxed for next week's performance."

"I would love to," she answered.

So much for that step, now I needed to call Zap and make sure the group could be there, especially Willie. I still didn't have any way to get in touch with Zap except by relay through the telephone number I was originally given. The Lulu who always answered remained a mystery. Since it was evening, I waited until midmorning on the next day to call. When Lulu answered, I said, "Hi, this is Daniel, and I'm trying to get hold of Zap. Is he there?"

"You mean Mr. James, don't you, White Boy?" It was the same confrontational tone that I had heard previously.

"I'm sorry, I mean Mr. James. Is he there?"

"You gots to leave a message, White Boy, you know dat," she responded.

"Can you tell him that I want to bring Brenna on Sunday to rehearse with the group?"

"I gots the message," and then she hung up. I knew from experience that I would get no additional contact, but Lulu had been reliable in the past so I figured that we should just take the chance and go together on Sunday. At least she would get to meet Zap. We only had a week to go, and this would be the last chance to rehearse.

We practiced together and separately and finally Sunday morning came around. "Don't you get real dressed up for this, Brenna. It is strictly informal over there on Sunday," I warned.

"What do you expect me to wear, Daniel? You know that I don't even own a pair of jeans. Everything I have is a little dressy, and it's too cold out for shorts."

It was a losing argument with her, so I just shrugged. She was going to wear what she wanted no matter what I thought. She fussed around and put out a steady stream of mumbling under her breath, purposely so I couldn't catch her words, while flinging things from her chest of drawers, deciding finally on black rather tight slacks and a sweater which was too large for her but did suit the moment. At least it hid her marvelous figure in folds of knit. Her hair was fastened back in a simple pony tail and her feet clad in black ankle boots bordered by light gray wool fluffs at the tops. Distinctively yuppie, but the best I was going to get, so I just nodded approval. Sweatshirt and jeans for me, as always.

We took her car and arrived about 10:45. As we entered, we noticed that the little stage was full of people moving about. They stopped and stared as we approached. "I see that you got my message," I observed.

"Yeah, man, we ready for action," Peaches said, grinning from ear to ear. "This be Willie," he said, pointing to a tall balding fellow holding his clarinet, who smiled and bowed politely. Zap was seated at the piano and nodded and smiled his gold-tooth smile. There was also a bass player behind his huge instrument and two guitar players. I had no idea what was coming, but they were taking this event seriously. They were all friendly, and each came up to shake Brenna's hand. All I got was a nod.

When his turn came, Zap stood and extended his hand to Brenna. "It's a pleasure to meet you. I am Solomon James, but you can call me Zap." He gave me an amused side look. He turned and spoke up to the group as a whole, "You guys get in your position and les run through *Sing Sing Sing* all the way to give Brenna a feeling of the piece before she sing."

There was a brief flurry of movement, and after a nod from Zap, seated at the piano, the drums started. The piece features clarinet and drums and has a nearly animal presence. They were a lot better that I was expecting and did sound nearly like the original Benny Goodman recording, especially Peaches on the drums. After the music died out, Zap turned to Brenna and said, "OK, you will come in this time after the clarinet and sing your scat part." Just then, the door opened, and we all turned to see who was coming in. It was Mill.

"Oh my God! Mill!" Zap blurted. He stood up and in his bent over way hustled over to meet her. She flung off her coat with her good hand and came toward us, stopping in front of the elevated platform.

"Think I might join in, Zap?" she asked.

"Well, bowing and scraping did work! I'm so happy to see you again, Mill," he said and extended his hand to help her up. They had a long embrace and then turned toward us with his hand over her shoulder and her arm around his waist.

"Let's do this together, Brenna," she said. Brenna walked over and affectionately touched Mill's shoulder.

"I couldn't ask for more, Mill," Brenna said. Her back was to me, but I knew her well enough to know that she was tearful. She wiped her eyes and turned to me smiling broadly.

Zap ambled back toward the piano, saying over his shoulder, "You girls get under the light, and we are going to do this thing right."

I was not part of this piece so I stepped off the stage to be front and center where I had the best view. Brenna and Mill held hands and swayed to the music in a charming and feminine way, waiting to come in. Mill's presence made the group either play better or somehow sound better. Someone should have made a recording of this moment and sold it.

The girls came in with their scat exactly on the nod of Zap who was watching while playing the piano. One of the guitar players, who was behind Brenna, reached over and quickly pulled out her hair clip causing her long bonde hair to spill out in waves. He was right. The effect was enchanting, because her hair was moving as she swayed and kept time with her body. They both tilted their heads back while singing and frequently smiled at each other and at me. When they stopped, Peaches' drums came in aggressively, and the girls held their position at center stage. The magic of this moment made Mill's disability and disfigurement disappear, and she was for the present, once more a young and beautiful singer. And there was no doubt she still was an impressive singer. Mill added some flourishes, demonstrating that Brenna still had some work to do this week.

Zap stood up clapping when it was done and was happier than I had ever seen him. He came over to the girls and said, "That was grand, just grand. Brenna, how about joining White Boy down there for a moment, and let me see if Mill still remembers some of our old stuff." Brenna stepped off and snuggled up to me. Mill was smiling and apparently ready for anything. Just before he sat down, Zap turned and said, "How about *The Way You Look Tonight*?" There must have been some meaning between them with this selection, because I thought that Mill was going to choke up, her eyes rolling in that way of remembering something potent from the past. She recovered quickly and nodded approval. Zap stared at her as if remembering the past himself. He looked around at his group and said, "If you know it, play it. If you don't know it, just keep still and learn." He returned to his old upright piano and started playing chords, establishing a mood. Without even glancing at Zap for direction, Mill started singing, and we could tell that this was her special piece. There was no one alive who could have sung it better. Outstanding was the only word I could think of to describe hearing them. Such emotion. When she finished, we all applauded briskly, even the bass player clapped around the neck of his instrument. Peaches was the only one who had joined in and was grinning with his accomplishment.

Zap stood, theatrically bowing low toward Mill. "I thank you from the bottom of my old heart. You haven't lost anything, Mill. I would have cried, but I was afraid of mussing up my piano." Mill stayed under the spotlights indicating her willingness to sing more. Zap picked up on this and asked, "Any favorites you want to do, Mill?"

"Remember *Stormy Weather*?"

"Yes, yes, indeed I do. I also know that these boys know it too. You want it romantic or quicktime?"

"I am feeling the love, Zap, play it slow," Peaches started a rhythmic beat, and on Zap's nod, they all came in. There were a few measures until Mill started singing. She was terrific, and there was no wonder that she had had a career at one time. I was sure that she could still have one if she wanted, but I had become aware that she was so uncomfortable about her appearance that she remained more or less in hiding.

Comparing Mill and Brenna wasn't really possible. Brenna, at the peak time in her life, was so attractive that it overshadowed and colored everything. She wasn't complete in her singing development but also had a different style than Mill. Both were good, but both together could only be described as "wow."

"I think that it's time for Brenna and White Boy to impress us and, please, Mill, stay and sing at least one more song for one who admires you so." Zap showed his gold teeth in a smile that was appreciative and pleading at the same time.

Mill smiled back at him and said, "How can I say no to such a flatterer."

Mill stepped off the stage, and we stepped up. I went toward the piano and heard Zap say what I expected by now, "Remember what I taught you, and I'm watching you for using any damned sheet music." He turned his back and went down to join Mill.

I could tell that the other musicians were not going to play and that was just fine with me, since I had not played with them before. Brenna stood under the light in a way that told me that she was ready to sing, so I started with a few simple measures using a slow rhythm as we had rehearsed. My attention was fixed on the keyboard, but I could hear her. She was as fantastic as I had ever heard, and listening to her sing the words to *It Was Just One Of Those Things* always went into my heart like a knife, but I never told her, because that is why she didn't want to sing it. Our love was not a fling, but if you live long enough you learn that everything is temporary, and you can lose the things and people you love the most. Life and death take it all eventually.

When we stopped, the formerly silent musicians started whooping it up and giving her the wolf whistle. Zap gave me a thumbs up and a wink.

Mill jumped up on stage and said, "Good, but we need to up the tempo. I would say if you were singing at 60, we need to turn it up to 90. If Cole were here, he would tell you that the piece is flippant, not serious. Love to be taken lightly. An up-tempo expresses that better and doesn't sound like remorse. He didn't intend remorse at all."

She pointed at Peaches, "Give me a bit faster beat and use some snares." He complied. "Faster." He complied. "Now all start again," she commanded. I started again trying to match the up-tempo. Brenna came in, and we seemed to be flying through it. I didn't like it as much. Sinatra sang it slow, and it sounded right. Mill, however, had her own agenda, and it didn't include feelings. She was satisfied and then nodded toward me and said, "Okay, Dan." At least I got credit for being alive and there.

Zap spoke up, "Wait a minute, Mill, let me try something." He got up on the stage and said, "You all heard the music, and I want you all in on this. Peaches, try just a little slower, if you please. Mill, would that be all right with you?" Mill shrugged. She had gotten what she wanted for her own reasons, and it apparently wasn't how good the piece sounded.

"Willie, you gonna start first. Play with the melody awhile and then Daniel, you come in with Brenna. When she's finished, the rest of you take off with it." Did you notice that he called me by my first name? I did. That means that he finally liked my playing. I had arrived!

As directed, Willie started, accompanied by just a little drum action, and as he got going on the melody, we got the nod from Zap. It was much better than before. The natural rhythms came out, and Brenna hooked on it better. She seemed brighter, more crisp. When we stopped, the group took off in a jazz interpretation which was more bizarre by the second. Well, that's jazz. Some like it and some don't.

Mill kept a deadpan expression, and I couldn't tell what she was thinking. When it was over, Zap came up to her and put his arm around her. "Just one more, Baby?"

She smiled at him and said, "Recall *Around Midnight?*"

"Of course, I do," he said, showing his gold tooth. He took my place and just winked at the other musicians. They would know what to do without direction. He played an introduction and then faded back to allow Mill to be the main attraction. They showed us how it was supposed to be done. There is a difference in professional and amateur, and we saw it. Both Mill and Zap were really good, and the band accompanied by staying in the background. When Mill finished, all of us, including Zap gave her a long applause. She gave a slight bow and jumped off the stage.

"Mill, you gonna be here next Saturday night?" Zap asked.

"You know I love you, Zap, but don't ask me that. I can't do it, and you understand that."

"Baby, you are so so good that it's a crime that no one can hear you. I wouldn't say anything to hurt you, Mill, but truly your voice is a treasure, and people don't care what you look like. Look how ugly I am, and I'm still up here playing music!" Zap knew it wouldn't work, but he had to try.

Mill was unmoved by his plea. "I've got to go, Zap. It's been great to see you again," she said, without any emotion.

"Will I see you again, Mill?"

"Probably not, Zap, but you never know for sure what will happen in life." A hint of a sardonic smile on the good half of her face briefly was visible, and she turned and left.

Are We A Band Yet? *by Alexander Francis*

Chapter Sixteen

A Surprise

*B*renna had three sessions scheduled with Mill in the week before our performance. During the first two, they mostly worked on her scat singing, especially since she was to do it alone. Brenna felt pretty good about what happened at the previous session, and I decided to go with her for the last one.

On Thursday evening, we went over to Mill's house and knocked on her door. When it opened, she appeared surprised to see me. "You were going to have me once a week, as I remember, and I am back again!" I reminded her.

"Of course, Daniel, you are welcome. By the way, I thought you played very well last Sunday." As we made our way into the living room, I was once again staggered by the enormous concert grand piano wedged into the small room. After we took off our coats, Mill said, "Daniel, can you play this and warm up while I have a talk with Brenna?" Absently, she handed me a small bunch of printed music.

"Sure, Mill," I said. They went into the kitchen, and I settled in to get a feel for the chords and timing. What a magnificent piano. I looked at it carefully inside and out, and from all appearance, it was brand new and in perfect tune. Gingerly, at first, I went to work on the chords. Using what Zap taught

173

me about chord tones, I started expanding the music. It finally dawned on me that I recognized what I was playing. It was *Laura*, made famous by the movie and sung by all the greats of its day. The piece lends itself to jazz chords and is a great slow, sleepy, romantic piece. I never liked the words to the song as well as the score.

In a few minutes, I felt as though I was as ready as I was going to be in just a short time. Just before the girls came back in, I pondered the choice of this song for a female singer, because it usually has been sung by males. However, somewhere in my distant memory, I sort of remembered a recording of Ella Fitzgerald singing it. They were all smiles as they came back into the living room.

As they approached the piano, Mill said, "I heard your playing, and you sounded ready; is that so?" I thought of some comebacks, but I just nodded. "Daniel, you start, and I'll sing first," Mill said. Brenna was studying the words on her paper and didn't look up. I started playing, and Mill came in about the second measure. It was putting me a bit off-balance to have her stare at me during her singing, but I tried to ignore her and pay close attention to my hands instead. When she finished, I saw Brenna smile and nod that she was ready to try. Brenna was up to the task, and although her smoky voice did not project as well as Mill's, it was ever more sexy. I noticed that they were both smiling at me.

"Daniel, you have come a long way; I enjoyed that. See... you can do it," said Mill.

"Thanks. Coming from you... well, it means a lot to me."

She put her arm over Brenna's shoulder and pulled her tight, "I have some news for you both."

Oh no, I thought, here it comes. I felt a wave of terrible dread sweep over me.

"There is a Canadian group, calling themselves The Terrence Star Jazz Band, currently touring the US. They have a booking at the Hollywood Bowl on Tuesday night. It is the big time for them and the chance to play with the best and be seen where it's important to be seen." She paused and looked at both of us with her expressionless steel gray eyes. We were listening. "They have a troublesome singer who has boyfriend problems. She hasn't been seen for three days, and they have alerted the police. The concert is very important for them, and they need a substitute singer on short notice. It happens that you are now up to speed on the very pieces that the missing singer sings, and I have already made initial contact with the manager of Terrence Star." She stopped again. We were struck dumb, and both of us struggled to understand the implications of what she was telling us. Mill continued, "Have I your permission, Brenna, to give the go ahead?"

"What does this mean, Mill? Can you please elaborate a little bit?" I pleaded. Brenna was unable to respond, and I felt her clutch my arm.

"It's this, kids. Brenna has the opportunity to replace the missing singer and sing with a group in front of both the cameras and a huge and important audience. The performance is a benefit for the poor of

North Africa, and I can promise that everyone who is anyone will be there, and there will be standing room only. She will rub shoulders with the current greats of performance, and she will get plenty of notice. This is the opportunity of a lifetime, and things like this only come once," she said with a level voice and the same hard look in her eyes.

Brenna finally spoke, "Am I really ready, Mill?" I intently watched her while she was speaking and could see the stress.

"Of course, you are ready. I am also on the line with this deal. My reputation is at stake, but I am completely confidant of your ability. Really, I think you are going to be a star. This is your big break, take it."

"I have never been to LA or Hollywood, Mill, and I don't even know who to go see when I go," Brenna said in a very small, helpless voice.

"All you have to do is say yes, Brenna. I am going with you and will be there at all times, except when you are on the stage, and I already have the airline reservations for us. We are leaving on Monday morning from here, and you will have Monday evening and Tuesday morning to rehearse with the group. You don't even have to worry about hotels, because you will stay at my place."

Now, I was dumbstruck. How could Mill have known that this unique opportunity would arise while admitting that the whole thing is already worked out to the last detail. Was there some foul play here? Mill has contacts, I've heard, but this was amazing.

"I have a question, Mill," I ventured. She looked at me without speaking. I could tell that she had an answer for any question I had and resented me asking. "What if the missing singer turns up?"

"Well, then Brenna and I will make use of our time by making contacts with the right people. That will happen nevertheless, but the singer isn't going to show."

This was a train we were on which had a destination and could not be stopped. The route was written in steel, and the train was accelerating.

"What is my role, Mill?" I asked. Again, she fixed me with her lidded steel gray eyes and said in a level tone, "Your role is completed, Daniel. You should be happy for her, because you enabled this to happen. You should kiss her and wish her well."

Brenna started to sob and wrapped herself around me, crying into my shoulder. I looked back and forth to the two women standing near me and realized that I had to let Brenna go. Every fiber of me wanted to keep her with me, but this instinct was selfish. I had to encourage her to go and fulfill her destiny, whatever the cost to me. If I went with her, I would only be a drag. I had made improvements in music, but we all knew that I was not nearly ready for a stage role and, in fact, none had been offered.

"Mill, what comes after this performance on Tuesday?" I asked.

"That, my young friend, is unknown. It depends on how she does and how she strikes people who have the power to make things happen. Anything goes." At this last reference to the old Cole Porter number, Mill gave me a subtle smile and looked to see if I got the connection. I sure did, but, at this moment, I remained as opaque as she was. Brenna had stopped sobbing but remained in my arms.

"She's going to go with you, Mill; I'll see to that," I assured her while caressing Brenna's shoulder.

"I think that we are done here, Daniel. You better take her home, and by the way, enjoy your performance Saturday Night," Mill said. I helped Brenna on with her coat, and we headed out. Before we got to the car, Mill called out, "Brenna, call me tomorrow morning, and I will give you some more details. Don't worry about clothing for the performance, because Saran Webber's outfit is there and is your size."

How convenient, I thought, even the missing girl's size is the same. It was like an evil force at play. The devil himself couldn't have done better.

Brenna was silent the entire way back to her apartment, but just as we pulled in to park, she turned her swollen face to me. "Daniel, I can't do this without you there. I can't even face life without your strength. Please help me."

Without thinking, I buried my face into hers, and we embraced and held on, kissing and crying together. I whispered in her ear, my nose full of her skin's natural scent and her perfume, "Dear, this is what we were working for. It's only a performance, and you have been certified by the best. Go and enjoy the experience. It will be the most memorable night of your life, and I promise that I will be there somewhere that night, and you will feel my presence inside you. You know that I am your biggest fan, and I want you to sing as if you were singing just for me. Don't worry, you can't shake me that easily. I will always be there for you as long as we are alive, you can count on that."

Inside, I was terrified both for her and for me. I knew that I had to inspire her to have enough confidence in herself, but I also understood that no one knew her fragility as well as I did. It was also obvious that I was not invited to stay with Mill and Brenna, and therefore, Mill wanted me out of the picture.

After we got back into her apartment, Brenna took my advice and went to bed for a rest. She was going to need a lot of support, so I called Mike to see if I could get the band to go out to dinner with us. He said that he knew that they would all want to go, and we arranged a time and place. After that was settled, I went online to find as much as I could about the Hollywood Bowl and perhaps get a ticket for myself. I quickly discovered that tickets for this fundraiser had been on sale for two months, and no ticket was available any longer at any price. I also scanned the long list of famous performers who were scheduled to perform. The event was taking place in the late fall just before Christmas, but the weather in Hollywood in December is usually temperate. I was startled to learn that the Bowl can hold a little over seventeen thousand patrons. It also dawned on me that Brenna could be gone for Christmas, if her performance was good enough. Again my personal loss struck me. My fear of losing her was going to become reality after all. Any chance of seeing her performance also would seem to be slim, and my only choice would be to show up just before the performance and perhaps buy a scalped ticket or just stand outside alone and listen.

It was a good idea getting together with our guys, even though we hadn't seen them for three months. They all came: Mike, Doug and Tom. They sat arrayed across from us in the big booth at the Shogun, sharing a large bottle of hot Sake, and keeping the conversation upbeat and brisk. They were boundless with praise for Brenna landing such a gig and so happy for her that it buoyed her, at least for a little while, and she smiled for the first time since hearing the news. They also promised to come to the Roundup on Saturday night and to hell with the risk. I wasn't too sure and told them that I better check with Peaches first, and after initial rebuttal, they all agreed that caution was appropriate. One look and I could tell that Brenna felt better, but she sat very close to me with our hips touching, and she would frequently reach for my hand below the table for a quick caress and squeeze.

Mike asked, "What did you two think of the recording you made?"

His question caught us by surprise. Brenna looked confused and said, "We actually haven't got it back yet, so we don't know how it turned out."

"Really?" Mike questioned, then turned to Tom. "Tom, didn't Pete tell you that his friend Harvey Silverman said that the recording turned out real well, and he was waiting to hear from Daniel and Brenna?"

"He did, and that was about three weeks ago," Tom answered. Brenna and I looked at each other, puzzled.

Mike asked, "Don't you have Harvey's number, Dan?"

His card was in my wallet, I remembered, and I dug around and found it, holding it up. "I'll call him on Monday and find out about this," I promised.

Brenna would be gone by then, I remembered, and my stomach knotted up again. Previously, I was only worried about our Saturday night gig, but now that seemed small and unimportant. My one-way airline reservation for LA didn't leave until Tuesday afternoon. The flight that Brenna and Mill were on was full. I would get there and only have time to rush over to the Bowl by cab. This kind of travel is the pits for me. Too many unknowns and I always stress out about details. We polished off the last of the sushi and another bottle of sake and adjourned outside to say goodbye. There was a cold drizzle and fog outside, and goodbye was awkward for everyone. It felt like our parting was to be forever. There were handshakes and hugs all around and, of course, tears from Brenna. As we drove back to her apartment, we were silent. There was nothing left to say.

Chapter Seventeen

Saturday Night Fever

As Saturday evening approached, the excitement and anticipation increased. We rehearsed in the morning, and since these were the very pieces that Brenna would be performing at the Bowl in three days, we took it very seriously. We did all that we could do, and I felt very comfortable that Brenna was ready. We both were upbeat and were able to keep a positive attitude.

Brenna had her long conversation with Mill and came away feeling better. She heard a lot of good things about the group she was to perform with, and about midmorning received a call from a Jeff Barnes who represented the band. He wanted to confirm with her that she was coming and was actually up to speed on the songs. The conversation was not long, and after she hung up, she was very happy.

We sort of lounged around making small talk the rest of the afternoon. We were both too stressed to eat much for dinner, and we found enough leftovers around to get by on. Brenna was reserving Sunday for packing, not that there was much to pack, given the many unknowns. I called Peaches as I had promised Mike, but he was not interested in extending any welcome to anyone other than Brenna and me. That was that for me, and I called Mike and advised him not to come at all, but that I would call him in the morning to tell him how it went. I didn't have any anxiety about going to the Roundup at night, because everyone we had met went out of their way to make us feel welcome, and besides, we had Peaches.

Nothing could keep Brenna from dressing up for her performance. One look at her and you knew that she was overdressed for a bar in a bad neighborhood. She wore a clinging low-cut red dress, heels and jewelry. I decided to wear a well-worn sweater and to fade into the shadows if possible. After dressing, we sat around and watched the clock. We were to perform sometime after 8 PM, and promptly at 7:30, there was a loud knock. When the door was opened, Peaches was standing there grinning, dressed in a black tux which made me feel underdressed. We asked him in, but he wanted to get moving. As promised, we were chauffeured in his immense black Cadillac right to the door of the Roundup. Before I could open the door, Willie came hustling out and opened it for us. I got out first and held Brenna's hand to help her out. The double doors to the Roundup burst open, and people spilled out, making a double line. We walked in like royalty to the applause, well-wishes and smiles of everyone present. I never imagined that this could have happened. I could see the stage in the distance, and there was old Zap under the light and dressed to the nines. His gold tooth glittering under the spotlights.

"Welcome!" Zap yelled into the mike which roared over the chatter of talk. The place was packed, with standing room only. Brenna and I were the only white faces in the room, but I couldn't have felt more comfortable. We ascended the stage, and there was only a foot between us and the front row of people crowding the stage. As I was helping Brenna take off her wrap, Peaches came to the mike and shouted, "Get back from the stage!" This was not a request, and the crowd moved back leaving about four feet of room. There was no more room to give, and after a sullen look around the room, Peaches sat down behind his drums. We could hear the expected cat calls and whistles at Brenna, and she smiled back at them. Zap came to the mike and tapped it to get some quiet. After the crowd at last grew silent, he spoke, "Brenna and Daniel are here to give you a preview of her performance on Tuesday at the Hollywood Bowl. In case some of you don't know anything about that place, I can tell you that it is as big as...well, as big as Hell. We have a new star among us, and I hope she will remember the little part we had in getting her there. I didn't tell her, but we are asking that she sing three pieces tonight for us, but first we are going to start with a piece that we love and Peaches especially loves."

At the mention of Peaches, the drums started a rhythmic roll and beat to introduce *Sing, Sing, Sing.* I moved over to the piano and stood to one side, while Zap seated himself. He gave me a wink and started playing. Willie came in for an extended solo on the clarinet, and at last, Brenna got the nod. She came forward under the spots, and we all knew that she was a new star. I could see her from the back with her long shimmering blonde hair swaying as she sang. The graceful motion of her hands and hips that had always been natural for her now had purpose. In my mind, I was seeing her as she would be on Tuesday night under the big lights and the cameras. She was captivating, tantalizing, perfect. The superlatives could go on and on. I was in love with her down to her molecules.

After her spot, she stepped back a little, twisted to catch my eye and gave me a smile. No doubt that she was ready for Tuesday and probably anything else. We had all done well by her, and she had worked hard for this moment. It was like seeing a bird take flight. The piece went on and on, and all the musicians got a spot in the light, but the night belonged to Peaches and Brenna. The crowd erupted when the music stopped and started to become unruly, until Peaches stood and glowered at them.

Zap came up to the center stage mike and bent down toward it, "The next one is an old tune, but probably most of you haven't heard it before. It was written about seventy years ago, but it is still sung and will always be sung, because it's still true. Listen to *It Was Just One Of Those Things* and enjoy." He turned to me and nodded in the direction of the piano.

This time I would play and be joined by the others as well. Brenna stepped up to the mike and waited. The room went silent in anticipation, the crowd and the musicians all waiting on the same thing. Me. I had a surprise in store for everyone, especially Zap, that Brenna and I had worked on. This piece has an extended introduction going on for about two pages before getting to the more familiar refrains. This section is rarely sung and more rarely played. I started playing the music just as Cole Porter wrote it, and I glanced up at Zap with a quick defiant look. Even though I played alone, I had everyone's attention. Brenna started singing at the right spot, and the other musicians joined in. I dropped back to chords and scattered leading tones and faded back. I kept playing softly and could only see her in my mind, because I had my back to the center stage.

Near the end, there was a repeat, and the other instruments became more noticeable. I turned to look just as she stopped, and I could see her wipe the tears streaming down her face. She bowed low to loud and sustained applause, and she twisted to the right and left and bowed in an acknowledgment of the other musicians, except me. She would not look at me, because her own words, the words written flippantly by Cole Porter seventy years previously describing a romance which had ended, had meaning to her and at this moment more so than ever. The pain in my chest was pretty bad, but I was happy for her and so proud of the way she could sing.

Zap sensed what was going on with us and intervened by striding up to the mike, brimming with control and confidence, "Come on up here, White Boy, and take your bow." There were many deep chuckles from the audience, but I got applause also. When I got there, I embraced Brenna and Zap both. He turned to the mike and addressed the audience, "Well, White Boy, you got to play your thing anyhow, but I didn't see any sheet music so I forgive you. You did sound good, and, Brenna, honey, you are going to shake LA up; we will feel the earthquake from here." Again, there was sustained applause. I realized that this was the first and probably only time that I would ever get to share a stage with Brenna.

Zap grabbed the mike again and said, "Brenna, I have a request for another song, and I happen to know that you can sing it." Brenna was looking expectantly at him with her eyebrows raised. Neither of us could guess what he was up to. "Dear, would you sing *Laura* for us tonight? Daniel will accompany you alone this time, and if I see any sheet music, he'll be called White Boy forever." The crowd loved this, and I bowed low to him, shaking my head and opening my hands, indicating no sheet music. Brenna nodded yes and smiled in his direction. We only had played this once before and had no music with us and no prior practice. This was a real spot Zap had put us in; just when everything was going well, he had to mess us up. My brain was cooking while I returned to the piano.

Zap tugged on my sleeve and whispered, "Start with B flat major and then do the four, five and one in dominant sevenths." I nodded that I understood; it was coming back to me now. Brenna was standing in the light waiting for me, her lovely head turned just enough to watch me. I hit the first chord ever so softly, and she came right in. At the end of the song, we were about to do a complete repeat when Willie's clarinet came in strongly, carrying the melody so beautifully. Willie and I went through it together, and then Brenna came back in for another repeat. We played it slowly and very romantically. Brenna was still full of emotion from singing *It Was Just One Of Those Things*, and her voice was still a little husky, but it added a lot to how she sounded. I wish that this night had been recorded, but I knew that all I would ever have would be the memory of it. The crowd was ours and went nuts. Zap couldn't get control or be heard, even with the mike.

Peaches stood up and went to center stage and bellowed, "We be going now. If any clown mother touches her on the way out, he going to wish he was dead." I believed him, and so did the crowd, which parted for us. We gave a final bow to the audience and the musicians, and we both gave Zap a long hug. Peaches led the way to his car waiting by the curb. There was so much comment from the crowd that I only heard snatches, but I did hear, "Come back again someday," more than once. We turned and waved as we exited, but by then the music had started back up, and we were forgotten as quickly as a door shutting.

Peaches was talkative and chatted back and forth with us all the way back. When he pulled up to Brenna's apartment, I offered a twenty for the trip, but he scowled and said, "No way, man, it be a pleasure and delight to play with you both tonight, and I hope we can do it again some day. Brenna... you go to LA and show who you are next week and remember us."

Brenna leaned into the front seat and gave him a big kiss. "You are so sweet, Peaches. I'm going to miss you."

Peaches rolled his eyes and said, "After a kiss like that, I'm not going to forget you, either."

"Goodnight, Peaches," I said, as his car disappeared into the night.

Chapter Eighteen

The Calm And The Storm

*W*e slept in late on Sunday, our last day together. We both knew that the past was behind us, and although the future was unknown, it would be different. Things were going to change from this day out, and for all we knew, we were spending our last moments in each other's arms. Part of me wanted to ignore what could happen and pretend that life would go on as always, but the other, the darker part of me, felt that Brenna was about to leave on a long voyage into strange lands and discover new worlds, forgetting the old one. We made breakfast together and sat across from each other, looking into our lover's face. I never grew tired of looking at her and seeing the flicker of emotion, whim and fancy move back and forth across her perfect features. During moments like this you have perceptive power which exceeds all other times. You know fully why you love someone, and you know that the love you feel can never go away and that no one can ever take her place. I am reminded of two lines from a haunting poem by Dylan Thomas, "Though lovers be lost, love shall not. And Death hath no dominion."

The phone calls started midmorning. Most were friends who wanted to wish Brenna well. A couple were strange, and after discussion, we felt they were feeler calls from talent scouts. Officially, Brenna had no manager or agent, and we assumed that until that happened, she was to be open season, the beginnings of a public life. She looked so small and helpless, so innocent, and I had no real clear idea of what was facing her. Jeff Barnes called again and wanted to be reassured that Brenna was still coming. He set up an appointment for her to meet her band and fellow singers on Monday night at the Hollywood Hilton. After she hung up, I could sense the anxiety coming to the surface again. Mill called and instructed Brenna to be sure to arrive at 5 AM at the airport Monday morning and to check in at the United desk for her ticket. Another attack of anxiety. I was doing my best not to talk about her trip or her singing. We went through her wardrobe to make sure she had enough clothes for several days. Jeff told her that a make-up artist would go over her before the stage performance and that a professional photographer would see her early on Tuesday before rehearsal, and he also reminded her that her costume was taken care of.

After all this preparation and stress, I secretly hoped that the original singer would stay missing and not spoil things by turning up at the last minute or, heaven forbid, turn up dead. It's amazing how you can use up time puttering around, but there was enough left for an occasional hard embrace, done as much for me as for her. I kept wishing that I could somehow memorize her taste and the feel of her lips on mine, but there is no substitute for the real thing.

The short winter day was fading rapidly as evening approached. I didn't want the day to end...ever. Perhaps we would wake up as in the movie, *Groundhog Day*, and have this tortured day to live over and over again. After a supper of commercial frozen meals, I insisted that she try to get to bed early. She was reluctant to retire, because it would end today for us. I knew that I wouldn't sleep, instead lying beside her and watching her all night, and I did.

The nasty alarm brought us awake like a knife in the ribs. This is the day. This is it. I stumbled into the kitchen and started the coffee while Brenna showered. Fortunately, time was in short supply, and we had no time to linger or feel regrets. After a quick small breakfast, we left for the airport. As anyone knows who travels today, there isn't a platform like the old train stations for a long goodbye. There is only the check-in area which is congested with other passengers, so our goodbye was painfully short. A hug, kiss and a soulful look and she left through the gate. In the distance, I saw her turn and look briefly back at me, and then she was gone. A huge weight settled down on me, and I struggled to get back to her apartment. Once there, the emptiness of it without her was killing me. I had to stay there, alone and lonely, overnight because of my flight the next day to LA. After preparing a little food and coffee, I tried to watch TV, but her face was before mine at all times, and her voice echoed in my head. When I tried to lie down, the lingering scent of her imbedded in the bed linens reminded me that she wasn't with me anymore.

I remembered our recording, and I dug out Harvey Silverman's card and called him. The secretary who answered took my message and said that she would try to get him to call back, but he was in LA at this time. Would he be at the concert, I inquired, and would he talk to Brenna without me there? No idea. I didn't want to dwell on what could happen, because I could tell that Harvey wouldn't mind fooling around with any attractive woman, and I resolved to kill him if he moved on Brenna. I had to stop thinking about those kind of wild imaginings, but I couldn't stop thinking about her. Her flight would arrive about 10:45 my time, and I fully expected a call or text from her. After the clock hands passed noon, I realized that no call was coming.

I called Mike and arranged to meet him and Tom for supper and cry on their shoulder. We met at a small blues club where the music is always too loud, making it difficult for me to talk to them in any serious way. They both were too excited about Brenna's big chance to notice my misery, which was just as well. Sympathy would have only made me more down than I already was. On the surface, we had a good time and a couple of beers which helped me a bit. We parted with the usual well-wishes, and I left to pack for the next day's trip.

Tomorrow came suddenly, and I sprang up to finish packing and eating. I made it to the airport early, forced to wait and worry how the rest of the day would go. The flight was uneventful and arrived at L.A. on time. I checked my phone as soon as I stepped off the plane. No messages, no missed calls. The concert was to start at 7:00, and it was just after 5:00. I had arrived at Bob Hope Airport, quickly found a cab at the departure area, and requested the cabbie, in my hurried, excited voice, to take me to a close, decent hotel.

He turned around and looked me over. "Sure, Bub." Without another word, he drove about a mile to a pleasant one surrounded by trees and a manicured lawn. "This OK, Bub?"

I answered that it was, but instructed him to wait for me until I checked in, assuring him that I would be right back. He agreed without complaint. I did a rapid check-in and requested the bellhop take my bag to my room, rushing back to find the cab still waiting. "Now, take me to the Hollywood Bowl," I asked, becoming more stressed and excited.

He lurched away, and we drove toward the Bowl through heavy traffic. "Going to the show, Bub?" he asked.

"I don't know if I can get in. I couldn't find any tickets, so I am taking my chances on finding a scalper."

"Why is it so important that you go?"

"Well, my girlfriend is singing there tonight, and I just have to be there to see it."

"You should check with the ticket office, because she should have left a pass for you. All the performers get some freebies," he said, watching in his rearview mirror for my response.

"Kind of doubt it, because she only found out about it this weekend, but thanks for the info."

"Scalping near the Bowl is illegal, Bub, but I know a place if you want to try," he said.

"Can you get there fast?"

"Right on the way," and the cab jerked around a sharp corner and entered a parking lot. A small crowd was gathered around some cars at the end of the lot. "Take some cash and go over there; you'll get your tickets," he said.

Hesitantly, I got out of the cab, leaving the door open so that he wouldn't be tempted to get away and leave me there. I found a couple of guys in dirty black tank tops, one hand full of tickets and the other full of cash. Other people were buying, and cash was rapidly changing hands. One of them spotted me and asked, "Wat you want?" He had large tattooed arms and a goatee.

"One ticket for tonight at the Bowl," I answered.

"All I got left is the upper balcony, but you can choose right or left," he smiled a gap-toothed smile and held out a couple of tickets.

"How much?" I asked."

"If you have to ask, you can't afford it!" he laughed, then said with a scowl, "Two hundred, take it or leave it."

I forked over the two hundred bucks and headed back to the cab. "Got it, thanks," I said as I flung myself in. The cabbie nodded and away we lurched toward the Bowl. It was now 6:30. Only thirty minutes to go.

I felt better about it. We pulled up to a long line outside the gates, and I paid the cabbie and gave him two twenties for his tip. Some patrons were dressed in tuxes and furs, others in sweatshirts with hoods, and in commonality, we all inched toward the gatekeepers. In the distance, one could hear the cacophonous sounds of musical instruments being tuned all at once. My ticket could have easily been bogus, but to my relief, it passed, and I entered the short path to the stands. The actual Bowl was far in the distance from the rear seat that I had, and I had to pick my way across several pairs of legs to get to it. There was a large projection screen set up above and behind the front stage so that the performers could be better seen. The place was packed, and I saw no empty seats. Several professional camera crews moved around near the stage like small military units installing a howitzer.

After I sat down, I decided to text Brenna. "I am here. Wishing you the best tonight. I love you." A couple of minutes later, the phone showed an answer, "Thank God, you made it; I love you always and forever. I am so nervous." I expected that she was, and I wished I was there to hold her and help calm her down.

The show booklet was being passed out from the aisles, and eventually, I got one. It had the schedule of events, articles about some of the groups and individual performers, and, of course, a large percentage had been devoted to advertisements. Brenna's name was not listed anywhere so I assumed that the change was too late to get into print. There was an article about Terrence Star Jazz Band and how they were the re-creation of Benny Goodman's band and style. They were slated to perform in the fourth slot and had three numbers. The *Sing, Sing, Sing* piece was first, followed by *It Was Just One of Those Things*. That one was Brenna's solo piece. It was happening, right here and tonight. My stomach did flip-flops. The third number was *It's All Right With Me*. That's another one we rehearsed with Mill at the last minute and also was our only recorded piece.

Could it be that this new, untested singer was going to have the starring role for her band tonight? No wonder Brenna was consumed by stress. I was far away, out in the back forty, with no way to help her. This assemblage of massive numbers of every type of human being was squatting in the stands, munching on frivolous food, and waiting to pass judgment on the one person that I loved. The facts held me in awe. The orchestra section was packed with the ultra-dressed, the privileged ultra-rich, but toward the back, where I was seated, they seemed to be the jeans and sneakers set. Well, I guessed I belonged to this group more than I did with the stars below. Too bad I couldn't see better.

I fingered the schedule again, reading each line one more time. There were fifteen groups or individual performers, the really big stars nearer the end. The performances were to start in a couple of minutes and go on until...whenever. While I was thinking it over, the lights dimmed, and the stage lit up. There was a small group of tuxedoed musicians in the orchestra pit, who commenced playing *No Business Like Show Business*, one of Irving Berlin's timeless hits.

The MC walked out to sustained applause, a spectacular lady on his arm, who was dressed in a long white flowing gown covered with sparkling sequins. He waved at the crowd and smiled broadly, also acknowledging the orchestra director with a little bow. According to the pamphlet in my hand, this was Ken Howard, president of the Screen Actors Guild, and his well-dressed companion was Lucille Myers representing Ray Hair, president of the American Federation of Musicians. They both spoke at length about what a privilege it was to be here in the company of so much talent and so forth and what a proud cause it is to help the hungry in North Africa. They were frequently interrupted by applause originating in the front row of the orchestra section seating. The large cameras panned back and forth over the front section of the audience, projecting their celebrity faces on the big screen to the wow of the lesser-born audience. An ongoing slideshow behind and above the speakers displayed the usual pictures of starving African women and children. The speakers also made a push for the audience to kick in more money for this noble and worthy cause, and volunteers were already circulating to pick up the checks or cash.

Dramatically, the curtains were pulled, and a rock band was visible onstage and on the large monitor, accompanied by the usual light show and loud music. They played one longer piece and again were hidden by the curtain. A small young blonde girl bravely strode out alone to the mike. She was apparently a recent winner of a popular televised talent show and was loudly applauded before and after her song, sung in the country style.

After she walked off, the curtain was again drawn back, exposing a large black grand piano, which was then pushed forward into position by stage hands. I consulted the listings again. This was a piano comedy act similar to the old Victor Borge ones. The performer, Richter Styles, strode out, waving at an appreciative audience, and put on a funny and entertaining show.

The time had come for Terrence Star Jazz Band to perform. I almost couldn't stand the pressure and wanted to hide my eyes. The piano was withdrawn, and the curtain closed. There was a moment of uncomfortable silence and then drums started faintly, as if in the far distance. The curtain parted slightly in the center, and a fellow in a black tux emerged and walked to the mike. The drums continued with the pulsating rhythm of *Sing Sing Sing*, but still slightly muffled and restrained.

"Hi, I am Terrence Star, and I would like say how much I appreciate being able to take part in this magnificent event and this truly worthy cause." He paused and looked about the room. The drumbeat continued growing, slightly more noticeable. "Benny Goodman first performed *Sing Sing Sing* in 1936 and also played it here at the Bowl the same year. This piece is in his honor." At that, the drums started louder, and the curtain withdrew all the way back.

The band was arranged like a comma with three dressed-alike girls in the center moving slightly from left to right, swaying in time with the drums. Was that Brenna in the center? It was too far away to tell. Just then the camera seemed to seek her out, and there was her smiling face in the large screen just long enough for me to know that it was her.

Terrence Star moved to the side, picked up his clarinet and started up the familiar melody to the murmured delight of the audience. After he finished, he backed up, and the singers started the scat singing, perfectly mimicking the old video we had practiced to. They sounded in perfect harmony and moved identically, heads up and arms in motion. I resisted the urge to come to my feet and watched, fixated on the screen in case I would miss a glimpse of Brenna. The lead went to the sax then to the trumpet and then finished with a prolonged flourish. Most of the audience came to their feet in a wave of appreciation and nostalgia. Terrence Star bowed low and extended his arm in appreciation of his troupe.

When the applause died a bit, he tucked his instrument under his arm and came to the center mike. "Now, I am proud to introduce our new member." He motioned with his hand, and Brenna came to the mike. God, I wished I could have been closer. She stood behind the mike looking so small. Her hands were held together in front of her, and she looked up to Terrance. He put his arm over her shoulder and leaned into the mike, "This is Brenna Kristen, and she has only been with us for two days, but as you are going to see, she was worth the wait.

She is going to sing an old favorite. Please welcome her!"

The crowd obliged with long, loud applause. Terrance withdrew to the side, and the spotlight was turned on her. She was dressed, like the other girls, in a long cream, low-cut strapped dress. There was a sash at her waist which hung lower on one side. The audience fell dead silent. I held my breath. There is an introduction to the piece, written by Cole Porter, which was meant for the Broadway stage musical but is rarely sung now. The band started up with the introduction, and the melody softly spilled out of Terrance's clarinet. All the instruments played subdued, allowing a lot of room for the singer. The spotlight stayed on Brenna and so did the cameras.

Desperately, I looked around me and found what I was looking for. In the lap of a lady two seats from me was a pair of binoculars. I tapped the gentleman on the shoulder and asked, "Could I borrow your glasses for just a second?" They looked puzzled but agreed and handed them over just as Brenna started to sing. I swung the glasses up to see her face upturned to heaven, her arms spread wide and from her came the voice of an angel.

When she paused, the instruments came into the foreground and Brenna stepped back out of the light. I was still watching with the borrowed binoculars. The cameraman seemed to not want to let her go, and the big screen showed her face in shadow while the music continued. Everyone there, including me, could see the tears streaming down her cheeks like little fireflies caught by the light. She held her head high and steady, but I thought I could see her lips tremble.

"Finished, fellow?" my neighbor asked. I reluctantly gave up the glasses.

He was giving me a hard look. "Know her?" he asked.

"My girl," I answered. I was opening my eyes wide to absorb the tears forming. He probably could see that in the light.

"I'm sorry; keep them till she's done," he said and handed back the glasses. I smiled and nodded thanks and put them up again.

The camera was trained on various members of the band, but frequently came back to Brenna's face. She appeared to stabilize a bit and stared forward, a small strained smile on her lips. When the number was over, during the immense applause Terrance moved to stand beside Brenna, and the spotlight and cameras followed him. He bent at the waist before her and kissed her hand then held it up like a prize fighter. The audience was on its feet, especially me. When the clamor died down, they walked together to the mike, his arm over her shoulder. I took a long look at Mr. Terrance through the glasses. He was tall, dark and handsome, just like the movie line. He showed a big pearly white smile with Hollywood teeth, his dark curly hair spilling over his collar. Trim at the waist and broad at the shoulders, Terrance was looking at Brenna as if she were a morsel to be devoured. I instantly hated him. Mostly, I was jealous. He was better looking than me, more talented and famous to boot, and he had Brenna and I didn't. I was down and out, just like I had feared.

"Folks, we are lucky tonight to get another song from Brenna." He stepped back away from her and said with a flourish, "Brenna Kristen!"

Brenna stepped up to the mike as before, but this time Terrance came up beside her without his instrument. On a nod from Terrance, the band started up Porter's *It's All Right With Me.* This was the piece Brenna and I had recorded but since had disappeared into Harvey Silverman's empire. Hearing this piece was especially painful for me, all the more so because of the words of her preceding song. Somehow, the planets had aligned to single me out for punishment tonight, and they were giving me quite a beating. The spotlight and cameras were focused on Brenna, and she was breathtakingly beautiful, wearing a radiant smile. This time, she was looking directly at the audience, as Mill had instructed. She started to sing and partially raised her hands to the mike.

As she finished, she stepped back slightly, and the camera went to Terrance's face, and he sang the second part. When Terrance paused, Brenna moved back to his side, and they sweetly looked at each other and finished the song together.

The applause was deafening. The crowd again stood and from what I could see over heads, the camera kept mostly centered on Brenna. Holding hands, they took a deep and long bow and moved back just in time to miss the closing curtain. As the applause died, so did I. I handed the glasses back to the couple on my left, and this time I couldn't hide the tears.

The fellow asked, "Say, you sure she's still your girl?"

I couldn't tell if he was trying to be offensive, but I had no fighting spirit left. "No, I'm not sure. Thanks for the glasses; I have to go." I pushed my way past the feet and into the aisle, headed for the exit as fast as I could walk.

After I emerged into the night air and took a deep breath, I decided to call her, and I dug out my cell phone and punched her in. After several rings, her voice came on and invited me to leave a message, and I did. "Hi. You were and are wonderful, and I am so happy for you. You are the star that lights the sky tonight. If there is any way we could get together, please let me know when and where and I'll be there. I love you. Bye."

I waited. There was a long line of cabs at the curb extending as far as I could see. I was nearly alone out there, with performances still booming in the background. I rested my back against a convenient tree and waited. Impatiently. I decided to text her, "Loved your performance; left me breathless; can I see you?"

I waited. Roughly ten minutes later the phone chirped a returning text. "Dearest Daniel, I love you. I am besieged by interviewers and have agreed to go with the band to Seattle tonight. No time to meet. Talk later, if poss."

There it is, boy; you are out of the picture. Might as well go home. I walked toward the nearest taxi, but just as I reached for the back door handle, a horn sounded, causing me to turn toward the sound, squinting down the long row of cabs. My cabbie friend from this afternoon was waving at me. I walked toward him, and he got out to open the door for me.

"How did it go, Bub?" he asked. I waited to answer until I was seated. Once inside, he twisted to see my face.

"Well, she performed and was a big success. She doesn't have time to meet me tonight and is going out of town immediately."

He continued to stare at me wordlessly. I had to do something to abate the nearly lethal pain I was suffering. "Say, if you could take me to a good blues bar, I'll buy you a beer and give you fifty bucks," I offered.

"I'll do that, Bub," and he started the motor. He drove what seemed a long way, as I sat in the back, mostly in a funk of silence, flopping around like a loose ball as he turned endless corners.

The bar was a little seedy but just what I wanted. Larry Ramirez and I occupied a back booth, away from the over-amplified noise from the little stage. Larry carried a US Navy tattoo on his left forearm and, once out of the cab, looked particularly hard. He was a much nicer guy than he looked and not only interested in my problems, but very sympathetic.

"Bad luck, Bub. To have a gal like that one and to lose her so fast... well it's just... and the assholes even changed her name!" He had no words which could adequately express his appreciation of my pain.

His girl had found another while he was serving at sea, and he never got over it. Listening to him and knowing how I felt at this moment, I knew that I would never get over Brenna either. Never. The blues being sung spoke straight to my soul, and the rhythm of the band matched my forlorn mood. Most blues songs are about lost love, and the one they were performing was exactly right on target. It made me remember our group back home, and I felt a sudden yearning to get back to playing and learning with them. I started noticing the musicians on the stage. The piano player was about the same age as Zap and had the same kind of flair. He was playing blues, not jazz, and I had never actually heard Zap play the blues, but after watching this musician for a few minutes, the similarity was striking. When they took a break, I took a long pull on my beer and informed Larry that I would be right back.

I went close to the stage and stood beside the piano player. He gave me a funny look and said, "Well, stranger?"

"I'm from the Midwest. I know a piano player who looks a lot like you. He is called Zap by his friends. Ever heard of him?"

"Zap? That do sort of ring a bell. Hey, Semore, come here."

An older black guy disengaged himself from the small group who were drinking beer and came toward us. He was the double bass player and was wearing a goatee and an old frayed linen vest. As he drew closer, the pianist asked, "Don't I remember you talking about a Zap boy you once played with?"

"Huh? Did you say Zap?" he asked.

I spoke up, "I know a Solomon James who goes by the name Zap. He is a very good piano player, but I have only heard him play jazz."

"Well, hell yes, I know Zap. We go way back. You know Zap?" He was smiling and jumped down on my level.

"He's been teaching me to play jazz. He is mostly retired but still plays some really mean piano," I said.

"Well, ain't that special!" Semore exclaimed, and slapped me on the back.

I motioned to both of them, "Come on back to our booth, and we can talk about Zap all you want."

"Only for about five minutes and then we got to git back to playing," Semore said.

The pair came with me to our table, and I introduced them to Larry, who had finished his beer. "You guys care for another beer?" I asked. They all agreed, and I signaled the waitress and pointed to the empty glasses. "Tell me about Zap, Semore," I asked.

"We got together just after the Korean War, and we already knew each other slightly, because we both served in that hellhole," Semore explained.

"I was in the Navy in Nam," Larry interjected and held up his tattooed arm. They admired his tattoo, and Semore rolled up his sleeve and showed his Semper Fi done in red and black.

"Aw, man, you were in the Core!" observed Larry.

"Sure was, brother, but I would have been happier if I would have been home with the ladies and didn't have to carry around some Chinese metal in me all these years," Semore said.

"Was Zap in the Marines also?" I asked Semore.

"Yep, got a medal too, then got blown up. That's where we met. In the naval hospital in Japan. We both pulled through and played together in New York for about 10 years and then went our separate ways. I haven't seen him for many years." Semore sort of looked away and was evidently nostalgic at this revelation.

A young woman came up to the table and stood there until we looked up. She was strikingly attractive with long brown hair and green eyes. Semore said, "Daniel, this is our singer for tonight. We call her Cute Chick, but her real name is Sharon. If you stay and hear her, you'll be impressed."

I was impressed. She was very curvaceous and certainly didn't look innocent, and she was looking right at me and smiling.

Larry reached over and put his big rough hand on my shoulder, "You are a stranger in a strange land, and you have deep wounds, but you should be careful, especially tonight." I looked into his sincere rough face, and he gave me a wink and a smile. "Don't you think I should take you back now so you can get your beauty sleep?" He was right. My mind was a fog, and I was searching for any comfort from my inner pain, so I wasn't in full control.

"We best get going, guys," I said, then continued, "Nice meeting you both, and I will be sure to tell Zap that I met you. By the way, I loved your band. Nice to meet you, too, Sharon. Perhaps we will meet again someday," and then Larry took me back to my hotel. He wouldn't accept my offer of money, because he said that he would still be parked at the Bowl waiting for the show's end, and anyhow, we were brothers in pain.

Chapter Nineteen

A New Life

I got off the plane in Chicago late Wednesday night. The trip was made up of mostly sitting in the airport waiting for someone not to show up so I could go home. While I waited, I checked my email, checked for missed calls, and looked for text messages. Nothing. I did the same thing when I got to Chicago. Still nothing. What should I do? There is no one to ask at times like that. After all, I am the expert in my relationship with Brenna, and I should have known what to do, but I didn't. There wasn't enough information to even form an opinion. I could imagine a thousand scenarios which could apply, but which was true? The anger and hurt boiled just under the surface of my skin. Couldn't she take just a moment to let me know that she was still alive? If she was going to forget me and move on, shouldn't she at least tell me goodbye?

Sitting in the Chicago airport, waiting for the regional bus, I decided to call her. For all I knew, she was giving her next concert right now, but what the hell, I needed to call. I did and got her sweet voice telling me to leave a message. "Brenna, I'm on my way back home, and I am thinking of you. Please call me and tell me that everything is going well. I'll always be there for you if you need me. I love you. Bye."

I decided not to text her in case she was singing. Tomorrow, I will talk to her come hell or high water. I made it back to my home about one in the morning and decided to go back to work and take some burden from my partner who had been fabulous in covering for me the past several days. I dragged myself in about eight and got started on paperwork. Still no word from Brenna, not a peep, not a thought. Hoping that she might check her email, I sent a short note asking about her and what was going on and that I sure would like to hear from her, etc. Still no word from her came back. The West Coast is two hours behind the Midwest so I had to wait until at least ten to try to call her again. Next time, I would text her.

A call came in on my cell, and I snatched it up, holding it with both hands. The screen showed that it was Mike. "Hi, Mike," I said.

"Hi yourself, dude. Don't you think that you should keep your friends informed about stuff?" he quipped. There was some irritation in his voice.

"I'm sorry, Mike. I should have, but I just got back early this morning. Brenna did her thing at the Bowl, and I got to watch from way back in the last row, but I haven't heard from her except a very brief note that she was going to Seattle with her new band. Nothing since."

"Are you down about it, Buddy?" he asked.

"No, I'm destroyed. I am a walking, talking zombie right now, and I am trying unsuccessfully to stay calm. That's the truth."

There was a brief silence as he thought of something to say, but there was nothing to add. "Did you know that there is a YouTube of her at the Bowl already out, and it has over nine hundred eighty-three thousand hits so far?"

"Mike, I am very happy for her, sincerely I am. This is what we were working toward, and I could see on Tuesday night that she was an instant celebrity. Only, I feel like I was discarded pretty quickly so my mood is real dark right now. I am very desperate to talk to her, but at this point, I don't even know if she wants to talk to me."

He paused again before he spoke. "There is an article on the news section of the online Rolling Stone which talks about her. I'm betting that she is completely bowled over by all the intense interest right now, and she may be confused or she may be getting some bad advice."

Yes, and I would know who is giving her the bad advice, either Mill or Terrance or both. Neither would like me back in the picture right now, or ever. "I don't know, Mike. I just can't think right now. I have to get back to work and let the situation sort itself out. If she calls me from the South Pole and wants me to come, I would do it. If she needs a heart transplant, I will be first in line. I can't help but feel that she is avoiding me. This is the longest period that we haven't talked in five years, and this is the most critical time of all. It's all on her end, though, because my feelings haven't changed a bit. The waiting is killing me."

"Maybe I can get hold of this Harvey Silverman for you and find out something," he suggested.

"Good luck. I have had a call in for him since Monday, but with no response."

"Hmmm," Mike murmured. "Look, I'll let you get back to it. Call me if you hear anything, Buddy, and I'll do the same. Keep your chin up. There is an explanation somewhere. I have seen you and her together, and let me tell you for certain that I have seen the love in her eyes. That doesn't just go away this fast." We said goodbye, and I resumed work, after checking my mail again.

When ten o'clock came, I put everything aside and picked up my phone. No missed calls or text. I typed in a short message, "Brenna, are you OK? I am getting desperate to talk to you. Love you." I waited, phone in hand, for a response. Still nothing.

I was just getting up to walk away when the phone rang, an incoming call. I snatched it up and looked at the number. Unknown source, it said. I answered anyway, and a familiar voice came through, "Dan, this is Harvey Silverman. I know that you were trying to contact me, but I wanted to find out what is going on before I talked to you. I apologize for the wait."

"Harvey, if you can tell me what is happening now with Brenna, I would be grateful. I know almost nothing."

"As far as I can tell, Brenna is still in Seattle. They had a big concert there on Wednesday night, and she was featured again and was wildly successful.

Terrance has pulled out all the stops to promote her, and he has hit some buttons that has brought out about everyone. She is being besieged by invitations, possible contracts, even possible suitors. Mill is with her and is preventing contact with most of the interested parties, including me. Terrance wants her to sign on with his group, and he has some justification, because he put her under the spotlights first. Mill, of course, wants in on any contract and has control of Brenna at this moment. Things I have heard make me think that there is something else going on with Brenna, because no one has seen her and the paparazzi are out in force hunting her. That scene during her first song with the tears was seen by everybody, and it made her look so pure and innocent, when combined with her voice, the package has made her really hot property."

"Yes, I was there and saw the tears. I almost had some of my own," I answered untruthfully. There were plenty of my own tears, rivers of them.

"You remember that I warned you about this, and it has happened on a scale that even I didn't anticipate. Do you think that she is strong enough to take all this pressure, Dan?" he asked.

"I don't know what will happen. I like to think that I am a stabilizing influence for her and understand her better than anyone else, but Mill engineered this very carefully for her own ends, and she has managed to exclude me completely. I can't even talk to Brenna over the phone, and she won't answer texts or email."

Harvey paused a little before commenting, "More than anything I have heard or surmised, this convinces me that something is wrong. I saw you two together, and I was sure that it would take a lot to separate you two. It couldn't have happened this quickly. To Mill's credit though, she is protecting Brenna from some pretty dangerous forces, not only the prying press. I know for a fact that Brenna has been invited to two separate Hollywood Hills home parties that normally are an opening to fabulous success. To attend something like that is also an opportunity for the jealous and the competitive to eat you alive, and to the predators, it's an invitation to their bedrooms. She needs at least a hundred thousand worth of clothes and jewelry and a lot of coaching and experience to even go through one of those doors. She is not ready for that world, for sure. By the way, Terrance Star's band usually plays in Canada, Australia and the UK, and they have been on nearly a constant tour. I got one recording out of them in a studio, but most of their albums have been live stuff from their gigs. The point is, that if she goes with them, you will never see her again, and that is what all the pressure on her is about right now."

"I didn't want to hear that, Harvey. I am feeling sick inside with worry for her, and of course, I miss her."

"Would you be prepared to go with the band to city after city and become a groupie?" he asked, knowing the answer.

"I haven't been asked, Harvey. In fact, officially, I don't know anything at all. I'm out," I responded flatly.

"If I could get in to the inner circle for a minute, I might be able to get some sense of direction and perhaps influence Brenna, but I am as out as you are. I think you know that Mill and I once had a fling, but you don't know that I ran away from her once I realized what she was all about. She is a formidable person and has really no limits when she wants something. What an amazing thing it has been to watch her catapult Brenna this quickly into fame. No one else could have done it, but prying her away from Brenna will be impossible."

"I have thought about it a lot in the past days, Harvey, and I think to Mill, Brenna not only represents financial enrichment but a chance to vicariously experience her own career over again. Mill is a force of nature, and Brenna is very vulnerable, innocent, and by comparison, helpless."

"Dan, I am not so sure about that. I was under the impression that she is very intelligent, so let's not write her off. By the way, I sent the finished recording of you and Brenna to Mill. A mistake, I now realize, but the intention was to solicit Mill's comment so we could jointly work on a path for Brenna. The finished recording has been test marketed in several cities but without any mention of who is singing. The DJ's tell me that it is a potential hit, because all the response so far is positive. We have been careful to only play it in the jazz venues and not in the general popular genre. I thought that your idea of playing the original music combined with melody chords during her singing was a novel approach, and it turns out to work really well. At the studio, we think you can make a commercial success with similar recordings, and you never know how far this could go. With all the current buzz about her, I am sure this recording would go big. If we ever get the chance again, we should meet and talk it over some more."

"That's big news, Harvey, and it could have made a difference in how all this turned out. Now, I am not surprised that Mill hid it from us. She had other plans and that explains my exclusion."

"One other question, Dan, which may be pertinent. Does Brenna have a passport? She is going to need one in a hurry if and when they cross the border."

I thought for a few seconds and finally remembered, "She has never been out of the country. To my knowledge, she does not have a passport, and I know for certain that she doesn't have one with her. I frankly don't know if she has a safety deposit box somewhere. She has some stuff in mine, so I doubt that she has one on her own. I am positive that I haven't seen a passport or birth certificate for her."

"That will be an obstacle for getting her to the gig next week in Vancouver. I will be interested to see how they solve it. They could drive her over to Vancouver, but she won't be able to come back in without a U.S. passport. Intriguing. She could get into a real mess unless she thinks about this with a clear head. Times are different today," he said.

We really had nothing left to say, and after promising to contact each other with new news, we signed off.

Chapter Twenty

Starting The Search

*B*ack to work with gusto, in part to forget my misery. Her face and the memory of her was constantly in my head, so much so that I was afraid of going insane. I found that I had no appetite for food, news or anyone's company and was short-tempered. About 3:00 in the afternoon, I checked my email and found a strange letter from someone called Michael. He identified himself as a bellboy in the Hyatt Regency in Seattle. The letter stated that he was given twenty dollars by a lady in a suite he serves and a note asking him to write me. He said that the lady had lost her cell phone and had no other way to contact me, but that she was okay, misses me very much and was going to try to call me as soon as she had access to a telephone. He said that the phones in her suite had been removed for privacy.

The letter explained a lot. She was essentially being held captive. Of course, she was being hunted by a variety of people for many reasons, and you could make a case for doing it this way to protect her. I hoped that it was more about being safe than being a prisoner though. I decided to exploit this source as much as possible, and I immediately responded to him, offering a steady stream of money if he kept me informed and would pass messages to the lady in question. He was quick to answer and must have been sitting right at his computer.

Michael wrote that since he had been given the note he was transferred to a different section of the hotel and ordered not to return to the previous floor, so he could no longer help. He offered to find out who replaced him and see if an arrangement could be made. I wrote back thanking him and told him that I was eager to proceed if possible. This helped me more than I could say in understanding that she wanted to contact me but couldn't. No telling when she lost her phone, but I felt certain that I knew who took it. Brenna likely didn't get any of my messages so she was in the dark about me also. I had such a longing to embrace her I almost popped with energy. She had not moved on, had not forgotten me. My mood changed dramatically.

I considered my options, the most obvious one would be to fly to Seattle and go to the hotel, demanding to see her. Most likely, I would be blocked like the rest of the lot wanting to get their hooks on her. The hotel may not even know her real name or even know that she's there. Apparently, even the bellboy didn't know her name. That approach wouldn't work. If I could get my friend, the bellboy, to get someone to lend her a phone, she would call me. I was sure of it. Everything depended on the bellboy following up for me. I wished there was someway I could put some money in his hands to give him incentive.

After some thought, I decided to contact the bellboy again, so I wrote him and asked for the lady's room number. He quickly responded and said that he could get fired for what he already did, and if I wanted any more from him, I had to get some cash to him. I had no clear idea how that could be done unless I went to Seattle myself. By the time I got there, Brenna could be in Canada. I had to figure out a better way.

Harvey never told me where he was while we were talking, and I wondered whether he was in Seattle or still in LA. I called Harvey's number and got his message box. I explained my problem and asked if he were in Seattle and if he had any ideas. The last time it took three days to hear from Harvey, so I decided not to wait too long. The other option was to contact a local private investigator who could employ someone in Seattle to deliver the phone. I had Michael's email address which could be used to track him down. I decided to give Harvey one hour to respond, but in the meantime, I would get hold of a local investigator to explore options.

Time was not on my side, and I also wondered, when I actually talked to Brenna, what she would have to say. Should I talk her out of this endeavor and deprive her of the chance to tour and become famous? There was no way to separate my longing for her from the right thing to do, if there was a right thing to do. I was about to launch an operation, but without knowing key facts, such as Brenna's intentions and feelings. Thinking about her situation, it seemed likely that she was being given a hard sell, using favorably selected facts and options, and was being isolated with an exaggeration of the dangers. I knew that Brenna needed protection and suspected that she could be easily lead to believe that those around her had only her interest at heart. But all I wanted to do was just talk to her and hear her views. Reluctantly, I was prepared to part ways with Brenna if it was the best thing for her. Talking to Harvey made me realize that Brenna suddenly had a lot of options, thanks to both her talent and the efforts of Mill and Terrance.

Waiting any longer was out of the question, it was time to act. I called Universal Investigative Agency's local number and told the receptionist that I had to talk to an agent right away. I withheld most of the facts but stressed that time was a factor. After a few minutes wait on the phone, a deep male voice came on. "Ross Simon here. What do you need?" I was prepared and gave him a very quick view of the problem. The short version was that my lady friend was not being allowed to talk to me and was being kept isolated in a hotel in Seattle. There was no kidnapping involved so I haven't alerted the police. What I needed was to get a cell phone in her hands so that she could voluntarily call me. Apparently this was not enough for Ross, and he wanted to expand on all the information so he had a clearer picture.

"Look, Simon, her name is Brenna Christensen, and we have been together for five years. We trained for months together when a singing break came out of the blue, resulting in her performing recently at the Hollywood Bowl and in Seattle. She is all over the

Web right now, and I mean, all over. She hasn't been allowed to talk to me, and they are going to try to take her to Canada for a tour. I have to talk to her. If you can't do it, I'll go elsewhere, but I don't have time to coddle you about it," I said forcefully.

"Well, hold on, fellow. I didn't say that I wouldn't help, but we have to be careful to be on the right side of things. Sounds like you need some help all right, but she is in Seattle, correct?" he asked.

"Right. That means you have to use your contacts to find the right man in Seattle to get over there and figure out how to get a cell phone in her hand and give her the opportunity to call me. If she doesn't want to talk to me, then I'll just have to live with it. Another thing, the band has an engagement in four days in Canada, and she has no passport, so there may be some funny business at hand."

"Well, the issue with her passport could be sorted out, but the border guys could give her a bad time when she tries to get back in," he said thoughtfully. "OK, I'm in. Let me make some calls, and I'll get right on it. Stay by the phone. By the way, this won't come cheap." I was dimly aware of what money fountain I had opened, but there were no other options at the moment.

"I'm waiting and depending on you, Simon. There isn't much time left, and I'm worried about her." I hung up and tried to work some more, but I kept the cell phone handy. True to his word, he called back in just short of an hour.

"Ross here, Dan. Got some info for you. We checked out Brenna first, and boy, you are right about the chatter about her. The YouTube of her performance at the Bowl has gone over a million hits, and there is a new one of her in Seattle, also getting lots of hits. I hope you won't be offended, but she is a real babe, and I don't blame you for not wanting to lose her. I'll get to the point. I have contacted a fellow called Mick Grundy. He is a legend on the West Coast. He was in Special Forces Black Ops and also a US Marshall for two years. I hear that no one argues with him, and he will absolutely accomplish any task, no matter what it takes."

I interrupted, "Say, we don't need violence here. The woman who is with Brenna is a cripple, and I doubt that anyone there is willing to fight it out over her."

"Won't argue with you there, fellow, but the best way to get things done is with more tools than you need. You shouldn't worry about this, and I think we should leave it to Mick. He is based in Tacoma and will go up there tonight. What was your contact's name?"

I looked at my notes and responded, "The guy is a bellboy named Michael, and he works at the Seattle Hyatt Regency. I didn't get Brenna's room number, and I doubt if she is even registered. Tell him to look for Mill Elbers' room, and I'll bet she is either there or close by." I also gave him Michael's email address.

Ross quipped, "What a coincidence, Dan. I'm sometimes called Mike, and there is a Mick and a Michael. That's auspicious!" and laughed. At that, I fell silent and was about to say something nasty when he continued, "Thanks, Dan. I would say to stay handy with your phone for the next couple of hours, and I will give Mick the go ahead. Talk soon." He hung up.

The die was cast. I just needed to calm down and think about what I was going to say to her. There is a sandwich shop on the way to my house, and I stopped for food. After getting home, I parked myself in a chair to wait, phone at the ready. I ravenously ate my sandwich and watched TV with the sound off. When I went to the restroom, I hurried back or took my phone with me. Time went by so slowly that I had time to think about Brenna. Her future was assured, if that's what she wanted. To that end, Mill was brilliant. I always knew that Brenna would be the one who would catch on fire, and I only had a dim dream of us doing it together. At times, we had a lot of fun getting ready, but it also had taken considerable hard work and not a little bit of money. I just couldn't hold her back. Thinking in a clear and calm way, I felt that I should gracefully bow out and get out of her way. Like Udi Gast told me several months ago, an attractive, intelligent woman has many options. The way Terrance was draped all over her, perhaps he would be the right one to take my place. Richard Bach once said, "If you love someone, set them free. If they come back, they're yours; if they don't, they never were." Good advice, but try to follow it. Unless someone mercifully removed my brain, I was bound to be in for a lot of agony. I continued to wait for her call. Dozing off I'm sure that I was dreaming about her, because when the phone rang I thought that she was waking me up.

When I got nearly conscious, I put the phone to my ear without looking to see who it was. "Hello!" I said, my voice a bit crackly.

It was Ross Simon. "Say, do you mind if we do a conference call with Mick? He has some news," he asked. My head was clearing rapidly.

"Sure, Ross," I said.

Momentarily, a deep male voice came on and said, "Hi, this is Mick Grundy." The voice was raspy and breathy and given with effort. "In case you are wondering, I took a bullet in the throat back when, and I talk funny. Hope you can get this," Mick said with effort.

"I understand you fine," I assured him.

"What's up, Mick?" Ross interjected.

"Well, first of all, there isn't a Hyatt Regency in Seattle. The email came from the computer services room at the Sheraton down by the Convention Center. There is no Michael there and never has been. That's a dead end. I looked for a booking for Mill Elbers and finally found her down the street at the Hilton in room 414. According to the desk clerk, she is to leave in the morning and has scheduled a pick up at 9 AM to go to SeaTac Airport. I checked the band's performance schedule, and they played at the Poncho Concert Hall two days ago. The band left yesterday for Vancouver. There is a lot of interest in finding Brenna Kristen out there, and I am not the only one looking. I have the room staked out and spotted a hired guard patrolling the hall, so I'm reasonably sure that she is in there. Before I go in, I want to know exactly what you want."

His voice seemed to need to rest, and he stopped. "Well," I started, "Brenna and I are long-term sweethearts and until last week were together nearly every day. Since she launched her singing debut at the Hollywood Bowl on Tuesday, I have not been able to talk with her. I think someone swiped her phone to keep her from speaking to me, and I fear that they are pressuring her to sign a singing contract. I don't know what she thinks about it or if she needs my support, but I am almost insanely focused on talking to her before she gets away from me forever. Please don't hurt anyone or scare anyone. Mill Elbers made her a star overnight and understandably doesn't want me to interfere. Just ask Brenna if she wants to phone me and give her a phone in a way that we can have a private conversation. If she doesn't want to talk to me, then you are done."

Mick responded quickly, "All right with you if I put a little persuasion on the guard?"

"As long as it's legal, and Brenna doesn't know about it, it's fine by me," I answered.

"Back to you later," Mick said and hung up.

Ross was still on the phone and said, "Don't worry, Dan; Mick's good at what he does. He will come through for you, but I wouldn't want to be the guard. Wait for the call, Dan," he said and hung up also.

Another hour went by and then my spine tingled when the phone rang. This time it was Mick only. The deep otherworldly voice said, "This Dan?"

I grunted, "Yes."

"Got some info for you. I got into the room after talking to the guard. He didn't want any trouble and was cooperative. He said that earlier today, a young blonde woman and this gal, Mill, left together and then Mill came back alone about six hours later. I believed him, but I wanted to check it out so I sort of forced my way into the room. Believe it, Mill is one tough broad. I usually scare people but not her. She denied everything, even knowing Brenna. I checked the room, and there are way too many clothes for one lady. Too many bags, too. Wherever Brenna went today, she didn't take luggage. After I left the room, I went to the lobby, and the manager checked it out and had no record of Brenna, and no one seems to have noticed her at all. I called a buddy in Vancouver, and he got hold of the manager of the Terrance Star Band...a man named Jeff Barnes, and he said that he knew about Brenna, but she had gotten strange, and they had to go on without her and that Terrance was pretty mad about it. He says that he has no idea where she is now. My buddy told him that the Seattle Missing Persons Task Force was looking into her disappearance, just to scare him, and it did, but he had nothing else to add. I went back to the room and confronted Mill again and threatened her with the FBI for abduction and kidnapping, but she just glared at me and told me to go ahead and do it. I don't recall meeting anyone tougher than Mill. I'll tell you this, unless Brenna turns up before Mill skips town, I will get the cops in on it, but in the meantime, I'll keep looking. Anything you want to add, Dan?"

"No, Mick, I have no idea what to do, none. Oh, one other thing. Did my name come up when you were with Mill?"

"Of course not," he replied.

After he hung up, I turned the scant facts over and over in my mind. Brenna went somewhere, but not to Canada, and went without her clothes. Where would a person go without clothes? And we hear that she was acting strange. Could she have become sick and taken to a hospital? If that were true, why would Mill hide it? The fact that Mill is leaving could mean that Brenna is leaving with her. After all, her clothes and bags are still there, but where are they going? If Mill had washed her hands of Brenna, she would have no more reason to protect her. She may have another deal in the works, and if so, they could be headed anywhere. Another question, if Brenna is free of Mill and out of the room, why doesn't she call me, because she did have someone try to make contact with me earlier. I sprang to my feet and paced the room. Logic wasn't enough to solve this riddle. I had to depend on my man on the ground in Seattle. It was late, and I was really tired from all the nervous tension, but I knew that I couldn't sleep. My brain wouldn't let me do anything but think about Brenna. Socrates said, "The hottest love has the coldest end." Is it the end for me and Brenna? Not yet, I told myself. Not until I found out what happened to her. I swore not to let this matter go until there was an end.

Suddenly, the answer came to me. If she had a mental breakdown from stress and was taken for treatment, if would fit with what we knew. It would also explain why Mill wouldn't say anything. News of mental instability was not going to help the career of a hot new star. Mill was still protecting her and at any cost. One word to anyone and all the media sleuths stalking her would discover it, and the news would fill the papers.

The phone rang again. This time it was Mike. I looked at the clock. Eleven fifteen. "Hi Mike," I answered.

"Did Harvey get hold of you today?" he asked.

I admitted that Harvey made contact and filled Mike in on some of what we talked about but not that she was missing. At this moment, I agreed with Mill that no one need know the reason she is missing or that she was missing at all. I told Mike only that I was trying to get her to a phone but was so far unsuccessful. I was vague, and he picked up on it.

"Listen, we are all sorry that you feel that your time with Brenna could be finished, but you'll get over it. Time will heal you, and we're all still around to help you. I know that you don't want to talk about it yet, but when you do, just call me. One last thing. You should check out Brenna's Seattle performance on YouTube. There is something there you need to see."

I was quick to respond, "No way, man. I am in enough pain without seeing Terrance's hands on her again. I couldn't stand it."

"Well, there is that, but there is also something else. Trust me, it will make you feel better. Go look at it. Tonight, Dan."

"Maybe," I said. "Maybe later."

After I said thanks and hung up, I thought about what he said. What if there was some message from her to me that I should know or would even prove useful in finding where she was? With misgivings, I got out my computer and soon found the video. In only two days, it had been seen over a million times. Has anyone ever become so popular this fast? She could name her price and get about anything now. I settled down to watch, however painful it was.

The first three numbers were the same as at the Bowl, except that I could see better this time. The video was taken illegally by someone in the forward sections to the right of the more elite orchestra section. The camera was shaky and often ducked behind some head to prevent being detected. It was good enough to see the show, at least. Brenna was wearing the same ivory dress as before, and she did look lovely, enough so that my heart ached when I saw her. When Terrance put his arm around her waist during their duet, I had a burning sensation in my chest and wanted to shut it off. This time, after their song ended, Terrance came forward to the mike and said, "This next number is a special request by Brenna, and it is not on your program, but it is another well-known piece by Cole Porter. It's all yours, Brenna."

At that, he did a bow and a sweep of his arm, and Brenna came to the mike and looked at the audience. The band was silent and was waiting on something. She finally spoke, looking right at the television camera straight in front of her. "I would like to dedicate this next number to someone very special to me who couldn't be here tonight, but I know that someday, someplace, he will hear it. To Daniel."

She put her hand to her lips and blew a kiss at the camera while smiling. Then, she stepped back a half step and started singing as the band followed her. It was *Do I Love You?*, another Cole Porter tearjerker if ever there was one.

I could tell that the audience came to its feet, because the view was obstructed with heads and clapping hands. The camera person must have held the camera over his head, and the picture resumed. She was bowing to the audience and smiling. I kept wiping my eyes to see better, but then the video abruptly ended. I never heard her sing more sweetly. We had never practiced that one so this was the first time I had ever heard her sing it, and no one could have ever sung it better. I rewound the video and played it three more times, and each time it had the same effect on me. Brenna, where are you? No wonder Terrance is mad. This was the break he was looking for. He had discovered a major new talent. Not only was Brenna on the way up but so was Terrance Star. All he had to do was to keep her.

After I recovered, I called Mick Grundy. He picked right up. "Mick here."

"Mick, this is Dan. I have some ideas. Can you talk right now?"

"Sure," he said. "I'm on my way to the University Hospital right now on a hunch and because of a tip. Go ahead, I'm listening."

"That is along the line I have been thinking, too. I think that she had a mental collapse of some kind, and she was brought in for treatment somewhere, and it's being kept secret to keep her name out of the mud."

"The cabbie that picked them up at the hotel brought them to the hospital that I am standing in front of. I checked, and this is the only major hospital that has a psychiatric unit in town. This has got to be the place," he said.

"It fits. One problem is that even you won't get any information from the hospital about an inpatient in psychiatry, and they usually lock the wards."

"Well, do you have any ideas?" he asked.

"No, I have to think about it," I answered.

"Then there isn't much left for me to do tonight, and since it is Christmas Eve, I think I'll go home. Let me know if you need anything or if anything comes up. I have to check something out, so I'll get back to you in the morning. Nite," and he hung up.

She was probably in the most secure place for withholding information in our society. Even prisons will admit whom they are holding, and there is no way in unless you are a treating physician. Hold it, I thought. I wondered if Dr. Gast might be willing to make a call for me. It was now one o'clock on Christmas morning, and this was no emergency for anyone other than me. I just couldn't call in the middle of the night. I dug around in my wallet and found the card he had given me in the hospital. Luckily, I didn't toss it. There was an emergency number on it, but I needed to wait until morning. It hit me that it was Christmas Day. I had no time to think about it until now. What a lonely feeling came over me, and fatigue settled in like a fog. All my energy was spent, and all my emotions had been wrung out until every bit was gone. I sat back in the recliner and fell asleep.

Sunlight came through the window directly into my face, waking me up. I looked at my watch and found it was already half past ten. I held up his card: "Udi Gast M.D., PhD, Board Certified in Psychiatry, Hospital Administrator," and then an emergency number. I rang it. A woman who had a strong German accent answered. I told her that I needed to talk to Dr. Gast, while apologizing profusely for calling on Christmas Day, as well as informing her who was calling and that I was calling about a Brenna Christensen. She was probably upset at the call and didn't give me a verbal response other than a little grunt of displeasure. I could hear the phone being put down. In a moment, the familiar voice of Dr Gast came on, "Daniel, a pleasure to talk to you. Merry Christmas. What brings you to call me this morning, please?"

"Dr. Gast, you told me to call if Brenna has a problem, and I think that she is in trouble.".

"Udi, please, if you will, Daniel. What is the nature of the problem?"

"I'll give you the short story for now, Udi. Brenna is in Seattle, and I have reason to believe that she has been admitted to the University Medical Center with some sort of mental instability. I don't know the nature of it or even for sure that she is there. I also don't know if she was admitted under her name or is using an assumed name. The problem is that she has recently acquired celebrity status and is being pursued by about everybody."

"Humm," he said, "why are you not with her?" I could visualize him stroking his beard.

"To sum it up, the agent who is managing her wanted me out so that she would have complete control of Brenna. We remain close, but this whole thing came up very quickly and was, and is, out of our control." I heard myself talking, but the answer did show my weakness in protecting her. I should have put my shoulder to it and never let this happen, but I was trying too hard to be nice and not to interfere.

"What can I do for you, Daniel?" he asked, with obvious compassion.

"Udi, you are the only one who can call the hospital and talk to her physician and find out what is going on. I am not a relative, and even if I were, they are not going to talk to me."

He paused, and again, I could imagine him stroking his beard. "You are probably right. I feared that her personality disorder was real, and this is exactly the circumstance which would bring it out. Enumerated, the key factors are the separation from a loved one and intense mental stress. When was she admitted?"

"I assume that it was yesterday morning," I answered.

He seemed to be jotting down some notes, and in a moment said, "She remains an intriguing case, and I will be glad to get involved on her behalf. Should I discover any medical information, legally I can't divulge much to you, but I can give you enough for you to act on. You do understand?"

I understood that this was the way it had to be, and I had no choice. At least I would discover if she had been admitted, and then, at least, I would know where she was. "I understand, Udi, and thanks a lot for this," I said. I gave him my cell phone number and left it up to him.

I got up and tried to find enough food in the house to eat, but I had been away for too long, and there wasn't much. Right after finishing my coffee, Udi called back.

"Daniel? Udi here."

"Hi, Udi," I said, trying to withhold any sign of impatience.

"There is a very nice young resident on duty there who was helpful. They had a Jane Doe admission yesterday morning, and the physical description matches Brenna. She was speaking with a curious French accent, but when they provided a French translator for her, she seemed not to understand what was being said. She has so far communicated very little to the staff and is being kept in a single room for her safety. From what I gather, there has not been a clear decision on diagnosis or treatment, and the holiday has been a factor since the senior house staff is away." He paused for a long time before continuing, "I would like to go up there and see her and assist with her care. Would you care to go with me?"

Oh, the joy. "Yes, I sure would. Do you mean that they have no ID for her at all?"

"That is right; there was no identification supplied with her when she was virtually abandoned in the emergency room. The usual procedure is to involve the police, who fingerprint and search the missing persons reports. I have no idea where that stands at the moment. Even without seeing her, I am convinced that the person they have is Brenna. Is there any next of kin that we can contact?" he asked.

"Udi, I am afraid that I act as next of kin for her even though there are no legal ties between us. She only has her mother left and that is another long story."

"That answer is enough. I would like to invite you to go with me, and I am going to use the services of the University to make bookings for you and me to go as soon as possible. I will continue to contact the staff there on her behalf so that nothing untoward happens to her until we arrive. There is a faculty member there, whom I have previously met, and we have some mutual respect, and I know that I can rely on her."

"Thanks so much, Dr. Udi Gast, for getting involved. I had run out of options, and this gives me some hope. I'll be ready to go at any time, and I look forward to your company." We hung up, and I realized that my work schedule would again be in disarray. Thank the heavens for my partner. I had a lot of making up to do when this matter got settled.

About an hour later, I received another call, this time from Mick. "Mick here. More info for you. This morning, I went to Elbers' room again, and she's gone. She left some clothes and luggage, and I made a careful survey of it and found a purse with Brenna Christensen's driver's license and credit cards and a little money. I kept the purse with me and had the bellboy come up and take the luggage down to the lobby storage until you figure out what to do. The room is rented and paid up for four more days by Mill Elbers. Did you hear any more about the hospital admission?"

"Thanks, Mick. I hate that you are working on Christmas Day, but I am glad to hear from you. There was a Jane Doe admission to the University Hospital yesterday, and the patient could be Brenna. There was no ID with her. There is a well-known psychiatrist named Udi Gast who is going to go with me soon to Seattle. He has met Brenna previously. When we get there, I will need her ID, but you better just hold on to it until we see that it really is Brenna."

"Until you call then," and he was gone.

While I was thinking of it, I dialed Harvey Silverman. To heck with the holiday, he was responsible for us going to Mill in the first place. Surprisingly, I reached him on the first try. "Hi, Harvey, this is Dan. Remember me?"

"You know, I was going to call tomorrow, but it's good to hear from you. Any news?" he quickly said.

"Some," I answered. "First, I want to know what you have heard and if you have been in contact with Mill?"

"I'll level with you, Dan. I've talked to Mill and Terrance. Both are upset the way things have turned out. Terrance has washed his hands of her and is looking to find a replacement singer. He's in for some disappointment if he thinks he can replace Brenna, and it doesn't look good for his image to lose her so quickly. He had the usual problems with Mill and her demands for more and more money, so he feels better at least without Mill in his life. He was told that Brenna had lost her mind, but he is keeping quiet in case someone blames him for it. Mill is currently in LA looking for contracts for Brenna, and she definitely has not given up. She told me that she put Brenna in a safe place and is going back for her in a couple of days. Other than that, she wouldn't talk about it, and I don't actually know what happened. By the way, I never was in Seattle, but I saw the video. She can go anywhere right now. The sky is the limit. I would like to talk to you both if you want to get out from under Mill's thumb."

"Thanks, Harvey. I don't have anything to add right now. I am going to Seattle soon, and I hope to see Brenna when I am there and work things out. I'll be sure and call you when things settle down. Sorry to bother you on the holiday." He realized that I wasn't open to giving out information, not that I actually had any, so he said goodbye and wished me good luck.

Are We A Band Yet? *by Alexander Francis*

Chapter Twenty-One

Seattle

During the flight, I had a lot of time to get better acquainted with Udi, who really was a perceptive and funny fellow. He kept things light and constantly reassured me that we were going to get Brenna back to normal very quickly.

"After all, I have with me the cure," he told me in a confidential voice and a sly smile.

Biting on the hook, and trying to picture some new marvelous pharmaceutical, I asked, "What are you bringing, Udi?"

"Why, it's you, Daniel. Bringing you two back together will be sure to generate a positive response." He informed me that he had talked to a Dr. Pamela Steward and had asked her to withhold any medication until Brenna is seen by them together. Udi refused to tell me what her progress had been, but reading his face, there had been no change. His medical residents had quickly researched Brenna using the Web prior to our departure. A large leather briefcase he carried contained a thick printout of articles about her. Although Udi had not seen the videos himself, the residents had, and he was well aware of the impact she had made on the music scene. We discussed how quickly the curious and the avaricious had gathered, and all of them were scouring the earth searching for Brenna. She had dropped off the surface of the planet, and the press was furious. One headline read "Where is Brenna Kristen?... Who is Brenna Kristen?"

Udi discussed how careful we had to be, if and when she emerged from the hospital, to shield her from unwanted contact. One photograph could be very damaging. Curiously, Mill had done the only thing she could have done to get help for Brenna and yet completely hide her identity. Brenna's fingerprints were not in any database and neither was her DNA. Mill was the only person to know the truth, that this Jane Doe admitted to the psychiatry unit was indeed Brenna. At this time Udi and I couldn't be sure that the person in question was Brenna. There are other possible things that could have happened, but I wanted to believe that we were headed in the right direction. We rode in silence while Udi busied himself with his paperwork.

At last, he put the work aside and fixed me in his focus. "Why haven't you married Brenna, Daniel?" A fair but blunt question delivered with a little impish smile.

"You understand that she lives in Madison and has a job that she likes, and I live in Rockford and have a job which is important to me. Marriage would be awkward, but I have asked myself the same question. I love her, and I believe that she loves me. The day will come," I said, returning a reassuring smile. "Since we are being blunt, Udi, tell me why you are in this country instead of Germany," I asked with the same little smile. Turnabout is fair play. He nodded his amusement at my question.

He stroked his beard and took a noisy breath, "The simple answer is that I got a teaching and research appointment that I couldn't refuse. The real answer is that I find the science of psychiatry in Germany, in fact Europe, to be fossilized. They just can't let Freud go. You Americans have no loyalties and research can take any turn. It's a freeform circus which produces results like no other place. Things may change, but for now we are very happy here, but sometimes we miss home and all the old traditions." He paused to rub his forehead and brow. "Another thing you don't know is that my grandfather was executed in Nuremberg as a war criminal after the war. My father served honorably in the German Army and was never accused of wrongdoing. I have grown tired of bearing that cross. Here, the war is forgotten for me, unless I watch some of your endless stupid movies about the war and the Nazis." We laughed together.

We arrived in Seattle about 6:00 AM on the third day after Christmas and the fourth day after Brenna had been admitted. As soon as we touched the ground, Udi called the hospital and talked to Dr. Pamela Steward and made an appointment for 10:00. Meanwhile, I called Mick and asked that he be there also and instructed him to bring Brenna's purse. We quickly checked into a hotel near the medical center, one that Udi's efficient staff had lined up, specifying adjacent but separate rooms. I was most anxious to get going, but Udi insisted first on a nourishing breakfast at the hotel. Afterward, we walked the short distance to the University Hospital entrance and arrived just five minutes early.

As we stood looking around like the strangers we were, I noticed a distinctive man headed toward us. His distressed green parka and knit cap attire was not unusual for Seattle, but it was his purposeful gait that caught my eye. I knew who he was even before he got close. Muscular, yet light on his feet, there was no mistaking Mick Grundy, and no wonder he got few arguments. As he came up to us, I noticed the end of a long scar on his right temporal area, typical of a craniotomy incision for surgical treatment of intracranial trauma. The right cheek displayed a long, old, depressed scar extending all the way across. Penetrating deep set, deep blue eyes and a beard stubble set off his rugged, square-jawed face. He seemed to know us by sight and walked up and stuck out his hand toward me.

"Dan, I believe. Mick Grundy." In person, his voice was striking, almost threatening. I shook his hand and put my hand on his shoulder to introduce him to Dr. Gast. "You the shrink, then?" Mick asked before I got a word out.

"Yes. You may call me Udi, please, and may I call you Mick?"

"Anything that makes you happy, Doc. You from Germany?"

"Yes, Mick. Is that a problem?" Udi answered in a low voice.

"No, Doc, just wondering. It fits," he said.

Udi appeared amused, but before he was able to continue this exchange, the hospital door opened and through it came a white-coated pair who walked hurriedly up to us. As soon as he saw them, Udi moved forward with his hand extended. "Dr. Steward, how good of you to meet with us."

"Please, Udi, it's always Pam to you," she responded.

Dr. Steward was no shrinking violet and very much in charge. She introduced us to her senior psych resident, Dr. Jones, who seemed less sure of herself. Both women could be seen to take special note of Mick, who hung ominously in the background.

"Shall we go into my office for some conversation gentlemen?" she asked and extended her hand to the door. She held the door for the three of us.

I turned in time to see Mick give a slow up and down visual inspection of Dr. Jones as he passed her in the doorway. We were led down a series of halls and eventually arrived at a suite of rooms dedicated to the senior hospital staff. Dr. Steward's office was large, thick carpet plush and lit with table lamps. Two large red leather couches and two leather armchairs occupied the center of the room. Dr. Jones remained standing as the rest of us sat down. Dr. Steward peered over her glasses and asked, "Who are you two gentlemen, and what is your relationship to this case?"

She was looking at Mick and me, the two of us sitting side by side on the same couch. Since she was already given our names, I realized that she was asking what were we doing here, our relationship or motives. Udi remained silent allowing us to fend for ourselves. Mick used his intimidating, level gaze at Dr. Steward but with no visible effect on her.

I answered for both of us, "Mick here is the investigator who tracked the party we are interested in to this hospital, and he has brought her ID with him to confirm or reject her as the same person you admitted four days ago. I am here because she is the love of my life, and I am trying desperately to find her and help her." While I was talking, Mick took out Brenna's pink purse from his jacket and found her driver's license with her photo. He stood and offered it to Dr. Steward with his thumb obscuring Brenna's name.

"This her?" he asked in his raspy voice. Dr. Steward and Dr. Jones leaned over the ID, studying it, and then nodded to each other, confirming that she was indeed the patient in question. What a relief that moment was for me. She was in this hospital, we had found her. Dr. Steward sat down again and looked at Udi, her eyes confirming his suspicions.

He leaned forward and said, "Now that we have determined who your patient is, Pam; there are some facts that you should know. I first saw her in the early summer in the University Hospital when she was admitted for emergency surgery. During recovery, she displayed some symptoms of a possible dissociative disorder. This resolved without intervention, but was troubling. I wanted to have follow-up interviews with her, but she resented my interest and was lost to additional diagnostic procedures or therapy. She recently engaged in two public singing events for which she has received wide acclaim and, resultantly, is being sought by some relentless people. No offense meant, Mick. She was abandoned here by her manager or agent, intentionally, to enable treatment, but mostly, I believe, to shield her from the carnivorous press. Her stage name is Brenna Kristen, but as you are about to learn, she is actually Brenna Christensen."

Dr. Jones put her hands to her mouth, her eyes wild. "You mean that she is the Brenna that has been in all the papers and the videos. I just loved her!" she said with delight. Dr. Steward apparently was not given to exclamation and looked hard at Dr. Jones over her glasses.

"Yes, that is her," Udi said, and continued. "And now you understand why we must tread carefully here. By the way, I am here to offer any assistance and advice you may need, but my ultimate goal is to get her back to Wisconsin for in-depth treatment in my own facility."

"So you feel that the pseudo-French she has spoken is a part of her multiple personality disorder?" Dr. Steward asked.

Udi quickly corrected her, "Possible disorder, I prefer to use. I have to see her first before I label her." Someone was knocking on the door, and Dr. Jones opened it slightly to converse with the other side. She closed it and turned to see all of us watching her, waiting on an explanation.

"There is a lady outside who insists on seeing someone in charge of our Jane Doe. She says that she is her mother."

My eyebrows shot up, and I could feel the other faces looking at me. "It's not possible that her mother is here. Be careful, it is a ruse," I warned.

"Daniel, would you like to go and see who it is, please?" Udi suggested.

When I got up, so did Mick. If the person was a pretender, Mick looked like he wanted to handle the situation himself. I hoped there was a better way to deal with it, but it was comforting to have him there. Again, we were led back through the long corridors toward the front lobby. Standing just inside the entrance door was the familiar visage of Mill. She looked shocked to see us emerge from the bowels of the hospital, the very last people she wanted to see.

She recovered quickly and took an offensive posture. "I should have known that you hired this brute. You should be ashamed that you resorted to this method after what I did for Brenna," she hissed with defiance.

"You mean after you abandoned the poor thing here without any ID or protection, instead of calling me. You knew that I would come running to be with her, and instead, you used her up and threw her away." I spoke with ferocious animosity while pointing to her with my index finger. Mick was silent but was a tightly coiled spring standing just beside my shoulder.

"I did not abandon her. I left her here for the excellent care I knew that they would give, and I came back today for her."

"Mill, you took her phone from her so that I couldn't contact her, and I'm sure that you pressured her to sign on with Terrance while she was locked in that hotel room with you. She had no protection from YOU," I yelled. People were watching, and the three of us began to notice. Mill was defiant, and I was angry. There was no middle ground.

Mick spoke up, "Mill should come to the meeting, Dan." He gestured down the long hall.

"What meeting," Mill asked.

"Come with us, Mill. You may prove useful," I said, and we all started to thread the labyrinth.

Mill and I walked side by side without speaking. Mick followed behind. I found our way back to the office of Dr. Steward, and we entered without knocking. Once in, Mill didn't look so confidant, surrounded by strangers whom she realized felt she had acted inappropriately with a sick dependent. Udi, in his European and charming way, smiled at Mill.

I informed the group that this was Mill Elbers who had been guiding Brenna in her singing events and who was the one who left her at the hospital. There was an uncomfortable moment of silence as the group assessed Mill, and she returned the stares, defiant and unafraid.

Udi spoke first. "Ms. Elbers, I am Dr. Udi Gast, and I practice psychiatry in Madison. From what I have surmised, Brenna is very ill, and we all should be interested in her well-being and not waste time in purposeless accusations. To that end, I would appreciate your account of events which led you to deposit Brenna in this facility."

Mill was standing in the middle of the room. She looked around again at each of us, gauging how to respond. I gave her credit for the vast amount of chutzpa she possessed. "If you know what is going on out there about this girl, you would understand better why I did what I had to do."

From the back of the room, Mick spoke up, "We aren't interested in you at the moment, the question was about Brenna. Stick to the subject." He was surprisingly loud for man with a damaged voice box. It got Mill's attention, and I saw her jump a little bit at the sound of it. She obviously had been afraid of him after all.

Mill stammered just a bit, "I had trouble getting her to do the Seattle performance. She had people pouring into the dressing area after she sang at the Bowl, and some of them were influential and couldn't be contained. Brenna was unable to deal with it and was terrified of a repeat experience in Seattle. She had no privacy, and the cameras were everywhere. Her hand was shaking so obviously that I took her phone away from her, hoping that it wouldn't show. I had the stage nurse give her a sedative which was too much for her and really put her out of commission. We hustled her out of there before the show ended when it would have been much worse. On the trip up here, she slept most of the way. The next day she demanded that she sing her song to

Daniel at the performance in Seattle, and we spent most of our time before the show going over it. We hid in the hotel to keep the press off of her." She stopped to gather her thoughts and to calm down.

"Keep going, that ain't enough," came from behind me.

Mill gave him an angry glance and looked menacingly at me before continuing. "Another problem was that I couldn't get her to eat anything. Nothing for almost two days. She was living off of the vending machine soft drinks. All she did was pace, pace, pace. For a time, I didn't think she was going to be able to make it to the stage. The only thing that kept her going was that last song. She told Terrance that either she sang it, or she wasn't going on at all, and he reluctantly agreed that she could sing it. She was right though, because her performance of that song alone will make her famous. After the performance, she collapsed, and we almost had to carry her back to the room. The next morning, I had problems getting her to wake up. When I finally got her up, she appeared confused, like she was on some drug. She didn't seem to know me or where she was, and when she did talk she had some sort of accent. She refused food or water, and I became alarmed, so I got in touch with the band manager who came over to look at her. He didn't know what to do with her either, and the band was already pulling out for Vancouver. He told me to get a physician to look at her and left."

She paused again and anxiously looked at Mick as if to prevent any comments from him. In a moment, and without additional prompting, she continued, "I called downstairs and had the hotel manager get a visiting physician to come to the room. He was inquisitive about the reason and preferred that we take her to a healthcare facility. I insisted that he find someone and to be discrete and quick about it. About an hour later, a young, inexperienced doctor showed up at the door. He examined her briefly but didn't get any cooperation from Brenna while doing so. She didn't want him touching her and wouldn't respond to questions. He said that in his opinion, she was having a mental breakdown, and we should go the University Medical Center. By this time, the band was gone, and I had no help with her and didn't know what to do."

This time she looked right at me. "You're thinking that I should have called you. By this time she wouldn't have talked to you either, and you were too far away to get here in time to be helpful. The other thing is...the reason I didn't want you there all along. Let's tell it like it is, Daniel. You know that you couldn't, or wouldn't, be able to follow her from city to city, and that's what it usually takes in this business. You knew that you had to let her go. I believe that you knew that all along, even if you don't want to admit it. What I didn't know was how fragile she is. I thought she would toughen up and accept what goes with fame in this country. It wasn't possible for her, she just couldn't do it. She isn't strong enough to take advantage of her talent and her good looks. I never had as much potential, and I don't know of anyone who has so quickly captured this much public attention. I was overwhelmed and unprepared for it."

Finally, she stopped. She had fascinated us with her dialog, and there was no immediate response from those present. She was right about me. I let this happen, and I knew Brenna couldn't take it. I was powerless to stop the process, and I couldn't bring myself to deny Brenna anything she wanted. We all were guilty. We let her down and look what happened.

Udi spoke up, "Thanks very much, Ms Elbers, for that clear description. That helps a lot in understanding the sequence of events."

Mill turned to Dr. Steward and asked, "Can you tell me how she is doing now?" There was a hint, just a hint, of pleading in her voice.

"That is something I can't do," Dr. Steward answered.

I got up and approached Mill. She had a spent look, a helpless look, all the fight and defensiveness she came in with were gone. She spoke softly and pleadingly, "What can I do for her, and what is left for me?"

"Your role is finished, Mill. There isn't anything you can do anymore for her. Come on, I'll walk you out, and we can talk some more," and I took her arm gently.

Udi spoke to me, "Daniel, I want to see Brenna before you do, and when you come back, just wait for us here. Is that all right, Pam?"

Dr. Steward replied that would be acceptable, and the three physicians also got ready to leave.

Chapter Twenty-One

"What about me?" came from the shadows in the room.

I turned and said, "I'll be right back, Mick, if you can wait for me."

"Roger that," he responded.

Mill and I walked arm in arm, but silently, back through the maze of interconnected hallways to the hospital entrance. In the lobby, I turned to face her. "Mill, I have lost my anger about this, and I can be reasonable about it now that I have had time to consider all our roles. We are all to blame for this. Brenna thought she wanted to succeed but didn't know what she was getting into and didn't know her own limitations. I am to blame because I let it happen, knowing her weaknesses better than she did. You are to blame because you are the only one who understood what was going to happen but didn't know Brenna well enough to anticipate her reactions. Udi is to blame because he foresaw her problem but wasn't forceful enough in pursuing treatment for her. Terrance, of course, wants what he wants. I also need to tell you that I'm in absolute awe how you got her ready and arranged to have her positioned for maximum effect. Brilliant, Mill, brilliant. It worked so well it was hard to tell it wasn't being ordained by God."

She watched me expressionless with those haunting gray eyes. She finally spoke, "I did my job, Daniel. Too well. I feel really bad for Brenna, and I wish from the bottom of my heart that she will be back to normal soon. I probably look bad for abandoning her, but I knew that she would be in good hands and safe from the press that way, and I intended to come back and assist her any way that I could, even by lying about being her mother. I left her ID at the hotel, and I had a guard out there to keep people out and to keep the room for her in case she had a quick recovery. I took a trip to LA to see some people about her who wouldn't wait for a second without screaming about it. She has offers from the Tonight Show and several daytime talk shows. This is the big time, Daniel. MGM contacted me about getting a signed contract before anyone else got to her. I never had Brenna sign any contract for representation so I can't make deals until she does, but I can easily get her several million this year for just the appearances. All we have to do is to keep her in the public eye right now, and there is no limit at all. Brenna is a gold mine for the moment, but the moment only lasts until the public attention drifts away. You have to hold on to it."

We looked at each other with understanding for the first time. I embraced her and she embraced me, and we had a long meaningful hug right in the middle of the hospital lobby with people streaming around us on both sides.

"What now, Daniel? What am I to tell all those hungry people?"

"Mill, I haven't even seen her yet. We have to wait until the shrinks have their say. I hope that when I see her and she sees me, we can get her to respond and back to normal. I have no idea what is going to happen next so I can't tell you what to do. Brenna is going to have the last word in this plan about her destiny, and she can't do it yet. I think you should go back to LA, and this time, leave your number with me, and I think you already have mine. We'll get together as soon as it's possible."

She dug around in her large purse and handed me Brenna's phone. The screen showed several missed calls and texts from me. Silently, she strode away, through the exit door and down the street.

Chapter Twenty-Two

Recovery

Mick was pacing when I arrived back in the office suite. He was obviously impatient and squared off and glared at me. This was one man I wouldn't want to take on in a dark alley, or any other place. "Mick, thanks for waiting. There is one more time that I will need some of your expert help." He looked questioningly at me without speaking. "When Brenna gets released from this place, and I don't have any idea when that will be, we are going to need some secure way to get her out without the press getting any whiff of it. Now that the hospital staff is aware of who she is, it's bound to leak out, and the wolves will be waiting."

"That's it?"

"Is there anything else I need to do?" I asked.

"What about Mill Elbers? Did you make up with her or something?"

"Until Brenna comes around to make up her mind and tell me what to do, I have no choice. Mill could still make or break her. Brenna has to decide."

He nodded and punched me on the shoulder. It hurt. "See you around, then. Call me, and I'll be there," he said, and walked out. I was left alone in the room waiting for the return of the three

259

physicians. I laid back on one of the couches and tried to calm down.

I spied a coffee machine on the left wall and sprang up to get some when the door opened and Drs. Gast and Steward came in. She assumed her position behind her desk, as Udi came up to me, slowly stroking his beard while looking at me.

"Want to see her, Daniel?" he asked. He raised his brow as if it there was any possibility I would refuse.

"Silly question, Udi.".

"You may be shocked by what you see," he said. "She doesn't look very good right now and hasn't been eating at all. Her physicians were considering a transfer to Medicine and tube feeding her when we arrived. She won't respond to questions from either of us. You are the last hope for us to bring her back quickly."

His warning struck fear in me, and I didn't offer anything in response. They had the legal power to admit her into a long-term institution if they wanted, and I would be helpless to do anything about it. I have briefly visited such places, and when I was there, I had the feeling that even a normal person would come apart in a psych unit if left there too long, not to mention someone actually sick.

"Come with us, Daniel, and see what you can do. Don't show emotion, just support when you are with her, and keep your voice low and soothing. Do not recoil from what you see. Do you understand?"

"I think so, Udi," I answered.

The three of us went down another series of halls and waited for the elevator. There was only small talk and none concerning Brenna. Dr. Steward used her key to engage the elevator, which then stopped at the psych unit. The elevator opened onto a small hall, a caged window was to the left of another set of closed steel double doors. With a wave of her arm, Dr. Steward signaled someone behind the cage who allowed us to enter. A penetrating scream riveted my attention, and I heard distant, guttural sounds from several locations. Some of the inpatients were wandering up and down the halls in bathrobes, and some wore street clothes. Some looked normal, others not so.

Dr. Steward acknowledged by name each patient we passed. "She's down this way in a private room." Following, we turned down a short hall and stopped beside a closed metal door. It had a small aperture window obscured by a sliding cover.

Dr. Steward peeked before she said, "It's all right to go in," and opened the door for us.

I was first in, followed by the two physicians. A sour smell of diarrhea or vomitus hung in the air. Brenna was on the bed in a seated position, but folded up, with her arms around her legs. Her head was down with her forehead resting on her knees. She was wearing a white robe which had faint blue stripes, typical of the hospital garments I had already observed on patients walking down the hall. The room was very small, with the toilet in a small open alcove to one side. Whitewashed walls and ceiling and yellowing asphalt floor tiles made the room seem more like a prison cell than a hospital. Brenna's beautiful hair was stringy and matted and seemed darker than I was used to seeing. She didn't move her position or even seem to notice us when we came in.

Dr. Steward informed us, "Well, that is how I usually have seen her. She has never responded to any of my questions. We tried to start an IV, but she won't allow it. Udi, if you hadn't requested that we withhold medication, we probably would have used forced sedation to allow hydration by now."

She and Udi exchanged glances, but I was too focused on Brenna to take in any meaning from it. Dr. Steward put her hand on her Brenna's shoulder and spoke to her, "Brenna, honey, we have a visitor for you whom I'm sure you'll want to see." Brenna didn't move or respond. Udi tapped me on the shoulder and motioned with his head for me to approach Brenna.

I knelt down in front of her, bringing my face closer to her level. Very gently, I touched her on the shoulder. "I'm here, Brenna."

At first, there was no response, then very slowly her head came up enough that I could see her watery eyes which were looking at me. Her lips were chapped and pale. I put some more pressure on her shoulder and let my hand glide slightly over her shoulder blade. In only four days, she had lost a lot of weight, because I felt bone there that I had never noticed before. She slightly shifted her upper body toward me, and I let my hand drop to her back.

She lowered her legs very slightly, as if she was making an effort to move toward me, "It's Daniel, Brenna; I have come to take you home." She continued to look into my eyes and then lifted her arm and slowly put it on my neck.

I could hear Dr. Steward remark, "Would you look at that!"

Brenna pulled me toward her, and as I got closer, I could smell her rank breath. She moved her legs out of the way, and her head came into my chest just as her other arm enveloped me. I eased my arms about her in an embrace and held her tight, my chin resting on the top of her head. I could feel her trembling and sobbing, but there was little sound from her. We held on, and I squeezed tighter and so did she.

"Oh, Daniel," she murmured.

"I'm here, Brenna, and I'm not going away from you ever again," I whispered.

Dr. Steward apparently couldn't wait any longer, and she said rather loudly, "Do you know your name? Tell us your name."

Weakly and hoarsely, Brenna replied without letting me go or looking at the questioner, "Brenna Christensen."

Speaking for the first time, Udi said, "Pam, lets you and I conference for a second, please."

I could hear the door opening, and they stepped into the hall with the door only partially closed. I could hear Udi speaking, and he seemed to be talking intentionally loud enough for me to overhear. "I feel that she is going to make a rapid change with him present and likely none without him. This bodes well for a rapid departure from this hospital under his and my care."

"Well, this is a positive change, but in my opinion she has to be kept here until she has an opportunity for a more complete recovery. She is obviously despondent and clearly ill. I cannot permit her to leave anytime soon," Dr. Steward said equally loud and somewhat assertively.

After a moment of contemplation, Udi's voice was heard again, "You know that I completely respect your judgment, and after all, you are in charge here. What I suggest is for us to leave them alone for a little while and see what happens. You can absolutely trust Daniel because he is head over heels in love with her and she him. Anyway, don't you want me to give a little impromptu presentation to your resident staff while I'm here? If so, this would be a good time to do it."

Dr. Steward hesitated, but because Udi was respected worldwide, she knew she shouldn't carelessly refute anything he said. Finally, she agreed, "Thanks, Udi, I think you're right. Come with me." The door closed the rest of the way, and I was alone with Brenna at last.

"This is one of the finest moments of my life, Brenna, to have you back in my arms again," I whispered in her ear. She had moved up, and we were cheek to cheek.

I could feel the moisture from her face running down my face toward my neck. "I love you, Daniel. Thank God you are here at last," she said and pressed harder against me.

"Are you ready to get out of this place soon, Brenna?" I asked. I could feel her head nod the affirmative. "I know you remember Udi Gast from Madison. He is here with me, and I think he is conspiring to get you out of here as soon as he can manipulate the doctors in charge of you." Again, she nodded her understanding.

Just then the door opened again, and I twisted both our bodies so I could see who was coming in. Our visitor was the young Dr. Jones, who came wearing a big smile. "Hi!" she said spritely.

I turned away from Brenna long enough to partially face Dr. Jones as Brenna continued to cling to me. "Dr. Jones, could you do me a favor?"

She beamed with the opportunity to become involved and brightly said, "Sure, anything!"

"Brenna needs to eat something. If you get the nurse to bring her some soup, I'll feed it to her myself." She nodded and agreed that that was a really good idea and started to leave. "And could you get one of them to come in to help me bathe her and clean her up a little? A toothbrush would be helpful." I pulled Brenna to me and put my lips close to her ear. "That all right, babe?" She nodded consent again.

After the soup was brought, I spoon fed it to her, small amounts at a time, but got the whole bowl in her as well as a small glass of hospital juice. Inspecting while feeding her, I noticed both how weak she was and how her flesh seemed to limply hang. A young nurse stopped by with plastic bowls on a cart, obviously intending to freshen Brenna up. "Sir, if you could wait in the hall, I'll work on her," she requested.

Brenna looked at me with a pleading face and shook her head back and forth. She didn't want me to leave her side for a moment. I didn't want to leave her either, and I told the nurse as much. "I have to be here for this, but don't worry, we have been close for years, and I've seen all of her many times."

The nurse gave a questioning look at me and then at Brenna and shrugged indifference. Together, we sponged Brenna down with warm soapy water and toweled her dry. I could tell that she was not yet strong enough to shower herself. Her greasy and stringy hair had to be cleaned, because I couldn't bear to see her like that a moment longer. "Brenna, let me help you stand, and let's try to wash your hair in the sink," I suggested. She looked willing, and with the nurse's help, we did a fairly good job of it. I brushed her hair as I had done many times before. The shine returned, and the difference it made in her appearance was striking.

Before the nurse left, I asked her if Brenna could have a cup of coffee. "Not without the permission of a doctor... but I'll ask," she answered before she left, closing and locking the door behind her.

Admiring our handiwork, I saw that Brenna had become a different person than her physicians had seen. She still had not said very much, but her eyes and gestures told me that mentally, she was very much with me. After a small knock, the door opened. A smiling Dr. Jones entered with a large Styrofoam cup of steaming coffee. "I got it from the doctors' lounge. Patients in this area are not allowed stimulants, but this is a special case!" She was more than delighted to be in the room with Brenna, and I began to wonder if she was one of her new fans. "Have you heard anything?" I asked, actually meaning the latest news regarding Brenna or her mysterious disappearance.

"I have, absolutely I have!" Dr. Jones gushed. "I am such a fan! She is so fantastic! All my friends talk about her constantly. The papers are full of stories about her, but no one seems to know anything!" She looked at Brenna with boundless enthusiasm and energy. Her buoyancy contrasted with Brenna, for she was nearly too weak to stand and only could manage a small smile back.

This young woman's interest gave me some concern. "Have you spoken to anyone about her, even to other people in the hospital?" I asked.

"Oh, no! I know better than to talk about a patient to anyone but Dr. Steward," she said.

"Listen carefully now," I told her with a steady stern look. "There are a lot of people who would like to know that she is in here. If you let even a shred of information out, the hospital will be flooded by the press and others, and it would be very bad for Brenna. If you are a fan, you have to help us disguise the fact that she is here. As far as her hospital record shows, and all your staff knows, she is still Jane Doe. We must leave it like that. Can't you help us out?"

She smiled broadly, "You can count on me!" I thanked her for the coffee, and she left, grinning as she went out. I was troubled by her intense interest and had doubts that she would live up to her promise.

Brenna slowly consumed her coffee, sip by sip, perking up a bit as the caffeine entered her bloodstream. I tried to engage her in conversation, with limited success. She wouldn't take her eyes from mine and followed me with them every step I made. I sat down on the bed beside her and took her hand. "Brenna, I have to ask you to do something important for me." She looked at me without expression, but intently, her eyes going back and forth between my pupils and my lips. "In just a moment, the physicians will return. You must remember to tell Dr. Gast that you remember him. Say, 'Hello, Dr. Gast. I remember that we met in Madison, in the hospital.' Can you remember to do that?" She looked at me with her focus changing from my left eye to my right.

Before she had a chance to answer, the door opened and in they walked. Udi looked from Brenna to me and back, giving me a wink and stroking his beard in thought. Dr. Steward put her hands on her hips and looked down at Brenna. "Quite a change since I left," she said. She looked at me and said, "Nice work, Daniel." While Dr Steward was trying to comprehend such a marvelous change, Brenna was sitting upright on the bed and alertly looking back and forth between their faces. I held my breath hoping she would remember what I asked her to do. Dr. Steward turned to Udi, who was behind her, and said, "Well, you promised results, but I haven't changed my mind about her leaving before I have a good grasp on what will happen to her outside these walls."

Just then, Brenna spoke, "How nice to see you again, Dr. Gast. I remember that I saw you last as a hospital administrator." That effort took its toll, and I quickly sat down beside her, wrapping my arm around to steady her so that they wouldn't guess that she could fall over.

Udi looked sheepish and shrugged to Dr. Steward. "My deceit catches up with me at times," he confessed. Returning his attention to Brenna, he said, "It warms my heart to see you come around, Brenna. You are going to be fine." He crooked his finger toward Dr. Steward. "Conference in the hall again, please?" She didn't look like she wanted to go out there again and instead lingered indecisively watching Brenna, but finally did join Udi outside the room. Udi managed to keep the door ajar so that I could overhear what was said.

Dr. Steward spoke first, "Listen, Udi, although I am impressed with what just happened, I am not about to let her out of here yet. There is no way that she could have this magical metamorphosis and have it be anything but fragile. I saw her in a near vegetive state for three days, and she needs supervision, counseling, examination and likely medication before she goes out in that world which is waiting for her like a pride of lions."

I could sense that Udi was stroking his beard. He would have a furrowed brow and be looking up to her with his head cocked a little in his peculiar way, figuring out his next move. "My dear Pam. If you went in there right now and asked this young lady to stay here, what do you think she will say?"

"Right now she will say no, I'm sure," she answered.

Udi then added, "It appears to me that she has regained her footing, however precarious it may seem to be to us. That means, my dear, that if we keep her, it will be against her will. The pride of lions you mentioned are right now prowling the streets, because they know she is in town somewhere. If they locate her... well, the hospital doesn't need that, does it?"

After a silence she finally answered, "No, Udi, I have been through that before with a celebrity patient. What do you suggest then?"

"Daniel and I will take your fascinating patient off of your hands. I will take full responsibility for what happens to her. She does need more time, at least overnight, to recover some strength and to be sure that she remains aware of herself, and I would plead with you to make an exception to the usual rule of excluding family in this unit after hours so that Daniel can be with her at all times until discharge."

Dr. Steward answered harshly, having figured out that she had been outmaneuvered. "She has a private room, but he'll have to sleep on the floor.

"I'm sure he would hang off the ceiling fixture if that's what's required. That's not a worry. Another favor, please?" he asked.

"Udi, you obviously will manipulate it out of me anyway. Just tell me what you want, and I'll try to see that it's done."

"Pam, under the unique circumstances of this case, it would be better to pretend that you never knew her name. The hospital record should remain Jane Doe. Could you do that?"

Dr. Steward responded, "In for a penny, in for a pound. Her records will remain unchanged. Do you have a time in mind for discharge, Udi?"

"I feel that she may be ready by 8:00 in the morning. I will meet you in the lobby and then we will make sure she is up to it. Now, I would like to thank you for your very professional manner and your personal warmth in this endeavor by inviting you out tonight to the finest restaurant in Seattle. You get to pick which one."

"Too bad you are married, Udi, unlike me. It's really too bad."

"You must understand, Pam, that we Europeans have an enlightened view of all that business, unlike you rigid and puritanical Americans. Can you ring my hotel for me when your schedule will permit?"

"Come with me, you old fox, I've got some more consulting for you to do first!" The door swung closed again, and judging from the sounds of their footsteps, they left together.

Are We A Band Yet? *by Alexander Francis*

Chapter Twenty-Three

Escape

We spent an uneventful afternoon together, and Brenna slept away most of it. Each time she awakened, I insisted that she eat and drink some more, and I got permission from Dr. Jones for her to try to stroll through the halls with my assistance. She became more normal as time went by. She started talking more, but we didn't discuss anything about her singing or Mill or anything about things which could make her tense. I did what Udi wanted and what I wanted and that was just to be close to her again and feel her touch.

I called Mick in the evening, "Mick, we are about ready to get out of here tomorrow morning. Can you help?"

The gruff voice that I had gotten to respect more and more answered, "I'll be ready, and I've been working on a plan. You should know that there have been five individuals in and about your hospital trying to buy information about Brenna. They are not dumb and money buys the same information as my fists, and they are plenty sure that she is in there, and they are watching. I spotted one of them when we came in this morning, but I didn't say anything to you. He is a PI like me named Elmo Burris, and he's filthy slimy. This afternoon I went to see him, and he'll be busy for a few days getting his teeth fixed. I checked the layout of the hospital, and I want her to exit from the loading docks on the west side. After that, we should drive the limo down to Portland, and you can fly from the airport there. It's only one hundred sixty miles down Interstate 5 and will take under three hours. Tell Dr. Gast to change your plane tickets to leave from Portland as soon as he can. Unless I hear otherwise, I will be waiting at the dock area at 9:00 in the morning with the motor running."

"Thanks, Mick. You have it all worked out like I hoped you would. I'm going to be here all night with her, keeping her company and getting her ready. Unless something comes up unexpectedly, we will be there at nine. Thanks, buddy."

I felt a load lift off of me. I decided to call Udi before he got out for supper so I punched in his cell number. He answered with a breathless and impatient, "Ja?"

I thought I also heard a woman's soft voice for a moment. "Udi, Daniel here. Sorry to bother you. I worked it out with Mick, and he wants to drive us to Portland in the morning to catch a plane, and he suggested that you should have the tickets changed. Is that acceptable?"

"Yes, Daniel, we'll work on it in the morning." He abruptly and uncharacteristically hung up. Something else to do, I surmised. The old fox is really an old dog.

I tried to settle in for the night. The staff had thrown in a couple of pillows and a blanket, but this was not good conditions for comfort. When I finally tried to lie down, Brenna insisted on holding my hand. She placed her face on the edge of the bed so that she could keep me in view. I had gotten a good deal of food in her over the past six hours, and she continued to improve. Her occasional wisecracks made me know how far she had come. Peering off the side of the bed at me on the floor, she remarked brightly, "Bet you'd rather be in bed with me, huh? Too bad for you."

I looked up to see a small grin on her face. Did you know that you can't shift positions or toss and turn while you are holding hands with someone above you? You can't sleep either. She had to get up and use the toilet twice, which was good because it meant that we were catching up with her fluid levels. Occasionally, the little cover on the door window would snap open then close with a click as the staff checked on us. Brenna got fed, but I didn't get offered anything. There was no way I could leave her long enough to go out for food. I was hungry, and my stomach was telling me so, and I was impatient for morning so we could get going. Home, how good it was going to be!

Morning at long last came, and I got up, stiff from my rest on the floor. I could catch a little sparkle in Brenna's eyes, and she was hungry, a good sign. Promptly at 7:00, her food tray was delivered, and she ate it quickly without any small talk.

Just as she was finishing, there was a knock at the door. I opened it to find one of the nurses holding a large paper sack. She said that it was delivered with instructions to give it to the Jane Doe in P441. I took it from her and found inside an old faded blue hooded sweatshirt. Instantly, I knew from whom and why it was sent. An additional cloak of invisibility for Brenna wouldn't hurt. I kept watching the time, and I was getting edgy about how to connect with Mick out back at the dock area.

About 8:30, I could hear familiar voices coming toward her room. When the door opened, I was not surprised to see Drs Jones, Steward and Gast come in. The final inspection was on. Brenna was sitting on the bed with her hands by her sides and slowly swinging her crossed legs. She was looking very alert, and I was sure that she could pass muster this morning. Good thing they weren't going to examine me.

"How are you this morning, Brenna?" Dr. Steward asked.

"Fit as a fiddle, Doctor," she said with a smile.

"Do you know where you are and why you were here, dear?"

"Sure do, Doctor. I'm here because I collapsed from the stress of the previous several days, and because Mill dumped me here instead of getting Daniel, as she should have. "

She continued to unblinkingly look directly at Dr. Steward after she spoke. Dr. Steward threw up her hands and said, "You win, Udi, she can go," and turned on her heel and left the room.

Dr. Jones continued to beam and said, "I'll write the discharge order right now, and you can get out of here this morning!" Udi was looking back and forth between Brenna and me, smiling and nodding his approval.

"I knew you could pull it off, Daniel, if anyone could. This doesn't mean, however, that she is done with the shrinks as you call us. We need to follow this episode up with some appointments when she returns home, and I want a promise from both of you about it." We reassured him that we would follow through, even though I doubted that Brenna would ever get around to it.

"Udi, what about the luggage from our hotel?" I wondered.

"Taken care of. Your investigator came to see me early this morning and took it all away. As you know, you don't argue with him, so I assume he will have it with him," he answered.

"Well, that leaves Brenna's luggage in the other hotel. We''ll have to swing by and get it also," I said.

"No, your man has that with him also. Quite a chap, that one," Udi said. "He also left this for you," he said as he reached outside the door and retrieved a paper sack. "I think Brenna will want this," and he handed the sack to her.

She peered inside and said, "Clothes, my clothes! Will you wait outside while I put them on?"

We both went into the hall and closed the door. While we were chatting, an orderly came to us with a wheelchair. "Miss Jane Doe here for discharge?" he asked.

"Yes, she is inside changing," I answered. "Do we have to use the wheelchair?" I asked both of them.

"Hospital regulations," they both answered.

I asked the orderly, "Do you know the way to the loading dock area?"

"You mean that you are going to take her out that way?" he asked with raised eyebrows.

"Yes," I replied.

"That's pretty unusual; I may have to get permission," he said.

"No, you won't," Udi intervened. "I am Dr. Gast, and I am authorizing it; in fact, I will be walking with you. You should understand that Miss Doe's ex-boyfriend may be waiting for her out in the lobby, and she is trying to avoid him." The orderly briefly thought about it and shrugged.

In a moment, Brenna emerged wearing her fresh clothes and the blue hooded sweatshirt on top. As she sat down, I pulled the hood over to cover her blonde hair. The sweatshirt was probably Mick's and was oversized which allowed the hood to deeply hide her face.

As we started to walk toward the exit door leading to the elevator, I saw Dr. Jones running toward us. "I just had to say goodbye and tell you what an honor it was getting to meet you, Brenna." She was loud and indiscrete, and I was wishing she would part from us. "You are going out the lobby in the front of the hospital, aren't you?" she asked no one in particular.

"Why do you ask, Dr. Jones?" I inquired.

"Well, my boyfriend is here and would like to meet you. I told him that I didn't think you would mind. You'll go right past him!" she squeaked.

"Of course that will be all right," Udi answered for us.

When we were safely in the elevator, I remarked, "The little creep sold us out!"

Udi looked sad and said, "That appears to be the case, and no telling who is really out there. If we can escape out the back way, we still have deniability on our side." The orderly was listening, but I didn't think that he got it, at least I hoped that he didn't.

We were led down several non-patient corridors and at last came to the loading dock. Mick was there and waved for us to follow. He opened the double steel doors to an inside loading area. There sat a large black SUV with blackened windows, looking like the kind the Secret Service uses or the President travels in.

While we were getting in, Mick gave the orderly a twenty and then said in his gravelly voice, "If I ever hear that you said a word about any of this, I'll come back for you." The words were menacing enough, but coming from Mick, it had the desired effect on the orderly who hurried off, very glad to be away from us, especially Mick Grundy.

Mick signaled someone, and the large door started up as he got in to drive. As we turned the opposite way from the front of the hospital, we could plainly see a small crowd which had gathered, with large cameras present everywhere. We turned south, heading toward our destination.

"Any chance you could stop for food before we hit the Interstate?" I asked. Silence. "Mick, you hear me?"

"Yeah, I heard you... There is someone following us."

We all turned around, but all we saw was what appeared to be normal traffic. I could see Mick intently checking his rearview mirrors. "I think there is only one back there, and he's an amateur. We'll find a spot to take care of him."

The rest of us looked at each other. We were all hoping that Mick didn't mean homicide, but with his background, you would expect him to consider it. The SUV continued south, and occasionally I looked backward, seeing nothing unusual. We suddenly pulled into a fast food parking lot which was nearly full. The move surprised me, because I assumed that our tail was still behind us.

Mick got out, ordering, "Wait here," and went into the building. I looked around and still saw nothing unusual. Suddenly, an auto horn continuously sounded. Mick returned, got back in and started backing up. I searched for the source of the horn and finally saw someone who appeared to be lying against his steering wheel. Mick explained, "He'll be OK; he just went to sleep for a short nap," and continued to drive. After a couple of blocks, he rolled down his window and tossed a set of keys into the road.

We were nearing the interstate highway, and I withheld my complaint about food. After we were on the way and leaving the Seattle area, Mick remembered, "Don't worry, we'll stop soon; I just have to watch for another tail first."

Miles and miles later, we finally pulled off the highway, stopping at a small family style restaurant. Mick got out first and, after studying the landscape carefully, decided that it was safe. What an interesting group we made: a singing sensation, a psychiatrist, a combat soldier and me. We all piled into a booth, Brenna and Mick seated across from each other on the inside near the window. They studied each other for the first time face to face.

"Are you a soldier of fortune, Mick?" Brenna asked him.

His hardened face softened into a smile, and he said, "If I am, I've missed out on the fortune. So you are what all the fuss is about." They continued eating and intermittently looking at each other with interest. "You are probably the best looking woman I ever sat this close to," he belatedly observed.

"Thanks, Mick," she said, "and you are the toughest looking guy I've ever sat close to." We had a mutual admiration society forming between these two. Brenna was still wearing her hooded sweatshirt and looked small, like a child was inside the big clothing. The waitress kept trying to catch a look at her face, unsuccessfully. I picked up an abandoned newspaper which was folded up in the corner of the booth.

There was a lengthy article with the title "Brenna Kristen... Where Is She." The interest in her was still there. Brenna and I sat with our hips touching and without looking at each other. We didn't need to look. The heat from her thigh went into me like a euphoric drug, and for the first time in weeks, I was happy and relaxed. Udi and Mick engaged in tentative and sporadic conversation. Mick lived in the physical world of violence and muscular strength, and Udi was entirely cerebral. I could tell from the conversation that each respected the other in his domain. Both types had been useful in the recovery and rescue of Brenna.

During a lull in conversation, Udi spoke to us, "Times like those we had in that august institution make me yearn for Germany."

I looked up at him with surprise, wondering, "Why so, Udi?"

"Well, because the tendency to use psychotropic drugs is so strong with my American colleagues. Medication solves all problems, you know. In Germany, we still have a lot of faith in the psychotherapy style of treatment which also includes investigation into the etiology of the problem and remedies which include a change of direction and involvement of family or loved ones. An example is sitting beside you. Without us, she still wouldn't know where or who she is. It makes me discouraged, you know."

"You proved your point to them. Perhaps some light was shed which will cause some change," I offered encouragingly.

"Unlikely, my friend, but thanks." Udi concerned himself with Mick who was silent and looking out the window, presumably for threats. "Do you ever have any doubts or hesitation, Mick?"

Mick looked his hard look at Udi and took his time answering, "It would be fatal if I did, Doc."

We finished up and left for the highway, our destination, the airport in Portland. There were no additional dangers, just the pulsation of the tires and the hiss of wind. Udi had changed the tickets and acquired one for Brenna. Mick delivered us to the departure area and parked. He asked if we wanted his company into the terminal, and we said that there was no need.

I asked him the necessary question, "Have you calculated all that I owe you yet, Mick?"

He turned to Brenna and said, "It was my pleasure to help get you out of trouble, and if you ever need me again, just call. By the way, do you know where Mill Elbers has her place in LA?

Brenna looked puzzled but said, "It's somewhere on Ventura near Beverly Hills. A house. I don't know the number."

"Mick, why do you want to know?" I asked.

"I think I'll collect my fee from Mill. She owes it to both of you, and don't worry, I'll get it out of her." Looking at him, I knew that he would. "Another thing you'll want to know, I put Terrance Star down on the hospital records as being responsible for Brenna's stay there. They will collect from him." We all laughed out loud. Poor Terrance, he will find the hospital more relentless than having Mick after him. We said goodbye and Brenna gave Mick a long hug. He looked sheepish for the first time since I met him.

Are We A Band Yet? *by Alexander Francis*

Chapter Twenty-Four

Home Sweet Home

My, what a wonderful feeling it was to stretch out on the couch with nothing to do on a Saturday morning. It had been only three weeks since we returned from the West Coast but already things were nearly restored to normal. Brenna had become her old self, back to teasing, tickling and wisecracking. She looked radiant and had regained all the lost weight. The clamor in the music press had calmed, but there was persistent interest, and her videos continued to accumulate hits. We had not heard from Mill, and I assumed with Mick after her for expenses, we would probably never hear from her again. As predicted, Brenna refused to see Udi Gast professionally, but I knew she had a fondness for him, and she said that she intended to invite him over someday for a meal as a friend. I resumed playing music for fun once more, and Brenna often sang as I played. This was as close to heaven as life gets.

Spoiling this moment of bliss, the phone rang and Brenna picked it up. "Hi, Harvey... no, not yet... well, I don't know... listen, Daniel is here; could you talk to him?" She handed me the phone.

"Hi, Harvey"

"Dan, so good to talk to you. I have some news, my friend, and I want to tell you both in person, could I come over there?"

"You mean that you're in town?" I asked, disregarding the obvious.

"Yes, I came from Atlanta early this morning just to see you both, and I am standing in the airport lobby right now."

I hid my amazement and said, "That will be fine, Harvey. Come on over, and we'll get some lunch ready. Do you need a ride?"

"No, I have someone coming to get me. Could you make that two for lunch?"

"All right, Harvey, see you soon." I hung up wondering who else was coming and what we were facing. "Hang on, Brenna, we have a lot of pressure on the way over here, and we have to stick together whatever comes at us. Are you ready?"

"With you here beside me, bring it on," she said, smiling at me. The obvious reason for this visit was to get Brenna signed to a contract with someone, probably Harvey. We knew it would have to be faced sometime. Might as well be today.

We had been hiding from this cloud for three weeks, but it was always out there, hanging like an ominous presence on the horizon. I picked up the phone and called for three large pizzas and a couple six packs of pop.

I took Brenna in my arms, and we looked eye to eye, our foreheads touching. "We have to talk this thing out before they get here, and we both know we have been putting it off, but today has been chosen as the day we face the future." She nodded yes and continued to hold my gaze. "I am acutely aware of what you went through out there, and I don't see the need to rehash all that stress, but we need to decide what you feel that you want to do and what you feel you are capable of doing. They are just interested in the ton of money dangling out there for the taking, but I am interested only in you. I will do anything for you, and I mean anything, but only if that is what you want. You must talk to me about it right now, before the pressure starts."

She moved to fully embrace me with her head buried in my neck, and she held on without words for a long tender moment then pushed away to face me. "I now know what it's like to be a star, even for a moment," she said. "I also know there is no place to hide from the public when you are a new face. When you are very young, it feels special when you are admired for your looks, but it is very tiring to be pursued and ogled by every man that you pass in the street. I don't like being an object or someone's idea of the perfect woman; I just want to be left alone to have my life to enjoy while it lasts. That much money! What could I ever spend it on that would mean anything to me? Where could I go and have a private moment or just walk down the street without people wanting to know every detail of my body or my life? I don't want fame like that. It's mine for the taking, the fame, the fortune and the adventure, but it's not for me. Anyway, I won't do anything that would separate us. I won't part from you again."

She drew me toward her and extended her neck back to lift her face to mine. I felt her hair caressing my hand on her back, and I felt her warm breath on my lips. I kissed her, and the world stopped for me. There was nothing beyond her. There was only her taste, her fragrance and her wonderful touch. If there was some way to suspend time, I would have chosen to stay with our faces together for a thousand years.

When the doorbell sounded, I fell back to earth and its realities. The pizza was here. Just after we put it on the table, the bell sounded again, announcing our guests. As my hand went to the door knob, I had a funny feeling that the expected may become the unexpected, and I was right. Harvey stood there with a broad smile, dressed in a tailored three piece pin striped suit complete with briefcase, and right beside him was Mill Elbers. I swallowed hard and blinked.

"Well, this is unexpected. Welcome and come in," I said. Mill, as usual, was not smiling and gave me a quick glance which seemed to me somewhat hostile.

Brenna came into the room and stopped with the sight of Mill. The two eyed each other for a moment and then both stepped forward for an embrace. Mill got out, "Brenna, honey, I'm so sorry," before Brenna cut her off with "Don't, Mill. There are no grudges or hard feelings, and I don't want to discuss it." They continued to hold each other by the shoulders for a long look.

Harvey spoke up, "How nice to invite us over. Ooh, I like pizza, my favorite." He was intent on breaking any ice and looked a bit uncomfortable. Brenna led the way to the dining table laid out with pizza, and we all sat down.

"How are things going for you two?" Harvey inquired.

"Good," I answered. "We are slowly returning to normal." I glanced at Brenna to gauge any feelings she was experiencing with Mill present, but I could see no stress in her face.

"Good weather for February," Harvey ventured. We all ignored him. We were all waiting for the moment when the topic at hand would be introduced.

Mill, blunt as usual, opened it up, "Brenna, I never have had a chance to tell you what has been going on. I was there when you left, and I have been center stage for you, and there is a lot to discuss." Brenna stared at her, then me, but was silent. Mill reached down into her large purse and pulled out a stack of papers. She stood and waved them in the air, saying, "All these are offers for public appearances. Money. Lots of money. This one," she said as she pulled one out of the stack, "is for The Tonight Show... five hundred thou just for a 15 minute appearance, as long as they are the first to get you. And, this one," she said as she extracted another paper from her stack, "is for The View, and they have it in writing that you get two hundred fifty thou." Her eyes bugged out a little at the effort, and she continued to stand and stare at Brenna for some sort of response.

Brenna remained impassive. Harvey spoke up, "I have to admit something to you both." We turned toward him for this new revelation. "I acted without your permission on something, and now I want to tell you about it and what has happened."

I already didn't like the sound of it, but my mind was occupied with what was going on with Mill and her offers of instant wealth. Brenna just sat there, and I couldn't read her at all.

Harvey continued, "With all this interest in Brenna, we at the studio decided to go ahead and release the recording you made using her stage name of Brenna Kristen. Dan, you are listed also but under your real name. I figured that you both needed time for recovery from the events on the Coast so we went ahead with the release without bothering you. Our reason was to feed into all that interest about her. The fact that your song is one of the ones sung on stage is even better. It's selling as a download right now, and the money is starting to come in strong. We went ahead of collections and cut you a check to get your feet wet, and I have it with me." He reached into the briefcase and presented the sealed envelope to Brenna. She took it hesitantly from him while watching my face for reaction. While she was opening it, he continued, "It's only fifty-thousand, but there's more out there. If you could cut several more recordings, we will be able to put out an album. The quicker you do it, the better. This will add an additional peak to the interest in you, especially if the recording keeps on selling as fast as it started. He paused for a breath. Brenna remained motionless with the check dangling in her hand. She kept looking at the check and not at any of us.

"That is great news, Brenna!" Mill said. "This increases the pressure on anyone who wants you to pay big bucks."

They clearly and definitively laid it out for her. A future of fame and big money was not a dream but real. Here it is, take it. Brenna looked at me and held my eyes for a long time. It was not my place to advise her on this. I refused to be a blockade in her path, and the decision was hers alone, and I made an effort to not express any emotion.

Suddenly, Brenna dropped the check on the table, turned her back to us and started walking toward the bedroom. "I need a minute," she said over her shoulder.

"Do you want me to go with you?" I asked. She didn't answer me but closed the door behind her, and we all heard the lock snap in place. We sat down at the table again. "Please, eat," I requested. "We can talk some more while we eat. She'll come back when she's ready." We silently picked away at the pizza which was clearly too much food for any serious dent we were willing to make. "She had a real hard time out there, and I know she won't want to repeat it," I explained.

Mill was still full of enthusiasm, "This is the most rapid ascent I have ever heard of. I would like to help her manage it and continue to rehearse with her to solidify her prospects, if she will let me."

"Mill, you didn't see her in that cell that she was stuck in. You didn't see this beautiful woman reduced to drooling, shriveled inside and out. They were about to start drugs and restraints on her, and

I'm not sure she would have ever come out again. We came close to losing her. You have to understand that she can't take that kind of stress; she isn't built for it and will never be able to handle it."

"Even if you are there, too?" she asked.

"Well, I could be closer than you let me be last time, but she will still have to be on stage alone, interviewed alone and pursued by the press endlessly. It's up to Brenna, but I am convinced that she will break down again under the stress." Mill sagged and looked off out the window.

Now it was Harvey's turn to pitch a deal. "Listen, Dan, Brenna and you have a hit with this record, and the public will clamor for more. All you have to do now is give it to them by making more recordings. You can do it right from here. Of course, Mill is right, to capitalize on it she should make some appearances or better still, some public performances."

"Harvey, I think what you offer is possible. We enjoyed making that recording, and I'm sure she'll do it again. She did perform on stage at the Roundup only three days before the Bowl performance and seemed to relish it, and I didn't see any stress other than her fear of what was going to happen in LA. Perhaps we can take it a little at a time, and give her time to adjust." I turned to Mill and said, "Mill, I'm afraid the stuff you want right now isn't going to happen."

A voice behind me said, "No, it isn't." It was Brenna. She had emerged silently from the bedroom and seemed to be in control again. She sat down and said, "Let's eat some of this pizza; I'm hungry." I laughed and gave her a quick hug around the waist and held her chair for her. As Brenna ate, Mill and Harvey sat and looked suspiciously at each other.

To break the ice, I spoke to Mill, "Mill, I thought that you weren't due back for several months?"

In return, I got a long stare from her lidded gray eyes. "I'm back to talk to Brenna. My mother passed away while we were in LA doing the show. I even missed the funeral, because I was occupied on Brenna's behalf in Seattle. I am putting my mother's home up for sale soon, and I won't be back again." Her voice was level with no emotion.

Brenna said, "I'm sorry for you, Mill. You have my deepest sympathy." There was sincerity in her voice, and it seemed to soften Mill a bit.

"I'm sorry for you also, Mill," I added.

"Thanks to you both. I don't hold it against anyone that I was gone. It had to happen sometime."

I watched Mill for a minute and finally asked, "Any hard feelings toward us, Mill?"

She thought for a second and said, "You mean about the monster you unleashed on me? I came home one night and found him standing in my living room. He demanded twenty-five thousand dollars in cash and said, 'or else', I was terrified." She recovered from the thought for a second, then added, "I got the Bowl people to pay up, plus some. They also stood good for the hospital fee that you tried to stick the band with. I came out OK too." She had a slight smile at the thought of profit on her end.

Chapter Twenty-Four

"Why would the Bowl pay anything?" I innocently asked.

"Because their nurse inappropriately and without supervision or consent gave Brenna a powerful sedative that night which caused some problems, as you know," she answered. We all exchanged knowing looks.

There was a very loud knock on the door. I got up to answer it and looked back at Brenna who was motionless, but I could see a small smile creeping onto her face. A huge familiar black guy wearing sunglasses was standing there. "Peaches! What are you doing here?" I asked smiling at him, and reaching out for a handshake.

"We here for Brenna," he answered in his deep resonant voice. I looked past him and saw Zap peeking back at me, smiling his flashy gold-tooth smile. "Hi, White Boy!" he said with a chuckle.

"Did Brenna call you guys this morning?" I asked.

"Yup," said Peaches.

"Well, come on in; I think there is a lot of pizza left," I said. They came past me while I held the door. Peaches playfully pushed my face with his clenched fist as he came by, and Zap gave me a quick embrace and a wink.

Brenna came running toward them and put her arms around Peaches first. I noticed that her hands were far from touching behind his back. She patted him on the stomach and asked "My, Peaches, have you grown?"

He responded with that deep "Ho, Ho, Ho" of his and smiled down at her, touching her gently on the top of her head with his big hand.

Zap wrapped his arms about her waist and picked her off the ground and turned her around in a complete circle. "Let me tell you, Baby... I saw your video and you are the ONE!" he said as he put her down.

She patted his face and said, "Thanks for coming on such short notice. You know Mill, but have you met Harvey Silverman?" She turned and pointed to Harvey who had stood and moved away from the table.

"I know Harvey Silverman by reputation as I'm sure he knows me," Zap answered while moving toward Harvey with his hand extended. After shaking hands, Zap turned to Mill and said, "I knew we would meet again, Mill. You can't get rid of this old trickster so easily."

Mill and Zap hugged, and as they were looking at each other, Harvey said, "Well, what a group you have assembled, Brenna. What does it all mean?"

Brenna ignored him, instead speaking to Peaches, "Eat some pizza, Peaches, and if you need more, we'll send out for it." Peaches grinned back at her and seated himself and started to dig in. The rest of us went into the living room and sat down.

Brenna spoke first, "Zap, tell everyone what's going on."

Zap cleared his throat and said, "Your friends, Mike, Doug and Tom, got ahold of me about three weeks ago and wanted some jazz lessons. We were joined by Pete, who I think is a friend of Harvey here. We have been going at it hot and heavy most every day since. Those boys have hot coals in their pants, and they work hard."

A voice from the kitchen said, "Dey sure do!"

Zap continued, "We are making a lot of headway, but we really need a piano player and a hot singer to make it happen." He grinned and winked at me and showed his gold tooth to everyone.

Harvey spoke up, "Are they any good, Zap?"

"They are getting there, and they are pretty good musicians anyway. It won't take long," Zap answered.

I looked at Brenna, and she smiled back. This was not new news for her, and she had been keeping it secret. My mind raced to catch up and to reason out any implications and to understand why Brenna chose today to have the news broken.

I had to know what was up, so I asked her, "Where do you intend to go with this, Brenna?"

Instead of giving me a direct answer, she looked at Harvey, "Harvey, don't you think that a real jazz band would help complete an album of songs for us? Some pieces I would want to do with just a piano, but I think some need a whole group. I saw that when I was with Terrance. We can put together a whole big jazz band. We even have a clarinet player. What do you think?"

"I'll have to hear you all play together first, but the idea is very good. I like it," he answered with some enthusiasm. "Zap, are you going to play with them?" Harvey asked.

Zap nodded at me and said, "I'm not against it, but Dan is coming along well. I think he needs some more coaching, because he has a tendency to slide back into his White Boy mode, but I think he is the one. Anyway, I'm too old, and I've done it before. Time for me to let it go."

We studied Brenna for guidance since it was obvious that she was calling the shots. She got up and moved to the center of the room. "The band, and of course Zap and his friends, invite us to a performance at the Brink tomorrow night." She looked at me and smiled, "Daniel and I will also perform!" My brow wrinkled farther. Harvey stood and came to her and put his arm over her shoulder.

"I am proud of you, Brenna. You have cinched a plan that will work. You will be with your friends and Daniel, and the stress will be manageable, and you are going to call the shots. It's a great plan."

Mill had been silent until now and she stood up also, "Are you going to throw away millions of dollars of a sure thing to put everything on this untested band of yours?"

Brenna turned to her and said, "Absolutely, emphatically, yes, Mill."

Huffy now, Mill wasn't about to let it go, "I have spent a lot of hours on your behalf, Brenna, and I am the reason, the only reason for your fame. I have nothing to show for it, plus all my contacts will dry up if I can't come through for them." I watched this exchange from the couch. Brenna was trying hard to be nice but firm, and I could tell that she wasn't going to back down an inch.

"Mill, dear, you have every right to feel that way, but I have one question for you that I need to have an answer to. What actually happened to the singer that I replaced in Terrance's band? Is she alive?"

This was the first time that I saw Mill stopped in her tracks. She cast her eyes around the room, a sure sign of guilt. She stammered as she answered, "Dear, I have no idea what happened to her. How should I know. She just didn't show up."

"How do you explain that we were working on her songs... her specific songs... long before she disappeared? You have to explain to us how you knew that she was about to take off," Brenna demanded.

Mill stammered and said, "Brenna, there was nothing illegal. I had a contact that had information that she was into drugs, and I knew that it was only a matter of time. I just got lucky. You just got luckier."

Brenna looked at her without answering. They both stood their ground. "Mill, I think that you and I have lost the trust between us that we would need to go forward. I do appreciate your skills both as a voice and performance trainer and as an agent; you have no equal. I haven't much to give you to replace all the money that you would have earned, and I didn't come away with anything out of all that either, except some wisdom." She went to the table and picked up Harvey's check for fifty-thousand and returned to Mill. "I want to give you this, but I want something in return." They walked together to the door, engaged in quiet conversation. After a short talk and a handshake, Mill put the check in her purse and left.

Brenna turned around and motioned to Harvey, "We can take you to wherever you want to go when you are ready." She smiled and crooked her finger at me. I got up, and we had a great hug with everyone watching. It was over, and the decision had been made.

"What did you ask her to do, Brenna?" I asked.

"Shusssh," she answered, and put her index finger across my lips.

Chapter Twenty-Five

Back Together Again

We wakened at dawn, or at least I woke up at dawn and woke Brenna up to be with me. She groaned and looked at her watch and groaned again. "What time are you getting up?" she asked.

"Now," I answered. "If you want to rehearse, we have to start early. Get up!"

"We can't this early... the landlady," she said and rolled back on her side and pulled the covers up.

She was right, but I had a lot to do. Luckily, I had my keyboard with me this time, and all I had to do is plug the earphones in and play in silence. I got up, and on the way past the kitchen, I turned on the coffee machine.

As I was setting the keyboard up in the living room, Brenna came shuffling in, rubbing her eyes. Her hair stuck out in four directions, and she had my old slippers on. "Can we eat first, please?" she asked. For her, the keyboard could wait, and we went back to the kitchen.

The early morning sunlight came in, horizontally lighting the room with warm yellow rays. During coffee, we sat and read the newspaper mostly in silence. "Are you ready to tell me what sort of deal you worked out with Mill?" I asked from behind the newspaper.

"No," she replied through hers.

"Surprise, then?" I asked.

"You'll see," she answered.

After breakfast we talked about which songs we were going to do. She did know about the activity of the band and must have been working on it as soon as we got back. She knew in detail which songs were with the full band and which were for just her and me. There were six pieces for me to work up, but four of them we had done previously. I finished setting the keyboard up and got out my music and earphones. The upright piano that we usually used sat in the corner looking lonely. As I played, I noticed that she was on the phone a lot, but I had much catching up to do, and I bent into the work at hand. About eleven, I was happy about the pieces... all Cole Porter, in case you are wondering... and decided to take a break and afterward encourage her to sing with me on a couple.

She didn't look in the least worried but agreed that it would be a good idea. There was a knock on the door, and she got it before I could get up. The man was dressed in coveralls and had others behind him. "Piano movers," he explained.

Brenna stepped back and pointed to the upright piano. "There it is."

"No, Brenna, they can't take our piano! What are you doing? We need it!" I complained.

"Don't worry yourself. Be useful and take down the keyboard to give us some room please," Brenna commanded.

What could I do? I bought it for her, and it was hers to do with what she wanted. I just didn't understand what she was doing. They came in and, in businesslike fashion, took it out the door and down the stairs. I looked out the window and saw our pretty little piano slide into the back door of a moving truck. Gone forever. I took down the keyboard like she asked and packed it away.

I heard a lot of puffing and heavy noise coming up the stairs and was beaten to the door by Brenna again, who opened it smiling from ear to ear. Through the door came a large black object which seemed to continue and continue like a long train coming out of a tunnel, pushed by four large men. The Steinway label came into view. It was a new concert grand piano and a Steinway to boot. When it got fully in, it seemed to take up the entire living room.

Brenna put her arms around me and kissed me on my cheek. "Daniel, this is my gift to you for all you went through for me. I know you loved this piano, and it's now yours."

"Is this the one that was in Mill's house?" I asked.

Brenna smiled. "Now you know the deal that I made. Mill got the check, and I got the piano!" It was an incredible deal. This piano was easily worth twice what Brenna gave for it, even used. "Mill said that she got it as a gift and since she couldn't even play it, she really didn't care. It saved her the trouble of selling it!" Brenna added. The movers finished uprighting it, and we moved it into the only position it would go. I gave her a long kiss starting at the top of her head and worked my way down to her neck. "Stop!" she declared. "First lunch, then practice." Rats.

When we arrived at The Brink, the band was already on the stage busily tuning their instruments. Doug was holding his long necked bass guitar, Tom behind the drums, Mike on the lead guitar, Pete with his sax and Willie with his clarinet. Zap was already at work on the small grand piano. The stage was full of sound equipment and mikes, and I saw Peaches helping move things about, when he looked up and spotted us. "They here!" he bellowed. The music stopped, and they all put down their instruments and started clapping.

"Welcome back, Brenna!" they yelled in unison. She and I met each of them in turn, and she gave each a kiss on the cheek while I shook their hands.

"Are you two ready for some action tonight?" Zap asked.

"Bring it on," Brenna replied.

Harvey Silverman came from behind us and slapped me on the back. "Knock them dead, guys. I am counting on you," he said over my shoulder.

The patrons started gathering amid the constant clink of drinks being served and the hustle and bustle of the waitresses. Exactly at 7:00, the lights dimmed, and Zap came up to the mike and surveyed and hushed the audience. "In case you haven't heard, we have a very, very special guest singer this evening. You get to hear what most of the country wants to hear right now, and you get to hear it first and live. Ladies and gentlemen, it is my deep pleasure to present Brenna Kristen and her band!"

There were about seventy people in the audience, and all of them were on their feet applauding and stamping in unison. Even the bartenders and waitresses were applauding. I caught the glint of several lenses along the back wall. The drums started first, then the other instruments joined in. I recognized a jazzed up version of Porter's *Another Op'nin', Another Show*. They played while Brenna confidently strode to the center mike in a bath of applause. Zap put his arm around her and raised his hand for the applause to stop. It took several seconds, but the applause and the band stopped about the same time. Brenna thanked Zap and turned to the audience with the mike in one hand.

"Thanks for that warm welcome. I feel so much better being here than standing in front of that crowd at the Hollywood Bowl." The applause started back in earnest and continued until Zap again raised his hand.

"I want to introduce the band, but first I want to tell Doug over there that we are a band, in case he's still wondering!" She got a lot of laughter from everyone, and Doug gave her a wave, also laughing as he did so. She went around introducing the band members one by one and then came to me. "Daniel is our piano player and the love of my life. If it wasn't for him, I'd still be out there in the ozone someplace." She smiled at me and gave me an embrace to the delight of the crowd. More applause. I seated myself at the piano and waited for my cue.

Zap introduced the numbers as they came up. First was *I've Got You Under My Skin*. We played and Brenna sang. My part was not hard, and I had a lot of time to look over at the band and Brenna with pride. She finally was the polished and experienced singer we hoped she would become. Radiant, with a sexy voice which had a lot of range, she brought the house to their feet after every number. We played the last announced piece, *You'd Be So Nice To Come Home To*, and during the number, she made sure to turn toward me so the audience could tell to whom she was singing. They loved it, and they loved Brenna as did everyone on stage with her.

The band was complete and, in every way, professional. I could see Harvey with both hands clasped together and held over his head in a signal of victory. Brenna had done it. She had a band that was hers alone, and she could take it anywhere in the world, and I had the feeling that she would.

When the music faded and the audience seated themselves again, Zap came up to me and said, "Get up, son, I'm going go play this next one." I looked surprised, because I thought that we were done, but I got up and got a pat on the butt from him as he sat. Brenna was watching from the mike and motioned for me to come forward.

"Daniel, this next one is for you and you alone. Would you please go down to the floor and stand in front of the audience?" I did as she asked, and the crowd made room for me. There was a hushed tenseness in anticipation. The band started a familiar tune, and Brenna stepped into the spotlight above and in front of me, looking at me the whole time. The piece was *Do I Love You?*, and she sang it just for me as I looked up toward her lovely face, wishing this moment would last forever.

The End

Afterward

While writing this book the first time, I carelessly used actual names and places because most of this story is true. Not the part about Brenna's sudden fame or the episode about the psychiatric hospital, nor the character, Mick Grundy, the leading man in three books I wrote later.

But too much of it was true, and facts about people I cared about had been divulged. It took some time and courage for me to admit to them that I had used my friend's real names in a novel. To my surprise, most, but not all, agreed to let the book go to the publisher as is, which I have done.

Some remarks regarding selected characters:

Solomon James passed away a year and a half before the book could be published but graciously gave me permission before he died to use his real name. He was delighted, to my surprise, and not least because I was able to portray him exactly as he was in life...full of talent and mischief. By the way, he actually did call me "White Boy" for three long years before I earned his respect. I miss him every time I sit down and play the piano.

The very real (and large) Peaches is another fine man who is both a fabulous drummer and a valued friend. Other members of that jazz group preferred that their real names not be used and I respected that.

Tom is really Tom but Doug was the name used by a guitarist whose whereabouts, as this is written, is anyone's guess. I changed Mike's name at his request.

There is a Harvey Silverman, in case you haven't heard of him.

Dr. Udi Gast, unfortunately, does not exist.

The real Brenna does have a voice coach, but she isn't Mill and looks and acts nothing like her.

That brings up the most important character of all, the one the book is all about. Brenna. I wrote the first version of this book using her real name, but at her request, I changed it to Brenna, and even now I can't read this book without mentally substituting the actual name of this wonderful woman who fills my life. This character is real, for sure, just not her name and I actually did spend two nights and two days hovering beside her bed when her appendix was removed. Most of all, she really does sing like an angel, loves Cole Porter's music, and even dances the Tango. It was a long valiant effort I made, on your behalf, to convince her that her story should be told, and at last, she agreed, and yet still loves me.

And now, in case you haven't guessed, I formally admit that I am Daniel and that I really do play the piano. You can invent the rest of my story all by yourself.

Alexander Francis

A Note of Appreciation

The worst and the best writers seek one thing above all others. A reader who not only reads their book, a work of astounding personal effort, but who shares his/her experiences with the world. We want to know what you think about our work. Truly we do. Of course, we want you to like it, and us, and will be so grateful if you take the time to give us even the smallest amount of praise. I really entreat you to do so.

If you have constructive criticism you want us to hear, please, out with it! Writing is such an isolating experience. I begin to live in my books and come to nearly feel that my characters are real. When someone criticizes one of them, I feel their pain. And some of my own.

But if you enjoyed this novel, I beg you on scuffed knee to give a positive review for me. I assure you that is the best way to see more of my work in the future.

Thanks again for reading this far.

Alexander Francis

Novels by Alexander Francis

Are We A Band Yet?
Mick Grundy...Spy Hunt
Mick Grundy...The Russian Connection
Mick Grundy...Elapid
Beware the Exit
The Green Scarf
Revenge of Jesus
Geminknot
The Copy Candidate
Memory Gap

Please visit afnovels.com

www.ingramcontent.com/pod-product-compliance
Lightning Source LLC
Chambersburg PA
CBHW051247210726
48287CB00002B/381